Critical praise for *Fiona: Stolen Child*

"Gemma Whelan's *Fiona* is amazing. It's a story of an Irish writer living in America who is collaborating on a film script of her own life which forces her to confront the lies and deceptions of her past, lies that have poisoned her relationships and walled up her creativity.

This is a richly textured novel, written with passion and style; an absolute delight to read."

—James N. Frey
How to Write a Damn Good Novel, The Long Way to Die, and *Winter of the Wolves*

"Gemma Whelan is a natural born storyteller with a brilliant eye for character and description. Her writing oozes with class."

—Peter Sheridan
award-winning Irish playwright and director

"*Fiona* is the captivating odyssey of a writer who, seeking fulfillment in Manhattan and Hollywood, is drawn back inexorably to face her roots in rural Ireland.'

Beautifully written, populated with memorable characters, possessed of a page-turning plot, the novel unspools in the imagination like a rich and wonderful film—and resonates afterward in the heart."

—Darryl Brock
If I Never Get Back and *Two in the Field*

"Set in the U.S. and Ireland, this fascinating novel within a novel poignantly illuminates the protagonist's heroic struggle to reconcile the complexities of her hopeful present with a haunted past, richly rewarding the reader with lustrous language and a spellbinding story!"

—Howard G. Franklin
An Irish Experience

Fiona

STOLEN CHILD

Gemma Whelan

To Lisa,
With all best wishes,
Gemma Whelan

GEMMA
Boston

First published by GemmaMedia in 2011.

GemmaMedia
230 Commercial Street
Boston, MA 02109 USA
www.gemmamedia.com

Printed in the United States of America

15 14 13 12 11 1 2 3 4 5

978-1-934848-49-4

Library of Congress Cataloging-in-Publication Data

Whelan, Gemma.
Fiona : stolen child / Gemma Whelan.
p. cm.
Summary: "A cinematic novel that travels between Ireland and America, following the life of a writer and her fictional counterpart as they wrestle with bitter pasts"--Provided by publisher.
ISBN 978-1-934848-49-4
1. Women authors, Irish--Fiction. 2. Authorship--Fiction. 3. Psychological fiction. I. Title.
PS3623.H455F56 2011
813'.6--dc22

2010035197

for Betty

PROLOGUE

Fiona held her breath as the lights slowly dimmed in the theatre. From her fourth row center position, she was aware of the red plush seats fanning out all around her and filled with expectant film goers. The smell of sweet buttery popcorn tickled her nostrils, candy papers rustled, bags crackled, and giant sodas swished up through plastic straws. People chatted and laughed, and the rhythms of the soundscape floated in Fiona's consciousness as she tried to settle, to center herself.

She looked up at the opulent art deco sunburst patterns on the walls; they helped her feel upbeat. Straight ahead was the tall silent screen that in a few short moments would start to unfurl a film made from her novel. She felt like a figure in a surrealist painting, floating above the earth, swimming in air, not able to touch down. She pressed her thighs into the velvety seat and her spine against the hard back to keep her body grounded. Her new shoulder length hairstyle caressed her neck like the touch of a lover. Her form-fitting emerald green silk dress was itself like a dream, all soft and luxurious against her skin.

She breathed in. She breathed out. She could barely contain her excitement. In one year, from June 1990 to June 1991, one revolution of the earth around the sun, her own orbit had been spun upside down and inside out. The lights faded to black. A moment of suspension, then the screen came to life and the credits began to roll. "Based on the novel, *Eye of the Storm* by Fiona Clarke." A storm arose on the screen. *1964*. Angry Irish summer skies. She could hear the suspended breathing around her, yet she herself felt surprisingly calm as she prepared to watch the film.

fiona

PART I

OLD TIES

CHAPTER ONE

THE STORM

"Life shrinks or expands in proportion to one's courage."
ANAÏS NIN

Fiona was content. She had slipped into an hypnotic rhythm induced by the gentle but insistent tapping of her fingers on the computer keyboard and the strains of Handel's *Arrival of the Queen of Sheba* on the kitchenette radio. Her long, slim fingers rippled with ease and grace over the keys, and the screen reflected back a faint image of her taut cheekbones, pale Irish skin and golden-lidded, moss-green eyes. She felt the caress of stray copper tendrils that slipped loose from the soft knot fashioned at the nape of her neck. Immersed in her review of a recent collection of short stories by Irish women writers, she was only vaguely aware of her surroundings, her tiny studio in a New York brownstone. The dark oak paneling and walls of bookcases, and the small multi-paned window high up near the ceiling which filtered in the waning evening light, were comforting in their peripheral caress.

The sharp splatter of raindrops on the window broke the spell. Fiona glanced up and noticed the sky over Manhattan had darkened. Distant thunder rumbled as hail pelted down violently on the tiled roof. She felt the same fear in the pit of her stomach that she always felt when a storm was brewing. She forced herself to concentrate on the keyboard, and to reason that the present assault on the window was only heavy rain and not shards of glass. It was almost June, summertime, surely it couldn't last too long. Now her fingers pounded out an arrhythmic beat as she struggled to stay calm.

Instead of words, images were forming. She was back in Ireland on the farm. It was over two and a half decades ago, summer of 1964. She was nine years old and crouched inside the secret treehouse in the trunk of the ancient oak with her five-year-old sister Orla. Lightning flashed, transforming bronze-haired, cinnamon-eyed Orla into an ethereal being. Thunder crashed and the girls thrilled with fear and excitement. They listened to the heavy rain which threatened to flood the earth and, at first, they felt secure within their own little fortress. A fierce thunderstorm had exploded with a fury that stirred them up and made them feel daring. Like *Alice in Wonderland,* which Fiona was reading to Orla, they were having an adventure.

"Will we count? Fiona, can we count, can we?" Orla tugged at the hem of her thin cotton frock.

Fiona forced herself to put on a brave smile. "All right. Ready?"

Orla nodded vigorously, breathless with excitement. "And in Irish, I want to count in Irish!" Orla was going to start primary school in September, and Fiona was teaching her letters and numbers in both Irish and English. She dramatically spread out all of the fingers of her left hand, and as the lightning flared they began to count in unison. "*A haon, a dó, a trí, a ceathair, a cúig . . .*" A fierce thunderclap shrieked through the air.

"That's five miles away, isn't it?" Orla was thrilled and clapped her hands. "Five seconds, five miles, isn't it, Fiona?"

"Right, it would be about at . . . Mullingar . . . I think." She tried to remember the maps of Ireland they drew in Geography class.

"We're safe here though, aren't we?" Orla's laugh tinkled in tune with the next huge storm blast, and she started to count loudly again, marking out the numbers on her fingers. "*A haon, a dó, a trí, a ceathair . . .*" Bang!

Fiona swept up *Alice in Wonderland* and the coloring book and crayons from the ground. "We're not going, are we?" Orla shrieked. "I don't want to go, please let us stay. Please, Fiona, please, pretty please!"

Before Fiona had time to answer, there was another lightning spike, and Orla started to shout out "*A haon, a dó, a trí . . .* Oh boy! Fiona, is it at Cregora yet? Do you think Mam and Dad are getting wet? How far away is Cregora, Fiona?"

"It's not nearly as far away as three miles. About two and a half, maybe."

"And Mam and Dad? Are they all right. Will they get sick?" Orla was working herself into hysterics now. "Is Mama coming home to us?"

Fiona gave her little sister a quick, urgent hug. "Of course she's coming home, you nincompoop! Mama is all better now. She'll never leave us again."

She watched as Orla moved instinctively for the doll, the doll in their mother's likeness that Fiona had made for Orla when Mam got tuberculosis and had to go away to a sanatorium for two years. The little girl clasped it to her chest.

"It's just a summer storm." Fiona tried to sound grown-up and assured. She wrapped the books and crayons in a plastic sheet and tucked them into the wooden shelf that formed itself out of the inner tree trunk. "And Mam and Dad are safe inside the chapel, so they won't get wet at all."

Orla held the doll ever closer. A sudden wind-blast ripped aside the first of the branches that shielded the entrance, and she screamed. Another onslaught stripped away the remaining twigs and leafy coverings, and the rain pelted in, dragged by the quickly rising gales.

"I don't want to chance making a run for the house." Fiona tried to keep the quiver out of her voice. "We'd get drenched."

"And would I get sick again? Have to go away again to that awful hospital?"

Fiona choked on her dread. The doll's face, which had an eerie resemblance to her Mama's, taunted her. She grasped Orla even tighter, shook her head and mumbled "No."

Another lightning flash. "One, two . . ." Orla's voice was high pitched with equal parts terror and excitement. The sound of the thunder reverberated in the hollow of their tree-trunk haven. The layers of burlap sacks that served as their carpet began to seep with moisture. The low wooden carton had initially protected them from the spreading wetness, but was now starting to disintegrate.

"Fiona, look, our floor!" Orla shouted hysterically. Fiona stared hopelessly at the darkening stains as their socks and sandals got progressively soggier. Orla shivered, and Fiona hurriedly slung the green tartan rug around her shoulders. "Here, this will keep you snug." She hugged her close. "You'll be grand. I'll mind you. I promise you, I will."

The rain turned to heavy hailstones. The sisters were trapped, a part of nature, and the storm gathered around them with a growing fury. On the next flash Orla buried her face in Fiona's chest. "One." It was an hysterical scream. "Tw . . ." The little girl abandoned her counting game as the burlap sacks lining their hideout gave way and they were exposed to the full fury of the elements. Fiona finally sprung into action. "Come on." She grabbed the old woolen rug, pulled it over both of their heads, took Orla's arm, and sped out of their collapsing fortress.

"We have to run like mad, Orla. Run, run, as fast as you can!"

Like a two-headed Irish colleen, with red and green tartan fringes flapping into their faces, they raced along the narrow muddy path. Fiona half pushed, half carried her little sister in the crook of her arm. Their sandaled feet sunk into the dank mass, and they had to haul them out with every footstep. As Fiona dragged her along, Orla snagged her toe in a clump of intertwined twigs and fell headlong into the spongy brown muck. She screamed as she swallowed the mud and spluttered it out, spitting and choking with fear and rage. In a flash Fiona was on her knees trying to extricate her from the slippery mess.

"Try to get a foothold if you can and I'll pull you up."

"I can't, I'm trying." Orla was crying uncontrollably. "Help me."

Fiona grasped her tightly around the waist, stood up straight, and yanked as hard as she could. A zigzag of silver brilliance sizzled across the gray sky, followed almost immediately by a deafening thunderbolt, as Fiona struggled to move them out of danger. A huge tug, a lunge forward, and both of them landed face down in the sludge.

Orla's screams merged with the low rumbles. She lashed out and started to slap Fiona's arm.

"Orla, stop it. I'm trying my best." Fiona snapped angrily, as she struggled to get a foothold and haul them both up again.

"But you're making me sick. It's all your fault!" Orla wailed at the top of her lungs. "There's muck in my mouth. It's yucky!"

Fiona sunk her feet into the soft earth with determination. She swallowed her heavy guilt at first failing her little sister and then getting angry at her. With gargantuan effort, she managed to drag them out and plow through to the end of the pathway. Orla was choking on her sobs. They circled the rising pond, bolted through the tree-lined lane, picked their way over the glimmering gravel, until finally, after an eternity, they were in view of the looming farmhouse. It rose up out of the white rain-shield like a haunted castle, gray and forbidding. Orla hacked and coughed. The outline of the slate roof was barely discernible, and the chimney stacks jutted defiantly into the angry skies. Fiona glanced sideways at her sister, hoping and praying she wouldn't get pneumonia, and pulled the soaking rug tighter around her thin shoulders.

"We're nearly there Orla. There's the house, look!"

Orla glanced up through her veil of tears and nodded when she saw the outline of their home. She shivered under Fiona's protective arm, and they ran the last few feet, through the yard, up to the front door.

Their twelve-year-old brother Declan, with his helmet of flaming orange curls, stood sentry stiff in the massive oak doorway and radiated a piercing glare of disapproval.

"You got her all wet!"

"I couldn't help it!"

"Where were you? What the hell took you so long?

"Would you get out of my way, Declan! I need to get her in and dried off."

In a flash, Declan reached over, snatched Orla, encircled her with his arm, and ushered her quickly into the safety of the house. Fiona, rooted to the spot, stood stock still in the pelting rain and stared hopelessly after them. The tartan rug flapped violently in the gale and whipped her bedraggled body.

Weeks later, Orla was dead.

■ ■ ■

Fiona fought against the memories and the continuing saga of her past. Beads of sweat stung her forehead, and she could hear her own arrhythmic breathing drumming in her ears. She struck hard at the keyboard, trying to erase Declan's stare from her brain. She desperately wanted to free herself from this onslaught that dragged her down and threatened to drown her. She was a writer, after all, and knew well how to shapeshift stories and situations, so she should be able to control them. The Handel oratorio signaled the triumphal welcome of the Queen of Sheba to Solomon's court. Outside, on the streets of Manhattan, the rain mercifully subsided, and along with it, Fiona's unwelcome memories. A jumble of nonsense words and symbols filled the screen, but she was safe again. She had managed, for now, to stop the images.

She slowly rose and began to circumnavigate her terrain. Nondescript cotton pants and top camouflaged her tall slender frame, as animal-like, she circled the small cocoon. Her nerves were fraught. She caught a glimpse of Joyce's *Portrait of the Artist as a Young Man*—the coming of age of her great countryman and expatriate written almost a century ago. She plucked it from the shelf and leafed through the pages, inhaling the aroma. "This lovely land that always sent her writers and artists to banishment." Joyce had said that somewhere. She spotted Edna O'Brien's *The Country Girls Trilogy* on a nearby shelf, replaced the Joyce, and thumbed through the Trilogy. One of Joyce's banished writers, O'Brien had to flee Ireland and the sexual repression of the 1950's when her books were banned. Fiona returned to the desk and her scattered notes. They were part of an in-progress review of a collection of contemporary stories by some of her favorite Irish women writers. Many like Mary Beckett, Fiona Boylan and Jennifer Johnston still lived in Ireland, although many others such as Elizabeth Bowen, Anne Devlin and Julia O'Faoláin had moved away and lived abroad. Were they happy in their exile, she wondered, or was there always a longing, an emptiness? Were they too plagued by unwanted memories, and did those memories interfere with their writing and their lives? Were they thrown off schedule? Did they miss deadlines because past memories invaded? Fiona took solace in the familiar paper and oaky smells of her own refuge. The tall wooden shelves housed her books and wrapped her 'round. Wood. Paper. Wood. A lifetime removed from that Irish childhood storm, in the depth of this American city, she had carved herself a place and crept inside. Safe. Unborn.

Still under the spell of the storm of past memories, Fiona drifted to the tiny kitchenette on the other side of the counter and put water on to make a cup of tea. Her hands shook as she held the kettle under the tap. She needed to calm her nerves, and the tea would help. She pried the lid off the Fortnum and Mason tea caddy and deeply inhaled the whiff of bergamot from the Earl Grey blend. The teacup rattled as she lifted it from the shelf above the sink and set it down carefully. She held on to the counter top to steady herself, and gazed at the purple gas flame as it leaped up and licked the sides of the old green kettle. She caught a glimpse of herself in the little mirror over the sink and saw that her hair had come loose—it spread like a wild and messy aureole around her head and made her think of Grace O'Malley, the Irish 16th century pirate queen. She had a vague notion that her second novel might be about this extraordinary Irish woman who had met face to face with Queen Elizabeth. But vague notions did not translate into solid writing, and Fiona was still unable to get started on that project as she knew she must. Instead she was writing reviews of other Irish women's writing. A safe remove.

The phone rang and jolted her from her reverie. When Fiona heard the Irish voice of her father's cousin Nellie on the other end, she froze.

"Fiona . . . is that you?" A whir of transatlantic noise hummed in her ear.

"Yes. Is this Nellie?" she asked, knowing right well it was.

"It's myself all right, pet." Fiona pictured her, standing in the entrance way of Fiona's old family home, beside the carved mahogany hall-stand, her shoulders slightly bent, silver hair glinting in the oval mirror.

"Is Dad sick, or . . . something?" Nell lived down the road and had been coming over a few times a week since Fiona's mother died two years ago.

"I'm sorry love." She stopped. "But he passed away this morning. Very sudden like. We're all in shock. Lord have mercy."

The moment froze. An explosion in her heart. Fiona could picture Nell perfectly now, in her navy-blue apron with the tiny white and yellow flowers and minuscule green leaves, one of the wrap-around kind that ties up with multiple strings at the back. The receiver slipped down on to Fiona's shoulder and pressed into the flesh above her breastbone. She could hear Nell's voice, muffled, as if it were struggling through a long, narrow tunnel.

"Fiona, Fiona . . . are you still there? Fiona, pet?" Fiona dragged the phone from her aching chest, slid on to a high stool by the counter and bolstered up the receiver with her shoulder. She focused on the image of Nellie's flowery apron.

"Yes, Nellie, I'm here. Dad? Our Da? Maybe I . . ."

"I know, I know. It's hard to wrap your mind around it."

"But . . . he wasn't sick or anything. If I'd known he . . . Does Declan know?"

"None of us knew, love. It was his heart, God help us!"

And Fiona felt an answering beat in her own breaking heart. It was his heart that killed him—just like Mam. Dead hearts. She heard Nell's voice reverberate, repeating "his heart, God help us!" in what sounded like a ghostly whisper.

"I came over this afternoon, as I usually do of a Monday, to clean and straighten up the house a bit . . . and . . . Yes. I rang your brother just a few minutes ago. I tried the two of yous earlier but couldn't get a line, and then I was rushing around, here and there, sorting things out. He's going to see what he can manage out of—California, is it he's at?"

"Los Angeles."

"Right you be. We're giving him a good wake, child. Plenty of fiddlers—he'd have wanted that. It's all set for this Thursday evening, and then we'll have the removal on Friday and the funeral on Saturday."

Fiona's chest heaved. "Nellie, you're great. You must have been on the phone for hours. It should have been myself and Declan . . ."

"It's the least I could do, love. Your father was good to me always. Lord have mercy on his soul. And your Uncle Frank helped when he could. He's in bits himself, poor man."

Fiona's heart convulsed at the mention of her uncle, at the thought of him touching her dead father. His brother.

"I'll get the first flight out that I can manage. Thanks, Nellie, for everything." She heard her own quavering voice echoing back, and it blended with the high pitched scream of the kettle, which hissed and whistled for attention.

■ ■ ■

The next two days were a confusion of phone calls and tickets and arrangements as Fiona scrambled to get a seat on a flight to

Dublin. She played Billie Holiday and cried. She attempted to write but her concentration was shattered, and she finally had to ask her literary agent Pam to get an extension on the review. Pam was sweet and concerned as always. Fiona contacted Mrs. Frawley, the supervisor for her office cleaning job, and arranged to get a substitute for the next few nights. She knew Declan was bound to call but she dreaded hearing from him. One of them should have called the other in the intervening days, but Fiona knew Declan was as reluctant as she was to talk. They were going to have to deal with each other, though—there was the house, the land and a myriad of other details.

Fiona pulled the old brown suitcase out from the back of the press—the closet. Closet was one of those words, like faucet, that even after ten years sounded so American to her. She found herself constantly doing little translations in her head. The Irish words were coming back to her now that the trip was imminent. The press was where you hung your clothes and also where you put the food in the kitchen. Same word for closet and cupboard. And she liked taps better than faucet. Faucet sounded so formal. The old case was well past its prime—it was the same one she had used to go to boarding school in 1967 when she was twelve years old. She opened it up and saw her name written in black felt pen on the inside of the lid—Fiona Clarke, Cregora 21378. It brought back a rush of memories, of parting, severing ties, leaving home, tears held back. There were torn strips where the veneer had scraped off, and the handle was coming loose. Past its prime is right! But it would have to do—it had gotten her over and back across the Atlantic a few times now.

She let the phone ring twice and then turned down the volume on Piaf's "Non, Je Ne Regrette Rien" before picking up. She and her brother exchanged the barest of greetings, yet Fiona was surprised at how emotional she felt on hearing his voice. It brought the reality of their father's death home to her in a profound way. She and Declan were the last of their immediate family—Orla, Mam, and now Dad, all gone.

"I have to be back by Monday," she heard him say, "so hopefully Mr. Stanley can come out to the house Saturday evening and read the will for us."

Fiona froze as the old suspicions came rushing back. Mr. Stanley was their father's lawyer.

"You've talked with him?" She tried to keep the distrust out of her voice.

"No, just to Uncle Frank—he's arranging it for us."

Fiona pushed back her mounting fear and rage. "What has Uncle Frank to do with it? He shouldn't have anything to do with the will."

"Well, he is the executor. He's Dad's brother, after all. And it should be fairly straightforward. I'm sure we'll sort it all out."

"What's there to sort out?" she asked. "It's the house and the land. We'll sell it and divide it fifty-fifty."

There was silence on the other end. "I'm not sure I want to sell it. Some of the land maybe—but I'm fairly sure I'd like to hold on to the house."

Fiona was gob-smacked. She had never known her brother to have any particular affinity for the family home or the land. He was a successful psychologist, had a good job at a Los Angeles hospital, was happily married and had a young daughter. "What on earth would you want to keep it for, Declan? Why would you ever want to go back to Cregora?"

"I might want to visit, have it as a holiday home, take Julie and the kids in the summers. Julie is expecting again."

"That's great. Congratulations! Is she coming for the funeral?"

"No, she hasn't been too well the first month or so. Look, about the house . . . we'll talk in person about it."

Fiona wandered over to the window and glanced out. "Right. Okay. I hadn't even thought about . . ." Her voice broke. "He was only sixty-four, Declan."

The phone was silent for several beats on the other end. Piaf crooned mournfully in the background. Then Declan spoke, echoing her thought. "Bad hearts."

She nodded in silent agreement.

EYE OF THE STORM

Excerpt from a novel by Fiona Clarke

Something died inside of me when Aoife died. For a full year afterwards, I lay awake in bed every night, stony-faced and dry-eyed, thinking about where she might be, full of the certainty and the finality of death. An eternity without her. But something also died inside of Mam and Dad. Mam seemed to be frozen—closed down, and closed in. Many is the time I came upon her, sobbing, as she looked out of an upstairs window, thinking she was alone in the house. And other times I would see her gazing at a photo of Aoife, mesmerized. Like she could conjure her back to life by the sheer act of staring.

I was convinced that Mam didn't want or love me anymore. When I got sick, she fussed too much over me, as if you could die from a few sniffles or a stomach flu. And the rest of the time she kept her distance, like she didn't want to be too close, or she thought I was bad luck. No one said a word, but I knew they all blamed me for not taking better care of Aoife. And it seemed to increase the old favoritism of Conor, as if he were more cherished now. Did I remind Mam too much of Aoife just because I was a girl? Could she never forgive me? Did girls die more easily?

And then there was Dad. He just got quieter when he was at home and seemed to lose a lot of the old fun. And he stopped playing the violin, forever. He would listen to music on his old record player, 45's and sometimes 78's. He'd sit alone in the parlor, not doing anything else at all, just listening. He often left the door ajar so the music would float up and around the house. But at those times when I heard Heifitz or Bach or Stephane Grappelli (I would get to know the music later), it never soothed my soul the way Dad's violin playing had. An inescapable loneliness hung about the recorded music. It had absorbed the sadness of my father's listening.

Sometimes Dad would let me ride with him on the tractor. I stood next to him, anchored by the huge rim of the wheel, holding on to the back of the saucer-like seat as we traveled in stony silence around the field. I could see the pores on his face, the spiky disheveled eyebrows, the redness of the toughened skin from constant exposure to the elements and the strain of hard work in the lines around his eyes. On the turns I leaned in to the roughness of his gray work clothes, and breathed in the comforting smell of clay and sweet sweat. I could also intuit the sad rhythm of his suspiration, and knew, beyond a shadow of a doubt, that he was thinking of the daughter he had lost, not the flesh and blood girl beside him.

Aoife's name was rarely mentioned in the house outside of prayer, and when it was, it was as if she was a little saint. I started to resent her, and to hate myself for that ugly emotion. While she was alive, Aoife had always been the favorite, and she was the one I adored, too. Now that she was dead, she was still the favorite—I didn't merit attention. Every night the four of us—Mam, Dad, Conor, and I—got down on our knees after supper and said the rosary.

"Thou, O Lord, wilt open my lips."

"And my tongue shall announce thy praise."

"Incline onto my aid, O Lord."

"O Lord, make haste to help us."

After the five mysteries, Dad would pray for "our dearly departed," and Mam always added "for our little angel." A big photo of her now hung in the kitchen next to The Sacred Heart of Jesus and The Blessed Virgin Mary, so that from the moment of her death it was implanted in my psyche that this was the kind of company she was keeping. According to my parents, she was an innocent who had died without the stain of sin on her soul, so she was seated at the feet of Our Lord and Our Lady in Heaven. This omnipresent triad became, for me, the Blessed Trinity. The Golden Child was now part of a new Holy Family—our Aoife had been canonized.

CHAPTER TWO

WAKING

"One must still have chaos in one,
to give birth to a dancing star."
NIETZSCHE

The west coast of Ireland was spreading itself out below in its green morning splendor. It presented an endless array of fields of different shapes and sizes, dotted with white specks of sheep in the first light of dawn. The Shannon Estuary, where the eponymous river which wound its way through the center of Ireland flowed into the Atlantic Ocean, appeared peaceful on this early June morning, and Fiona tried to simulate the calm in her own heart. She had slept fitfully and awoke feeling anxious. She dreaded seeing her father laid out. She dreaded seeing Uncle Frank and her brother Declan. She feared the memories. As the plane descended, she could make out the details of the stone walls which separated the fields and were a feature of the west of Ireland. Then the plane made contact with the earth and the entire complement of passengers broke out in spontaneous clapping. Fiona thought it a peculiarly Irish custom, applauding the pilot for landing the plane safely. Wasn't he supposed to do that? Wasn't it his job? Maybe it was the Irish outlook, the pessimism, and the surprise when things went well.

After fueling in Shannon, the plane set off at eight o'clock for the last leg of the journey to Dublin. Now the entire panoply of green hues was laid out below, and it was not an exaggeration to count forty shades. Fiona could make out fields and farmyards, towns and villages, cars snaking along the roads, the endless miles of railway tracks. This was her country, her homeland, and now a lump arose in her throat at the thought of leaving it forever. With her father dead, she would have no reason to come back. The plane swept over her county, Westmeath in the Irish Midlands, then over Dublin, out over the Irish Sea to turn around and head back in to Dublin airport. She fought back the tears and contradictory emotions as the plane touched down.

At the Dublin station, she boarded the train for Mullingar, several miles from her family's home. She sat back and did her best to relax into the soft seats as the train chugged along and the countryside flashed by, passing fields with contented grazing cows, serene horses and back gardens with washing hung out to dry. The passenger opposite read *The Irish Independent* and she caught a glimpse of an article heading, "IRA claims responsibility for London bombing." The endless Troubles. An attendant in his navy uniform and peaked cap came by with his cart of tea, biscuits and sandwiches. Fiona got a strong, sweet, tea and savored her first cup of the local brew. She braced herself for the scene ahead. Hopefully she could face Frank, get through the pleasantries, and act, as always, as if he had not stolen her childhood. Spend as little time as possible with Declan, honor her father and pay her respects. They would deal with the will, act professionally and leave the details to the lawyer. How bad could it be? The tea did not disappoint—tea made in Ireland always tasted different to her, and she inhaled some courage and comfort. Maybe it was the water. Or that it tasted of home.

■ ■ ■

Fiona stood, suitcase in hand, and stared up at the middle window of the stately red brick house. The lace curtains fluttered in the early afternoon breeze, and her heart missed a beat when she thought of her father, laid out up there, dead. Part of her wanted to turn right back around and leave. Glued to the spot, she saw the corner of the kitchen curtains drawn back. In an instant Nellie was at the door, and Fiona fell into her arms.

Fiona buried her face in Nellie's shoulder. As soon as she felt the solid arms around her, she melted into tears. Nellie let her cry all she wanted and then ushered her gently into the softly lit kitchen where Fiona sank into a chair. Nellie put the kettle on for tea. Through her tears, Fiona followed Nellie's slow, sure progress around the kitchen, getting out the cups and saucers and spoons, pouring the milk into a jug, filling the sugar bowl, checking the bread in the oven. All against the background of soft, murmured conversation. Daily rituals, unhurried and comforting. Rituals Fiona's mother had performed in this kitchen all through her childhood and which, for Fiona, possessed a simple, unspoken richness. Nellie hadn't changed at all in the two years since Fiona was last home. Her fine hair had been snow white for years now, and she had it tied in a neat bun at the back of her head. She wore her trademark wrap-around apron. This one was bottle green with burgundy flowers and brown leaves, and it had patches of white flour dust on the skirt. The sweet smell of fresh baked bread began to waft from the oven.

■ ■ ■

Sustained by the strong, sweet tea, Fiona kept a firm grip on her old brown suitcase and slowly climbed the wooden staircase which had seemed endless to her as a child, but diminished in length every time she mounted it since. She wanted to delay the moment. She let her hand trail along the sleek smoothness of the banister. The clean, strong, smell of furniture polish caressed her nostrils as she counted seven, eight, nine, and there it was, the creak of the floorboard on the second last step. This creak had taken on a terrifying significance when she had started to listen in dread for her uncle's ascent. Ten steps to the first landing, now she counted them for herself to try and allay her fear of seeing her father's body. Turn right around and one, two, three, four steps up to the top landing, where the window looked out across the fields, a reprieve, then left through the door to the long landing and her parents' room on the left. All the floors were carpeted now in a downy teal that replaced the checkered linoleum of her childhood.

The door to her father's room stood ajar. A figure got up off her knees, blessed herself, and, as she left, muttered something softly to Fiona like, "Sorry for your trouble." Fiona wasn't sure she knew her, probably one of her father's many friends and acquaintances who were keeping vigil over the corpse. A corpse was not to be left alone at any time. Someone was supposed to stay to keep the spirit company until it was ready to leave the body—and that could be a long while after official death, so the saying went. Fiona's heart leaped when she thought of the old belief, that she might now be the keeper of her father's spirit. The neighbor moved so fast—a flash of gray—that Fiona didn't have a chance to see her properly or respond. Gone, like a will-o'-the-wisp.

Fiona's senses were assailed as she moved towards the doorway of the darkened room. A faint trace of frankincense filled her nostrils, lingering from the final sacred church rite of Extreme Unction. Dozens of white votive candles flickered and cast yellow shadows on the blue fleck wallpaper, lending an air of unreality to the scene. The full-length blue and gold curtains, sewn by Fiona's mother, were drawn tight so as not to let in any early afternoon light. Fiona braced herself as she forced her eyes to look. On the bedside table was a small statue of Jesus of the Sacred Heart, and a tiny St. Bridgit's cross. Her Dad had a great devotion to the Irish saint—allegedly the first (and only) female bishop of Ireland. His worn, leather-bound prayer book was there, too, and corners of holy-pictures and memorial cards of the dead stuck out from its pages. Fiona could picture her father reading his prayers, remembering all the friends and relatives, his wife and child included, who had gone before him, as he fingered his rosary beads and moved his lips in silent supplication. Although she herself no longer practiced the religion of her childhood, she envied her father the belief and the solace rituals provided him.

Through the smell of the sacramental incense, Fiona detected a faint aroma of Molton, the tobacco her father smoked in an occasional pipe. She had a memory flash of herself as a little girl, curled up in the warmth of his lap, as he read her the story of the Irish hero, Fionn mac Cumhaill, and the Salmon of Knowledge. Whoever ate the famous salmon, the story went, would gain all the knowledge in the world. Fionn did not catch the salmon himself but was given the task of cooking the fish and a stern warning not to taste it. While cooking, he burned his thumb, instinctively put it in his mouth for relief and was imbued with boundless wisdom. He became a brave and fearless warrior. Her Dad also told Fiona that her name was the female equivalent of Fionn, and that Fionn and Fiona both meant fair, or bright.

For the child Fiona, the magic of her father's words as he read to her was connected to the comforting tobacco smell which clung to his woolen pullover. She recalled the sound of his beating heart, the wondrous tale unfurling and a sweet sense of safety. Fiona smiled and hoped her Dad had thoroughly enjoyed a long and languorous last pipe.

Her smile released Fiona from a frozen posture. She finally put down her suitcase and let her eyes rest on the figure on the bed. The black, highly polished shoes, Irish size 12 (about 14 in the U.S.), the carefully pressed gray suit, white shirt and blue-gray tie, the shiny black rosary beads in his joined hands. The very same hands that had tilled the fields and coaxed beautiful melodies from his violin. Finally, the face, still strong and handsome, weather-beaten from a life of farming, much of the hair still red and thick except for the gray at the temples. He looked fit and sturdy, younger than his sixty-four years. Far too young to die.

Fiona knew that she should step over the threshold and go to him, but her feet were rooted to the spot. She wanted to think he was just asleep, and she wondered if his spirit had left his body yet.

Then, as she stared harder at the still face, she noticed the creeping pallor and was hit with the certainty that she was in the presence of death. A pounding cramp spiked her abdomen as she doubled over and sank to her hunkers. It was the same sickening hurt in the pit of her stomach that she had felt crouched in the corner of the bedroom she shared with Orla, all those years ago, after the storm. The bedroom that was just on the other side of this wall.

They were all around the bed. Mama, the Doctor dressed in black, Dada in the background, and Declan like a good elder son beside his Mam. Orla's fever-wetted, golden curls were flung out on the snow-white pillow, and she looked pale and lifeless. The doctor crouched over her and put the stethoscope to her chest to listen to the labored breathing. He whispered something to Mam and started to put away the instruments in his rumpled black bag.

Nine-year-old Fiona watched it all, everyone moving as in a dream, and she hoped she was invisible. She saw Mama pull the covers gently up to Orla's chin and then begin to show the doctor out. The doctor left, and Mama followed him, but not before she turned to Fiona and gave her a look that said, "You should have known better, she's your little sister and you should have known better." Declan, standing close to his mother, also looked at Fiona and echoed the accusing look. "Stupid girl," he seemed to say—his favorite taunt. "Silly, stupid girl."

In twenty-five years, Fiona had never managed to rid herself of her feelings of terror, guilt, and shame. A lifetime later, as she crouched in the doorway of another chamber of death, those accusing eyes were still boring into her.

■ ■ ■

Fiona thought that if she just stayed on course and navigated her way through the crowded room that she could avoid both Declan and Frank. The latter was nowhere in sight, but she could see her brother out of the corner of her eye. Why was he always so cocksure of himself, while she could never manage to be gracious even on the surface—to put on the face to meet the faces that you meet? He seemed so natural and relaxed out there, so skillful working the crowd, and he just off a plane from Los Angeles. He would have made a great actor or politician, if he hadn't become a shrink. Fiona felt pulled down by the blackness of her proper black dress and hoped that she was invisible. She had managed a few hours of fitful sleep before Nellie had knocked gently on the door to tell her it was time. Now, she pushed her sorrow and terror to the back of her consciousness and forged ahead.

The sounds of the room ebbed and flowed as Irish accents rose up and floated and shimmered and then descended. Fiona could make out the distinctively confident tones of her brother and, somewhere behind her now, Uncle Frank's lilting voice. She also heard the rising notes of a fiddle which played one of her Dad's favorite, old-time, Irish tunes, "The Minstrel Boy." A singer began the familiar opening lines—"The Minstrel Boy to the war is gone. In the ranks of death you will find him. His father's sword he has girded on. His wild harp strung behind him." It must be coincidence, she thought, that the fiddler chose this Thomas Moore song, seeing as her Dad hadn't picked up a violin himself since Orla died. Unless Declan had remembered. The whiskey was flowing, and baked ham and brown bread and fresh apple tarts were piled onto people's plates. A proper Irish wake.

Fiona had almost made it past the overflowing oak table and

round the curve to the kitchen when she and her brother were trapped simultaneously by a neighbor.

"My condolences Declan, but thank God it was fast—we have that to be thankful for."

"Thanks, Mr. Cusack," Declan replied simply, and before he could continue Mr. Cusack turned to her. "And is this your lovely wife, Declan? I don't believe I've had the pleasure." Fiona turned beet red.

"This is my sister, Fiona," Declan explained. "You must remember Fiona—she lives in the States, too."

"Well, glory be! Little Fiona! I think you were in knee socks the last time I saw you."

Fiona felt her color deepen.

"I was home two years ago, 1988, for Mother's funeral," she said.

"Oh, aye. God rest her soul. Grand woman, your mother. Your father was lost without her." He made the sign of the cross in respect for the dead.

"And is your wife here at all then, Declan?"

"She's in the early stages of pregnancy and feeling a bit off-color. Her doctor advised her not to make the long trip." Fiona detected the concern in Declan's voice.

"Well, I hope she'll be better, now, God bless her. But, isn't it grand for the two of yous, Declan and Fiona, to be living in America." Mr. Cusack droned on, and Fiona knew that he probably had a notion of them living nice and cozy, side by side, as if America were a little place like Cregora.

"I live with my family on the West Coast," Declan explained. "My sister lives in New York, on the East Coast."

"Oh, aye, aye, to be sure," Mr. Cusack nodded. "It's a grand big country over there, isn't it!"

"It's big all right." Declan agreed.

"You'd fit our little country into it many times over now, wouldn't you!"

And he slipped away leaving them alone in the midst of the crowded room.

Her brother hadn't changed much in the two years since their mother's funeral. He was almost six feet tall and solidly built with perfect carriage. His hair was a toned down version of the orange mop he sported as a child, and the close cut and California tan accentuated his strong chin and deep gray-blue eyes. He dressed with a casual elegance; his dark gray sports jacket and tailored pants perfectly suited the occasion. Fiona felt frumpy and pale by comparison.

"Nellie has done us proud." He broke the ice.

Fiona nodded.

"And everyone turned out for Dad."

Fiona quickly surveyed the room. "I hardly know anyone anymore. Where are they all from?"

"Around. The village. Dad was well liked, even if we weren't the most social of families—at least after . . ."

Orla, name unspoken, presence felt. Fiona felt the pushed-back fear tickling her insides, threatening to break loose.

"Stanley is here." Declan changed the subject. "He said tomorrow afternoon after the funeral would work for him to read the will. He knows we both have to go back, so we need to attend to business."

Fiona nodded. It seemed a bit indecent to have to deal with inheritance issues so soon, but there didn't seem to be a choice.

"And you still think you want to keep the house? Hold on to it?"

"It's our heritage, Fiona. Dad's family has been here since 1850—just after the Famine."

"I always thought you wanted to get away—you went farther even than me—all the way west."

"Well, maybe I've changed. Having a daughter . . . I'd like Una to know where she came from."

"But we weren't happy here." Fiona spoke *sotto voce*. "It's not like we had a blissful childhood. Why would you want to revisit bad memories?"

"Isn't that what you did in *Eye of the Storm*? Plough over that old territory?"

"Everything isn't therapy, Declan! My novel is just that, a novel!" She looked around uneasily to see if anyone had noticed her slightly raised voice, but the room buzzed with conversation—everyone engaged in their own chatter. The band launched into a rendition of "Fiddler's Green."

"At any rate," Declan continued, seemingly unruffled, "maybe I can buy you out. I couldn't do it right away. I'd have to figure something out, but eventually I could pay you your share."

"But you'd still be here. As long as you're still here, there'll be ties." She paused. "Knots." Her heart was racing.

"And we did have happy times here, Fiona. It wasn't all gloom and doom."

Before Fiona could respond, a tiny, white-haired woman, chin thrust forward, propelled herself like a dynamo into her path with outstretched hand.

"You must be Fiona," she announced, more a statement than a question. "I'm Mrs. Connelly from the far end of the village. I knew your father well, God rest his soul."

Fiona extended her hand as she reached back in her memory to find a match for this neighbor. "Thanks, Mrs. Connelly, thanks for coming."

"Lord, I wouldn't miss it for the world, child. Your father was a grand man, one of the best. He always talked about you two." Mrs. Connelly continued in a gushing stream, not pausing even for breath. "Every time I'd see him he'd give me the news from America."

Fiona was taken aback. "I didn't write as often as—" she started to blurt, but Mrs. Connelly was on a roll.

"He'd tell me about the stories you wrote and the things you published—he was proud as punch to have a daughter who was a writer—seeing as he always wanted to be a writer himself but didn't get the chance, like."

Fiona was dumbfounded by this information, completely new to her.

"I run the little bookshop down there, you know, next to the chemist. I bought out Miss O' Shaughnessy when she got a bit long in the tooth. Your father and I had great chats about books."

Now Fiona was starting to make sense of the picture, and she had just opened her mouth to fashion a reply when Mrs. Connelly interjected.

"And this must be your brother, Declan!" She swiveled to face him. "Still handsome as ever—Lord, but you were a beautiful baby!"

Fiona concocted an excuse about checking on the food and made a beeline for the kitchen. She was reeling from the encounter with Declan and also from Mrs. Connelly's monologue. Here was a neighbor from the other end of the village who knew things about her father that she herself did not even have an inkling of. He had never mentioned any desire to write or expressed any pride in her chosen profession or her tiny amount of success. As far as Fiona could remember, he had always been generally disapproving of the writer's life. He thought it was irresponsible for a grown woman to spend her time scribbling away, supporting herself mostly from cleaning offices, with nothing to show for it but a few stories and one book. A waste of a fine university education, is what he used to say.

Fiona unnecessarily shifted plates around and rearranged scones on serving dishes. Declan had always been the pretty boy, good in school, and now successful and well established. He had trained in a solid and lucrative profession and had a good job working in the psychiatric unit of a hospital. He lived in Marina del Rey, owned his own home and had apparently a nice settled family life. The American Dream. By comparison, she herself still felt adrift, cut off from family and ties, struggling to get a firm foothold in her career, raw and unsettled in her emotions. She could more or less control it all in New York. Everything had been going along fine in her safe haven, stashed away in the hugeness of the city, and now she was back in the thick of it, both Mam and Dad gone, leaving only herself and Declan. Her heart pounded with the heaviness of their shared grief, but the barrier was too wide. She could not extend herself to him. It was too confusing, too overwhelming. Her country, her family, drowned her.

The final words of the song emanated into the kitchen, "I'll see you someday on Fiddlers' Green," and Fiona recalled that the Fiddlers' Green of the title was where fiddlers went to die, a kind of heaven—a fitting place for her father to go. She choked back the tears and wondered why he hadn't kept up with the violin when he loved it so much. Fiona associated her reading to Orla in the hideout with her Dad's faraway melodies. "The Gypsy Rover" was one of her favorites, and when he played the melody she would sing the words in her head. "The whistling gypsy came over the hill, down by the valley so gaily. He whistled and he sang 'til the green woods rang, and he won the heart of a lady." And in her mind's eye she pictured the colorful gypsy, romantic and carefree, able to win the heart of a beautiful girl with his whistling, as her Dad was able to win hers from afar with his magical playing.

■ ■ ■

At about one in the morning, as they put the finishing touches to the clean-up, the house was eerily quiet. Emptied of its visitors, the stories and praises and songs seemed to linger, still, in the rose pattern on the heavy wallpaper, the strong lines in the dark wood floor, the family photographs which graced the walls. The old house was filled with the lived life of her parents and drove home to Fiona the sad finality of their passing. As she returned the china to its place in the dresser, she was conscious of her brother and her uncle moving around behind her, putting things away. She worked in silence, breath held, as Frank and Declan exchanged the occasional pleasantry. She hoped that she would not be left alone with Frank and would escape with the small talk they had exchanged during the course of the wake.

Her tasks completed, Nellie bustled out of the kitchen, removing her many stringed apron, just as Declan opened the Jameson and brought out some whiskey glasses.

"Will we have a night cap? Frank, Nellie, Fiona? In Dad's honor."

He was already pouring in anticipation. Frank eagerly reached out and claimed a glass, Declan poured one for himself, and, after a moment's hesitation, Fiona said yes.

"Nellie, a wee dram?"

Nellie laughed. "No thanks, Declan. I think I'll head off home—tomorrow maybe, before you go, I'll raise a glass to your Da."

"I'll walk you home, then, Nell." Declan set his glass aside, and Fiona's heart skipped a beat.

"Not at all pet, shur' it's only down the way a bit. I'll be grand."

"Arra, I'm not letting you out there on your own—never know who might run away with you!" Declan replied jokingly.

"A cow or stray sheep maybe!" Nellie laughed. "Sit there and enjoy your *uisce beatha*."

But Declan had made up his mind. "I'll be back in two shakes of a lamb's tail. Come on, I'll get your coat."

Fiona felt her tears well up again as she hugged Nellie goodbye out in the hallway.

"Hush, hush, *macoushla*." Nellie soothed as she rubbed Fiona's back. "He's gone to a better place, by the grace of God."

When the outside door banged shut, it hit Fiona that she was now alone with the person she hated most in the world. Maybe the only person she truly hated.

She and Frank sipped their whiskeys in silence for a while. Frank's resemblance to their father was uncanny, unsettling. He was slighter in build, but had the same strong jaw line and the same red hair, though Frank still had his moustache. Fiona thought his dark green eyes were harder, colder.

"And I believe the writing is going well then, Fiona? Any more novels?"

Fiona winced. Not having a second novel in the pipeline was a sore point.

"Not yet. A few stories. I'm mostly working on reviews at the moment."

She noticed that Frank had already made a dent in the whiskey.

"I read your novel, you know. Very good it was. A fine read."

Fiona nodded. They sipped in silence. She knew that Frank was not much of a reader of fiction—here he differed hugely from her dad who loved to read. Frank had read the local newspaper every day of his life and was always well informed about current events. Fiona recalled walking by his bakery and waving to him on her way to school. He would smile broadly and wave back as he turned the pages of the paper. He had never shown the slightest bit of interest in fiction.

"Nice characters. All nice people."

"It's all . . . well, I based it on what I know of course, but . . ."

She stared at him and then immediately averted her gaze.

"A nice story of growing up on a farm, in Ireland."

Fiona wanted to scream. She wanted him to stop using the word nice. She knew he had only read the book to see if there was a character based on him, and if so, if he was "nice." And there was. And he was.

Silence.

"Your father made me the executor, you know."

She nodded.

"Declan said you wanted to sell the house."

"Yes."

"But he wants to keep it."

"Right."

Frank cleared his throat and partook of another sip of whiskey. "Well, that could be a sticking point, you see."

Fiona was puzzled. Her old fear of Frank came coursing back. Frank looked at her and fingered his mustache, as if he were contemplating a problem.

"It's like this. Your father put in a stipulation that the two of yous need to agree on what to do about the house and the land. He didn't want you split on the issue."

Fiona made a supreme effort to try and keep calm. She looked at Frank.

"Why on earth would he do that? He knows we don't agree on much. He knew . . ."

"And that's why he wrote that in the will. He wanted the two of you to make up, to see eye to eye, come to an agreement."

"But, but . . . if we can't . . . we obviously want different things." Fiona's frustration was rising with the fear in the pit of her stomach.

"It mattered to him." Frank sounded infuriatingly calm and collected. "And that's why he asked me to help. To be a mediator in a way. To help you to work it out."

Fiona tried to keep her voice even. "Mediator? In what way? How can you do anything if Declan and I can't agree?"

"Well, you see, your father gave me the power to cast the deciding vote, if you like, in the case of a disagreement. It's not what he wants, but if there isn't a way to work it out, whoever I side with—having spent good time, mind you, listening to both sides—whoever I side with will get their choice."

Fiona fought the urge to stand up and scream.

"What did Declan say when you told him?" Her voice came out small and squeaky. Childlike. "He must have been furious."

"Oh, I didn't say a word to Declan yet. It's our little secret, Fiona."

The word sent a maelstrom of emotion swirling through her head and entire body. She wanted to say—how can it be a secret? What's secret about it? He'll find out tomorrow when the will is read.

"Our secret is that I will be on your side. I can put the pressure on to sell all and divide it between you. I can break the tie if the two of you can't agree." Frank paused and looked at her. "You'll be free."

Fiona was wrenched with a confused mix of emotions. Frank was backing her up to buy her silence on a topic she couldn't speak of anyway, his childhood abuse of her. He was the only one she had ever spoken to about her hesitation in getting Orla out of the hide-out during the storm. She felt bound to him, locked in that exchange of secrets, and he knew he could count on her paralysis. She had made "him" nice in the novel. He who had stolen her childhood was offering her freedom. And she would take it, because she needed more than anything to get out and leave it all behind. *Tabula rasa.* A clean slate. She gulped down the rest of her whiskey, welcoming the punishing heat in her throat and the temporary sense of distance it afforded her.

■ ■ ■

Fiona recalled the long nights after Orla's death, the lonely nights when she cried herself to sleep under the blankets. She shed no tears, her ducts were sealed, but it was crying all the same, a dry, soundless crying from despair and loss. Her parents told her Orla had gone to heaven and was happy. She tried to imagine her in the presence of God, little baby Jesus and the Virgin Mary. Downstairs, she could hear the grown-ups talking. She couldn't hear their words, but she could register the tones of their voices and the cadence of their talk. Mam spoke softly and brokenly and her voice lilted with a slight sibilance; Dad's voice was low and sad and tried to be strong; Uncle Frank's was a bit higher than Dad's, shaky and halting. Uncle Frank visited a lot now, every Friday and Saturday night and often during the week as well. He would bring a fresh loaf or two of bread and his smell of the bakery. Fiona had noticed another smell when he bent to kiss her cheek. It was sharp and pungent and unpleasant. It was the same smell Dad had sometimes if he went out to the pub on the weekend, which he now did less and less. He didn't have the heart for socialization and music any more. Now, they sat down in the parlor, with the fire lit to keep away the autumn chill—and cups of tea, and whiskey for the men, to keep away the inner chill. They were a shattered group with a magnetic pull towards each other for a comfort that was beyond their grasp.

Fiona remembered the visits of the adults to kiss the children goodnight. Sometimes one or both of their parents would come up, sometimes Uncle Frank. They would go in to Declan in his room at the top of the landing, and then they'd come through the other door into the next landing, past her parents' empty room and into hers. After lights out they usually closed over the outer landing door so the light wouldn't keep her awake. Fiona preferred it to be left slightly ajar as she liked to hear the rise and fall of the droning voices, sometimes the television sounds. Noises helped to hold back the cold empty silence.

Her parents' goodnight kisses had become more automatic and robotic since Orla's death. They still leaned over, brushed against her cheek and pulled up the clothes to her neck if she had fallen half-asleep. Sometimes one of them turned out the light and the other would check on her when they came upstairs for bed. Uncle Frank started to do that, come in to say goodnight if he came upstairs to use the bathroom. He'd bend down and kiss her cheek, and she'd smell the bakery smell and sometimes that other smell she came to associate with the yellow whiskey. When Fiona had confided in Frank her guilt over her part in Orla's death, all he had said was "Hush, hush. It wasn't your fault, little one." Fiona knew it was, but was grateful that she had been able to share the secret, grateful that he still loved her in spite of her sin. He'd often whisper something soft like "Goodnight, little Fiona, sleep with the angels." Sometimes, he too would adjust the covers so she would be warm, and then he would leave the room and cross back down to the bathroom. A little later she'd hear the flush and his footsteps going back downstairs to join her parents.

The night his breath went into her mouth she thought it must have slipped over from her cheek by accident. He whispered "Goodnight, my little one" as he leaned over in the half-dark. Then, his mouth was over hers, and it was hard to breathe. She was afraid to move. His breath was heavy and strong, and then she felt his hand go down to pull up the sheets, but it went under the blankets and her nightdress and Fiona froze and stared at the sliver of the moon as it peeked through the almost fully drawn curtains. His beard and face were in the way, but she could see around the blur of the hairs, and she studied the shape of the moon intently. It was hardly there. Like a thin sliver of an arc—suspended. And for an interminable moment the fingers fumbled and his breath grew harsh and urgent and he breathed out abruptly and pulled back with a start. She could feel his stare though she did not look. All her attention was on the moon. Just as suddenly as the onslaught began he was her kind uncle again and pulled the covers up gently around her neck and whispered, "It will be our secret, Fioneena. We will keep each other's secrets." And he touched her cheek and left. Closed over the door, visited the bathroom, flushed, and went back down the stairs.

It was the first of many visits.

EYE OF THE STORM

Excerpt from a novel by Fiona Clarke

"Which of you wrecked the bike and left it stuck out in the ditch?" Dad took another gulp of soup. "Sheila? Conor? It had to be one or the other of you. I saw it out there just before I came in."

The two of us glared at each other as if each expected the other one to speak. Naturally, I was waiting for Conor to own up as I had just seen him flying around on it ten minutes before.

"Sheila did it."

I was gob-smacked at this bare-faced lie and jumped in to defend myself, but Dad cut me off.

"Don't lie, Sheila. You need to own up to what you do."

I continued to protest but Dad wasn't listening, had decided little sweet-faced, butter-wouldn't-melt-in-his-mouth Conor was telling the truth.

"I don't want to hear any excuses. You need to learn the value of things, of property. That bike was bought for both of you with money earned from the sweat of my brow and you won't be getting another."

We ate the rest of the meal in silence. The succulent lamb, one that Dad had reared himself, fresh turnips and parsnips, flowery new potatoes with lashing of runny butter. All spoiled for me. Through the mouthfuls, I thought sadly of the poor old bike lying in the ditch out back. And I thought of Conor's lying mouth that I'd give anything to wash out with carbolic soap. My stomach knotted up and I couldn't finish my strawberry jelly and ice cream. Mam caught me moving my spoon around and told me to clear my plate, and then Dad threw in the starving babies in Africa. So out of guilt and obedience, I scraped my dish clean and felt even sicker.

■ ■ ■

I found Conor out in the barn about an hour later. There he was, happy as Larry, lying flat on his stomach in the straw with all his metal toy soldiers lined up on slabs of wood, ready for battle. He was simulating noises for his warriors and so didn't hear me come in and creep quietly up behind him. I dropped to the ground and started thumping him on his back as hard as I could. "Liar! Liar! Liar! Liar!" I shouted, getting more vehement with every thump. He just started laughing, made a few maneuvers with his soldiers and then pushed me away so that I fell over sideways onto the straw.

"I'm not a liar," he said, nonchalantly, "because people always believe me."

"That's because you're pretty and won a baby contest with your lovely red curls and innocent face!" I knew this would get a rise out of him. He was fierce embarrassed about the baby contest he won when he was six months old.

"Don't you call me pretty." He snarled. "Boys aren't pretty!"

I picked myself up and brushed off the stalks from my shoulders.

"Pretty! Pretty! Pretty!" I teased. "Pretty Conor, pretty Conor!"

That did it. He sprung up and roughly grabbed my arm. "Take it back," he ordered. "Say you're sorry and take it back. Just 'cause YOU're ugly!"

I felt a stinging behind my eyes but forced myself to not cry. I knew I wasn't pretty. I knew that.

"Sticks and stones . . . " I started, but he twisted my arm even harder. " . . . may break my bones . . . Ouch, let go, you're hurting me!" I tried to disengage my arm but he had a solid grip.

"Not 'til you say you're sorry, Ugly Face! Say it!" He gave my arm another fierce twist, and I honest to God thought it was going to snap. Still, I held out. "But words can never . . . ouch!"

"Go on," he goaded. "Say it, say you're sorry!"

A further unmerciful twist, and I couldn't take it any more. I thought my very shoulder would pop out of its socket. "All right, all right, I'm sorry," I squealed. "Let me go!"

He released me, and I reclaimed my arm, all red and sore and twisted. I jumped up and headed for the door, holding onto my aching limb. At the barn door I turned and threw a parting shot back at him.

"You're a liar and a bully, Conor Flaherty, and I hate you! I'll hate you forever!"

He just chuckled and went back to his lazy afternoon soldiers.

CHAPTER THREE

TIME PAST

"Time present and time past
Are both perhaps present in time future
And time future contained in time past."

T.S. ELIOT—*Burnt Norton*

The night of her father's wake, after Frank had left and Declan gone up to bed, Fiona tarried in the kitchen. She heard Declan's footsteps fade as he ascended the staircase and stepped onto the landing. Every inch of this house was familiar and intimate, each sound resonant of both tender and terrible encounters. And Mam, Dad and Orla seemed palpably close.

The deep silence which descended when Declan closed his bedroom door reminded Fiona of Good Fridays when she and her mother polished the silver cutlery. They, like many Catholics, observed three hours of silence between twelve noon and three o'clock, the time that Jesus hung on the cross. They sat side by side at this very table and slowly and methodically burnished the silver with a soft cloth and silver polish. It was one of her favorite moments in the whole year. Time slowed down. The mantle clock ticked. The cloths swished. Fiona and her Mam's breathing were barely audible. From time to time, they caught each other's eye and smiled. The tines of the forks were challenging, but the most difficult were the egg spoons. Something about the sulfur that turned the spoons greenish. The gentle motion back and forth was soothing in its rhythm. It was a magic time for Fiona when she could love her mother completely without ever exchanging a word. Just a sweet, serene, shared silence.

Fiona took the whiskey glass she had refilled, lifted the big latch on the yard door and stepped out into the night. There was nothing like it. This cool fresh air and the clear night sky. Having lived in New York City for ten years, she had almost forgotten how crystal clear a night sky could be, how startlingly brilliant the moon and stars, how profound the silence.

Fiona walked through the yard, crunching the gravel on the path, aware of every sound and of the feel of the soil under her feet—her family's land. Soon she stood by the huge oak tree at the top of the cornfield, and by the light of the moon she saw that the structure of the tree-house was still intact. Nature had carved it—a rounded womb-like chamber—out of the giant trunk. It was a perfect hide-away, and as a child, Fiona saw the possibilities. She had built an elaborate camouflage system of leaves and twigs and branches, casually placed against the opening as if by chance and nature. She had hauled crates and apple boxes and used burlap sacks to line the inside, making it into a cozy secret home. She knew somehow that this was the place. The place to make her private domain. The place to escape from the pain of her mother's absence when she went away to the sanatorium. The place to cradle Orla.

The adult Fiona was still able to squeeze inside. She sipped her whiskey and recalled Orla waiting for her to come home from school, her curly golden hair like a halo round her luminous face, the big brown eyes waiting and hoping for further adventures. They were far enough away from the house that it felt like a real hide-away, yet near enough to hear Dad if he called them or practiced the violin. The day of the storm it felt as if they were trapped in a separate universe, the distance to the house impossible to cover. At that moment, as if cued by her recall of that past storm, the heavens opened. The rain began to pound without warning on the earth, the lightning illuminated the interior of the treehouse and the thunder rumbled like the growling of the gods. Crouched inside the ancient bark, Fiona felt nine years old again, hearing the same sounds and staring at the vision of her sister encircled by light. She remembered with a sharp stab of pain. Like a birth pang, it seemed to come from deep inside her, ripped away with an unmerciful fierceness from that secret place where she had tried to bury it all and make it disappear.

■ ■ ■

Fiona and Declan watched Frank and the pallbearers as they moved their father into the handsome mahogany coffin. Since the conversation with Frank the night before, Fiona's head had been in a swim as she anticipated the inevitable showdown at the reading of the will. They lifted their father off the bed, laid him down in the satin-lined box, waited respectfully until Fiona and Declan gave a signal, and then closed the lid. It was eerily reminiscent of their mother's removal not so long ago. It was all happening so fast, a last glimpse, and then gone. She wondered if Declan remembered Orla leaving the bedroom next door in her tiny white coffin, so small it seemed like a toy.

She relived the two earlier journeys as they traveled through the house and down the stairs to the waiting hearse. Fiona felt a momentary stab of pity for her uncle who sat in the seat in front of Declan and herself. He was staring out the window looking desolate, lost in thought. No doubt he, too, was reliving the series of deaths more than twenty-five years ago which had wiped out his small family and his hopes for the future. As their father's hearse wound its way around the familiar roadways, a sharp drizzle began to fall.

After the memorial mass, the pallbearers mounted the coffin on their shoulders, steadied it and marched to the graveside. Declan, Nellie's husband Ignatius, and Frank were in the vanguard. As Fiona stood facing the black hole that was her father's grave, she could see her sister's tombstone with the inscription: "In Loving Memory of our daughter Orla. Died September 7th, 1963, aged 4 years." And her mother's: "For my loving wife, Anna. Died February 20th, 1988." She caught a glimpse of her Aunt Rita's grave and that of the little baby buried with her, and she became aware that Frank was making an effort not to turn towards it. Fiona was afraid to let herself cry in public for fear of unleashing the floodgates. The neighbors huddled against the lashing rain. The priest droned on as he recited his incantations, and the mourners echoed back his blessings in response—"everlasting peace," "in the bosom of Our Savior." Fiona watched the pallbearers lower her father's coffin on ropes into the gaping hole. She shuddered at the sight of the black earth as it moved in mesmeric slow motion, separated out like strands of dark cloying hair and landed with a thump on the wood below. The mourners drifted over to the family, shook hands, whispered soft words and began to filter away from the graveside. A small hilly mound of fresh brown earth rose up, leaving only traces in memory of the man below.

■ ■ ■

They were seated formally around the heavily polished oak table. Mr. Stanley, the family lawyer, Frank, Declan and Fiona. Declan was fuming. Fiona tried hard to act surprised and puzzled. Frank was poker-faced. Declan glared at Mr. Stanley as if the unwelcome clause was his fault.

"Well, can we agree to disagree?" he was grasping at straws. "What if Fiona and I decided that it's okay for me to buy her out so that I can keep the family home?"

Stanley shook his head. "I'm afraid not. It's stated clearly that you both have to reach consensus on whether to keep the house and land, or to sell. And the house must remain in both of your names until such time as one of you dies, or you mutually agree to sell it. Your father wasn't concerned with your holding on to the property, merely that you attain agreement regarding the outcome."

Fiona tried hard to look neutral as she knew what was coming.

"And," Stanley continued, "if there's a failure to reach an agreement, Mr. Francis Clarke is designated to act as intermediary in an attempt to negotiate an understanding."

Declan was flabbergasted. Fiona could see that he was struggling to maintain his composure. He now turned his ire on Frank.

"Can you enlighten us about this, Uncle Frank? What exactly will be the nature of the intermediation?"

Frank smiled disarmingly, and Fiona felt a wave of guilt and shame for having anything to do with him.

"It's all very simple, Declan, really. Your father wanted me to help out, that's all. His wish, you know, was to have his children happy and in accord. I'll try to help if I can."

Before Declan could reply, Mr. Stanley intervened.

"Excuse me. But we need to continue with the formalities of the will, so I need to record both of your wishes and then proceed from there. If I may?" And he politely looked towards Fiona.

"Fiona, could you please let me know your preference regarding selling or keeping the land and the property?"

Fiona cleared her throat and tried to sound firm and convincing. She had been rehearsing this for hours in her mind. "I would like to sell it. Both the house and the land." Despite her best efforts her voice quavered.

Mr. Stanley recorded her response and then turned to Declan and posed exactly the same question.

"I want to keep it. I'd like to keep it all. And I'm in a financial position to eventually raise the money to pay my sister the market value for her half of the property."

Stanley duly noted Declan's comments and then looked at Frank.

Frank cleared his throat importantly and looked from Fiona to Declan. "Do either of you have an opinion regarding each other's choice? I'm not saying this will have any bearing on the outcome, mind you, but maybe it will help us reach some common ground."

Fiona hated him more by the second. He was a wolf in sheep's clothing. She hated herself for feeling even a moment of compassion for him earlier that day at the funeral. In her mind, he was a mean and devious man, but he also held her in thrall. And she had to escape his clutches.

Just as she was about to speak, Declan asked if the two of them could have a moment alone. Stanley nodded, and he and Frank walked towards the kitchen, closing the door behind them.

"Fiona, I have no idea what Dad was up to, but it seems really pointless to hold us hostage like this." Declan was livid.

"Well, I can see his point" Fiona rejoined. "This is the only big joint decision we'll ever have to make, and he wants us to try and agree. Mind you, I think that's a tall order. Just saying I understand his impulse."

"Yes, but look at our choices. We have to agree to let it go completely or to co-own."

"And I want to let it go completely. Declan, can't you see how much better that would be? Your life is in the States now. And you could buy a house here in Ireland if you want to come and visit. A house somewhere in the countryside, if that's what you want for your family."

"No, I want this house!" He was vehement. "You'll get what you want either way. You'll get the same amount of money eventually and can use it as you want."

"But not my freedom. If you stay here you will keep the family connection."

"But you won't have to come. I mean you'd be welcome if you wanted to, but there would be no obligation."

"But I'd know you were here. That your children were here. Here in this house."

"And why is that bad? I know there are a lot of bad memories, Fiona, but there were a lot of happy ones too, if you'd let yourself remember them. We're a new generation. Our children are a newer generation."

Fiona was struck by his use of "our children," the mere mention of the possibility that she might have children. She flashed on the memory of Declan serenading her with the song about "dying an old maid in the garret."

"But the memories. They're ingrained. Maybe as a psychologist you believe they can be excavated and purged . . ."

"Or maybe as a writer you believe the same thing?"

"I write because I have to. I always thought that if I didn't have to spend so much time making ends meet . . . I honestly never even thought about our 'inheritance'—Mam and Dad were so young. We're only in our thirties." Fiona choked up at the thought of both of her parents gone—and so much unfinished business.

Declan nodded and then indicated the door. "They're outside, waiting."

Fiona tried to get her emotions in check.

"I don't want to give up this house." Declan resumed. "I can't let our past, our history vanish just like that."

"Our past is locked in my brain, in my body. I want to let the house go, be free."

"You are full of contradictions, Fiona. I know that a part of you loves this place; a piece of your heart is here. And yet you want to fling it away. My past and my history are here, too, not just your version. I can't let you throw it away so blithely."

"We're at their mercy then."

"Yes. The lawyers. And Uncle Frank. I find it hard to believe Uncle Frank would let all that Dad worked for just vanish like that, pass into the hands of strangers."

Fiona was affected by Declan's passion. It seemed like his desire to hold on to the home of their childhood was equal to her need to be rid of it. She realized that she didn't know him, her only brother, now her only surviving immediate family member. They had grown into strangers and established separate lives, and now they floated in this same orbit around the planet of their home. Declan was part of the pain, specific and general, that was trapped in the fabric of this house, and she was aware that in letting it go she was letting him go, too.

■ ■ ■

Her victory felt hollow to Fiona as, up in her bedroom, she wandered about putting the finishing touches to her packing. This was her old bedroom, the girls' room, the one she had shared with Orla. The wallpaper was the same—pale blue with a light rose flower pattern. The double bed against the back wall had a wooden headboard with an inlay design of leaves which Fiona and Orla had delighted in tracing with their fingers.

Frank's voice reverberated in her head. "All I'm saying is that I can see Fiona's side of things."

She folded the black dress into the battered brown suitcase, and her brother's heated response echoed in her head.

"And you can't see mine—the value of keeping the property in the family?"

Beside the wardrobe, a tall bookshelf held some of her books from childhood, school and university, a collection ranging from Louisa May Alcott, through the Brontës, Jane Austen, John Keats, Samuel Beckett and D.H. Lawrence. Her *Alice in Wonderland* stood next to a poetry collection of T.S. Eliot. Fiona opened up the book and read the inscription, "Christmas 1962, Love to Fiona, from Auntie Rita and Uncle Frank." Her godparents.

"Your father's wish was that if the place were to stay in the family it would be owned by the both of you—not just one of you. So what you want, Declan, is not one of the options. What Fiona wants is."

Fiona had a sudden memory of a younger Frank, smelling of fresh baked bread, and of Auntie Rita, small and thin, always by his side. Her legs were the same shape all the way up and looked like twigs. Her head always reminded Fiona of a round rosy apple that had just been polished up with a soft cloth. It was tiny and heart shaped, and there were two big pinkish red spots right in the middle of her white cheeks. When Fiona asked her Mama why it was that Aunt Rita and Uncle Frank didn't have any children, she said that it was because God hadn't blessed them with any yet. Aunt Rita had two little babies who were born before their time and then died, and, please God, they might be able to have a healthy baby yet, Mama added. When Aunt Rita gave Fiona *Alice in Wonderland* for Christmas, she was very bubbly and happy and the pink circles on her cheeks were even brighter than usual. When Mam came back home from the sanatorium in February she told Fiona that her aunt was going to have a baby and that, God willing, it would arrive in the summer. And it did, a little girl, full term, dead two hours before birth, strangled by the umbilical cord. Aunt Rita died half an hour after delivery.

Frank started to drink heavily after the untimely deaths. Fiona wondered if he had had a shot or two of whiskey while in the kitchen with the lawyer that afternoon. His voice had been excitable and his color a tad high.

"Would you not think of selling up, Declan, and moving on with your life in America? It seems like the sensible thing to do."

"Are you supposed to take sides, Uncle Frank? I thought your job was to mediate?" Declan could barely control his rising anger. He turned to the lawyer.

"Is it possible to sell the house to my wife Julie?"

Mr. Stanley shook his head. "I'm sorry, Declan, but your father worked with me to be sure his wishes were crystal clear. There's a clause that specifically states that the house can not be sold to another family member. So, I'm afraid the two of you will need to come to terms with the conditions. You do have three months from today." His voice was calm and measured. "Talk in the meantime, back in the States. You have until the end of the summer. And I'll provide you both with complete copies of the will."

"Yes, yes." Frank was excitable, "but wouldn't it be better to get it settled now with the two of you in the one room? I think your father would have wanted that."

Fiona sensed that Frank was the one who wanted so desperately to put the past behind him. She recognized the edge of panic, carefully controlled, as one recognizes oneself in a cloudy mirror. But Declan was not going to cooperate.

"I can get other legal counsel if I wish. I'll consult my lawyer. And I can wait three months."

It was his right. And anxious as Fiona was now to move through the window of escape that had presented itself, she realized that three months was not that long to wait. She had plenty of work to occupy her, and maybe she could actually get started on that second novel.

She plopped her copy of *Alice* in the suitcase and then picked up her mother's tea cozy that she had found in a kitchen drawer. Her eyes brimmed with tears as she let her fingers travel over the textured linen and trace the pattern on the hand-embroidered cloth. She had very few mementos of her mother—part of her ongoing effort to avoid the past, to keep memories at bay. She explored it thread by thread, as if it were a map. Deep pink and purple flowers with yellow centers, pale green stalks, carefully wrought. It was a miniature garden sown by her mother's hands. Then she picked up her father's diary. He had willed this to her and his violin to Declan, the only personal items he had assigned specifically in his will. She untied the brown shoelace and selected a page at random.

"May 15th, 1961. Just got back from the sanatorium. It breaks my heart to see my lovely Anna so weak and worn out. She's fighting as hard as she can, but the doctors aren't hopeful—then again they gave her six weeks to live over a year ago, and she's still hanging on for dear life. She's heart-broken that she can't see the children, but it's too dangerous, and of course the doctors won't allow it. She's afraid they'll lose all memory of her, and today she said that maybe that was for the best, so they wouldn't be so torn up when she died.

Fiona was mesmerized. That her father had written down some of his innermost thoughts and feelings and that he wanted her to have access to them. She read on.

"I got the shock of my life when I got back and saw Fiona and Nellie huddled over a doll that Fiona was making. She got this notion a while back of making a doll of Anna, so Orla wouldn't forget her, she said. So, I went along with the scheme and got her the bits and bobs to make a doll. Nell has been helping with the cutting and so on, though Fiona herself was already a fine little seamstress for a child who just turned seven. What put the heart crossways in me was the sheer likeness, the doll was the spitting image of Anna. It was as if she captured a bit of her spirit while making the imitation—uncanny it was.

Little Fiona gave me a big hug and proudly showed off her handiwork. Then she announced that she and Nellie were going to the shops on their bikes to get some trim for the doll. She said Orla was having a little sleep and Declan was keeping an eye out for her, as he worked on his crossword puzzles. She has the whole household organized! And she's a resilient little lady. As she was leaving she informed me that she didn't need any money because she had some left over from last time, and then she thrust the doll in my arms.

'You can mind Mama 'til we get back, Dad. That way you won't be lonely!'

My heart was aching all over again as I slipped Nell a few pounds. I sometimes wonder how much heartache a body can endure."

Fiona closed the pages gently, pushing its secrets back inside. Her father's private grief. She was struck by her Dad's characterization of her, her sunny disposition and determination. Her resilience. Where had all that gone? She slipped the diary inside her mother's tea-cozy—she would save the rest for later.

She felt a soft, blurry sensation all over, a vagueness. Fiona discounted it having anything to do with the generous shot of Irish whiskey she was nursing. She had taken to having a glass at night while she was here—it gave her comfort. But this sensation, it came from something else. She felt they were in the room with her, the spirits of this old house. They seemed to be all around. They didn't follow or frighten her, they just hovered, and cast a gossamer thin veil over her head and form and clung to her body.

She nearly jumped out of her skin at the sound.

"Sorry, did I frighten you? I knocked several times, and you didn't answer." It was Declan. His voice was cold, formal. "I'm going to be leaving early in the morning."

Fiona noticed that her brother was carrying a glass of whiskey, too. Was this place and each other's company turning them both into sots?

"We have to work it out, don't we?" she offered.

"We have three months. I plan to fight as hard as I can. Frank is on your side, so I seem to be outnumbered, but I plan to explore all legal avenues."

Fiona looked him square in the face. "I'm going to fight my corner, too."

Declan nodded. "I'll try to contact you in a couple of weeks." He looked tired. "I'm a bit pre-occupied with Julie at the moment. She's still not well, and she's all on her own with Una." Declan's voice catapulted Fiona across the Atlantic, and she had a stab of regret that she had never made the effort to visit her brother's family. She realized that their daughter Una must be about seven by now.

"When is she due?"

"December, around Christmas. Actual due date is the 23rd."

The day before Orla's birthday, Fiona thought. She had been a Christmas Eve baby.

"Maybe we can work it out over the phone?" Fiona suggested, unconvincingly.

"Or meet up with Frank half way?" Declan countered, jokingly.

"In Kansas City?" she smiled, and placed her hands over a set of imaginary guns in imaginary hip holsters—remembering the game of Cowboys and Indians they had often played as children. She realized that Kansas City really was about half way—as children these names had mythical resonance, not clearly connected to a concrete place.

"How's about Dodge?" Declan laid his glass on the chest of drawers and matched her gesture by letting his hands hover over his own imaginary pistols.

"At High Noon?" she proffered.

"With pistols drawn!" They spoke in unison and drew their guns simultaneously. They held the stand-off for a minute, fully cognizant of the real tension beneath the game. Then they released their hands, lifted their whiskey glasses, took a drink but did not toast. Declan said goodnight and started for the door. As he was leaving Fiona called his name and he turned back around.

"I think," she said, "that we should both have our hearts checked."

He stared at her for an instant and then realized what she meant. A momentary softening. "Yeah. But they didn't have any history, did they, either of them?"

Fiona shook her head. "Not that I know of. But we do now."

Declan nodded, and left.

Fiona reached for her Eliot collection and sought out her favorite passages from *Burnt Norton*.

> *"Time present and time past,*
> *Are both perhaps present in time future,*
> *And time future contained in time past."*

She thrilled at the mystery of the lines, the confusion, the deliberate mixing up of past, present and future. Like Alice hurtling down the rabbit hole and landing in Wonderland.

> *"Footfalls echo in the memory,*
> *Down the passage which we did not take,*
> *Towards the door we never opened,*
> *Into the rose-garden."*

Fiona added this to her collection in the suitcase, clamped it shut and laid herself down to rest.

EYE OF THE STORM

Excerpt from a novel by Fiona Clarke

In the middle of my second term at St. Catherine's boarding school, I failed the first ever exam in my life—Science. I was mortified. All through primary school, I was among the top three in my class but never attributed this to any cleverness on my part. Neither my parents nor teachers had ever paid a compliment or passed any remark at all to indicate that this was good, bad or indifferent. And I wondered if maybe I really was stupid like Conor was always saying I was.

I was summoned to the Reverend Mother's office. Such a summons was an indication that you had done something particularly bad, so bad that the ordinary nuns felt it needed to be attended to by a higher authority, and that higher authority was The Very Reverend Mother Mary Assumpta. Since all nuns were married to Jesus, hence the middle name of Mary, I assumed that Mother Assumpta must have the status of one of the principal wives.

The first thing I noticed, after I knocked on the door and walked in, was the abundance of books and piles of papers strewn about the office. For some reason, I found this comforting in my terror. There were a few holy pictures on the walls, one of Jesus and Mary and one of the namesake of the order, St. Catherine. My eye also picked out a plaque which denounced the Seven Deadly Sins. I could recite them in my sleep—Pride, Covetousness, Lust, Anger, Gluttony, Envy, and Sloth. The brief comfort I had garnered from the sight of the books vanished in an instant. I had definitely been guilty of Sloth.

The Very Reverend Mother Mary Assumpta, in full headdress and regalia, unfolded from the chair as she extended herself to her impressive height of six feet, and towered over the thirteen-year-old me. She was a large woman with rosy cheeks—her face and hands being the only parts of her body visible in the habit. To me, and every other girl in St. Catherine's, she was the epitome of the dragon. We were all terrified of her, more because of her physical size, commanding presence and fierce reputation than any first-hand knowledge. The Reverend Mother's legend was probably the greatest deterrent to wrongdoing in the whole school, and it was every girl's hope to never have to set foot in this office. And here was I, shivering from fright, getting a private audience, and me not even at the end of my first year yet.

"Now, Sheila," Mother Assumpta began, and she raised her head. "Now, Sheila," she repeated, and I was mesmerized by the chin that came wiggling out of its hiding place beneath the wimple and passed over the stiff white collar as if trying to set itself free. For all the world, it reminded me of a swan extending its neck, and I had to stifle that thought immediately, or I knew I would giggle for sure. Then I'd really land myself in hot water!

"You are a very intelligent girl," I heard the voice say and went into shock. "You are a very intelligent girl, but you need to apply yourself."

I was stunned as the neck settled back down on its stiff rest. I stared at it, but it had lost its entertainment value. I felt numb.

"Did you hear me?" Mother Assumpta was asking, and I managed an almost inaudible, "Yes, Mother."

"And what did I say?" she inquired, as if not at all convinced that I had.

"That I need to apply myself." I all but whispered.

Mother was clearly not satisfied with that answer. "And what else, before that?" she prompted, and it was gentle, not pushy.

I was rooted to the spot, and my tongue felt thick as if it were stuck to the roof of my mouth. I couldn't possibly answer that question. It would imply some acknowledgment of something about myself that I wasn't able to own. I turned bright pink with embarrassment. I felt my lunch turning into a round hard ball and wanted to clutch my stomach to push back the ache.

Mother Assumpta persisted. "What else did I say? Can you tell me what I said?"

"I don't know, Mother," was the best I could manage. A kind of lie, but then again, I didn't really know.

"I said you were a very intelligent girl."

Simple words, but earth-shattering for me. I had no concept of my own abilities or capabilities, no way of consciously assessing my intelligence.

"Yes, Sister . . . I mean Mother," I stammered. But it was not an affirmation, merely a rote reply.

"Well?" the Reverend Mother persisted. "Can you say it back to me? Have you lost your tongue, child?"

Now I had to grasp my stomach. The little ball had developed spiky edges, like a medieval ball and chain.

"Do you have a stomach ache, Sheila?" the nun asked, and I shook my head first "no" then "yes."

"Do you want me to call the nurse for you?"

This time I just shook my head "no."

Mother Mary Assumpta let out a little sigh and then motioned to a chair. "Sit down, Sheila."

I sat on the edge of the wooden chair, and Reverend Mother sat on her throne behind the desk. The interview was clearly not yet over.

"Do you believe you are a good student, child?" she began. "Do you believe you are intelligent?"

I thought for a moment before answering. "No, Mother."

"Even if I tell you so," Mother Assumpta continued, "and have reports from all of your other teachers, too?"

I looked down at the floor. I was absolutely mortified and couldn't possibly talk about this.

The Reverend Mother tried another approach. "Sheila," she began yet again. "Do you have any idea yet what you might want to do? You're very young, but do you think of what you might want to be?"

I had no hesitancy this time and blurted out. "I want to be a writer."

She seemed pleased with this—probably because it proved that I hadn't lost my tongue entirely. "Oh? A journalist? Playwright?" she asked.

"I'm not sure yet," I ventured. "Maybe a journalist. I'd like to travel."

"Good, good. That's good." Mother Assumpta assured me. "Now you know," she went on, "that you're going to have to work hard to be good."

"But I write all the time." My words were coming out in an excited jumble now. "I have notebooks full of things—stories and poems."

"That's very good child, very good. But I also want you to apply yourself to your lessons. You'll need good marks in your exams to get on. All right?"

I nodded happily. "Yes, Mother. Thank you," I wasn't exactly sure what had happened yet, but I felt a lot better.

Mother Assumpta looked at me for a moment then nodded her dismissal, and I got up to leave. As I headed for the door, I glanced at the wall plaque, and, just then, I heard her calling my name.

"Sheila," the Reverend Mother asked as the neck began to float up

and out again. "Sheila child," I saw her glancing in the direction of the plaque, "what do you know about Pride?"

She's examining me on the Catechism, I thought, and answered right away.

"That it's a sin, Mother."

"Ah!" Mother Assumpta proclaimed, triumphant at last. "So thinking you're good is a sin? Having pride in yourself is a sin?"

I knew this was an obvious question but answered truthfully anyway. "Yes, Mother."

"Well, I would like you to try and have a little bit of pride in yourself. I promise it won't be a sin."

As I gratefully made my escape, I heard Mother Mary Assumpta deliver an audible sigh, caught a glimpse of her shaking her head in frustration and, out of the corner of my eye, saw her pick up a strip of black cloth and drape it ceremoniously over the plaque.

CHAPTER FOUR

GHOSTS

"What doesn't kill me makes me stronger."
NIETZSCHE

The Fiona Child raced from the room and away from the burning stares.

"I'm sorry," she cried. "I'm sorry, I'm sorry."

She headed for her tree, her safety, her cocoon. She wanted to feel the safeness of her things around her. Wrapped around. The wood, the warmth. She wanted to go inside. Go in.

"I'm sorry."

The cry ripped from Fiona's throat, and she woke with a jolt to find herself in her loft bed in her own apartment in New York. She lay still and tried to compose herself as the memories receded to the back of her consciousness. They didn't disappear like ordinary dreams. These memory-dreams floated away from the surface of her thoughts but rested on the background canvas of her mind. They were becoming more and more corporeal in her present life in the here and now. She fought back the panic and tried to shift her awareness by staring at the cracked plaster on the ceiling, in particular one tiny triangular piece that dangled precariously above her eye. She remembered her writing deadline, threw back her summer sheets, dragged herself out of bed and climbed down the wooden ladder. Pam had gotten an extension on the short story review, but Fiona still needed to focus in order to meet the new deadline. She had the same ritual every day. Strong black coffee. Ease in.

She was almost out of coffee but made three-quarters of a mug anyway, and, still wearing her long white cotton T-shirt, she carried the brew over to her work-station. She already had worked her outline and notes before she got the call about her father, before Ireland. So, she had gotten a good start on these stories and expected it to be painless. She read her notes and then turned to the screen, her fingers poised, at the ready. Nothing. She re-read her notes, started again. She hit the keys, but instead of words images danced before her—the treehouse of her childhood, the storm, the flight from the storm with Orla, the shadowy figures gathered round the sick-bed. Was this from her novel or her life? From the screen of her mind these pictures burned onto the computer screen, the very concrete surface that she used to write. They had followed her here to New York, one thousand leagues across the sea. They had ridden on the crest of the waves and slipped into her private domain.

Fiona's heart pounded as she banged on the keys—letters, figures, symbols, anything in any shape or form or order. An incantation. An exorcism. A banishing. She pounded with all her might until her fingers started to give way under pressure and she slowed down and finally stopped. She sat and stared at the crazy quilt of nonsense.

■ ■ ■

Later Fiona escaped to buy coffee beans and muffins in the hope that a disruption in her schedule might get her back on track. As she reached the ground floor, her neighbor Saul emerged from his apartment, stuffing papers into his briefcase. He beamed when he saw her and held the door open as they stepped outside. Fiona smiled to herself as she caught sight of his rumpled curly hair.

"The near or the far office?" Fiona asked mischievously.

"Near!" Saul laughed. "I don't have a lecture today. You heading to 'my office?'"

"Yeah, just for supplies, though." The local bakery was Saul's second office where he met people to discuss new research ideas.

"Have coffee with me. My meeting is not for another thirty-five, forty minutes."

Fiona was tempted, out of loneliness, and frustration too. But that wouldn't be fair to Saul.

"I can't, sorry. I have a deadline tomorrow, and I'm way behind." She gestured to the stuffed briefcase. "How's your work?"

His laugh tinkled. Saul always reminded Fiona of a leprechaun. An extremely brilliant, Jewish leprechaun who was a physics professor at NYU.

"Good, good. Some new ideas brewing. You know, the usual!"

Fiona did know. Saul's sparkle and freshness made her hover on the brink of saying 'yes' to his repeated invitations over the last eighteen months. But she kept her armor sealed.

The aroma of baked bread and freshly brewed coffee met them as Saul held open the glass door to the bakery.

"Dinner, tomorrow after your deadline?" he suggested as they entered.

Fiona laughed and shook her head. "Thanks, though, Saul. Good luck with the next invention!"

Resigned, Saul sprawled his briefcase and papers on a corner table to stake his claim.

■ ■ ■

When she returned, Fiona saw the red light blinking on her answering machine before she closed the door—two messages. One would be from Pam. She put the water on to boil, ground the mixture of espresso and Colombian beans, set up the coffee pot with Melita filter and got out her favorite gold and teal pottery mug. Her rituals. Only then did she approach the beckoning signals across the room.

"Hello, you have two messages."

"Hi, Fiona. Pam. Hope all went as well as possible in Ireland. As you know, I got an extension on the review, but they do want it by Thursday. Let's talk. Hope you're okay. Oh, you might get a call from a Sean Collins—remember the option on the novel? Surprise, surprise! Later, kiddo!"

Fiona pounced on the rewind button to see if she had heard correctly. Her novel? Couldn't be! She let the machine play on.

"Ms. Clarke, this is Sean Collins. Your agent, Pamela Long, may have mentioned I was in town. I'm the director who optioned your novel for a movie about a year and a half ago. I'm in New York until Sunday and would love to meet with you, if possible. I can be reached at (212) 829-237 . . ." Fiona's heart missed a beat. This couldn't be happening. She played the message again to convince herself she hadn't imagined it. Still, she had to ring Pam, who was with a client but assured her it was true. Fiona listened to the message once more, saved it and headed back to her whistling kettle. She poured water over the ground coffee and stared as it turned to a dark brown soggy mass against the white filter, sending up deliciously aromatic vapors.

She began to circle the room. Her head was spinning with excitement. Was it really possible that someone thought her novel was good enough to make a movie from it? She swirled back and poured some more water into the filter and started to hum with happiness. Things were starting to look up. She put on Stephane Grappelli to match her upbeat mood and hoped it might help her get back in her writing stride. Pam sounded over the moon about the news.

When Fiona turned on her computer, the amber letters beamed back at her. They looked strange, too bright, too much. She laughed at herself. Away for a short while and the computer, practically an extension of herself, felt like an alien. She opened the file she was working on and started to read over what she had already written. She had to concentrate because the words kept jumping and running together. But she got to the end and then raised her fingers, poised, ready to continue. Nothing.

It was way past noon when Fiona made the second pot of coffee and distracted herself by starting to unpack. Her battered brown suitcase lay in the middle of the floor where she had left it the night before. Her eyes fell on the photo album. It had been in her old bedroom at home, and something had possessed her to pick it up and put it in her case. She was entitled to take it, of course—she knew Declan had lots of the old family pictures—yet it had felt like an illicit act. Fiona ran her fingers over the textured linen cover and the imprint of four dark brown leaves on the upper left hand corner. The album was bound with a golden cord and frayed at the edges, revealing the natural off-white linen. Beside it in the case were the T.S. Eliot poetry collection, *Alice in Wonderland* and her Mam's tea cozy with Dad's diary sleeping inside. She pushed back the tears brimming at the surface for the loss of both of her parents.

The coffee cups, the dirty plates, the cartons from last night's take-out—they still sat on the kitchen counter when Fiona was getting ready to leave next evening. She had slept badly. She felt she had been through a war, fighting all the way. She woke up several times, terrified at the thought that she might never write again. It was what she lived for. She spent the day organizing, moving her files around, scribbling notes, drinking too much coffee. She had everything lined up and had just turned on the computer and actually written a few words when she looked up at the clock and saw that it was almost 7 pm. Damn!, she thought. Just getting started, and I have to rush off and clean a blooming office building! She closed her file, saved the little bit she had written, logged off and raced out.

When she arrived back at 11 pm. Fiona went straight to the computer, launched an attack on the review and managed to break through the wall that had foiled her previous efforts. It had been a sheer act of force, of will, and she hadn't enjoyed the writing at all. But she tore through the material, forced her brain to formulate a coherent response and was grateful she had done so much of the legwork before Ireland, so that she had strong, lucid notes on which to base her opinions. She had finished at 4:30 am and set her alarm for 9 before she collapsed into bed.

The following morning, Fiona stood a long time under the shower in the hope that she could shake utter exhaustion. Her head ached and her eyes stung from lack of sleep. Her whole self was disoriented from having had to force herself to write, to wring out the words in a painful and excruciating process. She enfolded her damp body in a huge soft bath-towel. Writing was a love, a passion. Yes, it was hard work and labor intensive, but she never had to tie herself in a knot before to turn out a review. She dressed in an ankle-length, pale blue cotton skirt and a loose fitting silver-gray blouse. She placed the wide-brimmed straw hat over her pulled back hair, perched her sunglasses on the bridge of her nose and decided she felt sufficiently covered for the world. She threw the review into her book bag, loving as always the weight of her work on her shoulder, and headed out to see Pam.

Fiona's spirits lifted as she stepped out of the door of her brownstone. She loved everything about this building: the graceful dark bricks, the large six-paned windows with the generous ledges that emanated an air of having been looked out of for countless decades, the classical portal, the sense of belonging on this street with other buildings of similar age and history, and the ability to preserve an aura of peace and tranquility within a stone's throw of bustling Manhattan. The whole street possessed an air of domesticity and a whiff of late spring into summer. Fiona passed a long row of houses, similar mostly to the one she lived in, two stories with a basement, steps leading up to the entranceway, the lawns separated by wrought iron fences. White lacy curtains wafted in the wind as a hand opened out an upstairs window to let in the early summer air. A gray-haired woman leaned out of a second-story window to water the African violets in a window-box, and as she caught Fiona's eye, she smiled broadly. Fiona smiled back. She remembered Sean Collins' voice on her machine. Near the end of the row, someone on the ground floor belted out a Cole Porter tune on the piano. Fiona picked up her pace and let a skip creep into her step.

"The way you wear your hat, the way you sip your tea, the mem'ry of all that . . ." And she joined in, *sotto voce*, "No, no! They can't take that away from me!" as she skipped, barely perceptibly, down the street.

Fiona smiled to herself as she passed the small brass plaque which read "Pamela Long, Literary Agent." She mounted the familiar stairs, passing several offices on the way up. At the top she was drawn into Pam's small, but bright and airy space, where the light filtered in through the skylight, and various plants rambled along the walls and up to the ceiling. Filing cabinets bulged with papers and the centerpiece—the large oak desk—was piled high with papers and manuscripts.

Pam was searching for something among the pile of rubble as, at the same time, she jotted down notes in a yellow pad. Just seeing her there, with her dynamic persona and quick assured manner, made Fiona feel right. The cool, linen-textured oatmeal pants-suit set off her dark Italian skin and her laughing green eyes. The cut of the suit complimented her trim shapely figure.

"Hi. Made it." Fiona greeted her.

Pam gave her a mischievous smile. "Barely!" She teased. "You look shattered. Up all night?"

"As usual. Well, worse than usual." Fiona admitted.

Pam gave her a quick, strong hug as she whispered in her ear,

"I'm so sorry, Fiona, about your Dad." Fiona nodded thanks and swallowed the lump in her throat.

"Coffee?"

"Sure, I'll get it."

While Pam resumed her search, Fiona headed over to the coffee area where a fresh pot was percolating.

"The sooner you become a full time writer, the better." Pam had put down her pen and looked over at her. "You'll get some sleep, and we'll both be rich!"

Fiona laughed as she poured the two mugs, putting cream and one sugar in Pam's. "Don't hold your breath." She handed Pam her mug and plunked into a chair opposite her desk. Pam searched through her papers as she imbibed a mouthful of creamy coffee.

"Ah. Here we are." She pulled out a sheet with handwritten notes. "This won't make you rich, exactly . . . but . . . it's a start."

"What?" Fiona asked, searching for a clue in her face. "What, Pam?"

Pam pulled herself up to her full height of five feet nine and a half inches and expanded her chest. She breathed in deeply and spoke on the exhale. "I just got a *New Yorker* assignment," she announced, "and it's tailor-made for you. They want an Irish story."

"*The New Yorker*. Oh, Pam!"

Pam laughed, a sparkling, joyous laugh. "Isn't it great?"

Fiona had a moment of panic. "Oh, my God. Pam. What'll I do?"

Pam laughed. "What do you mean? You'll write it of course."

"But, I . . ."

"I wouldn't ask you to do it if I didn't . . ."

"I don't want to let you down." Fiona finished.

" . . . if I didn't know you could."

"And Irish," Fiona went on. "I don't know."

Pam laughed again. "You're too much, girl! You are Irish. You've already written an Irish novel."

"That sold all of a few thousand copies." Fiona reminded her.

"It's a start; it was decent enough for a first novel." And, you've got yourself a movie deal . . . that gives you a certain *cachet,* baby!"

Fiona laughed. "Isn't that amazing, too? Do you think it will actually happen? Maybe that guy is some relation using an assumed name who thinks he's been maligned in the novel and is trying to get back at me! Sean Collins—Irish name. Why not pick something successful or big or something?"

"I'm sure he sees the potential. And of course he'd be even happier if you'd work with him on the script."

Fiona got up abruptly and started to pace. "You've talked to him?

"Yesterday. He said he called you but hadn't heard back."

"You know me and the telephone. I probably wouldn't even own one if it weren't for your endless nagging!"

Pam laughed. This was a teasing game between them. Pam as the Wicked Witch of the West—or East, forcing the little Irish girl to face up to the big bad technology, to remember that she was living in the nineteen nineties, the last decade of the twentieth century.

"But you did have a phone as a child?" Pam queried.

"No . . . well, not as a young child because we lived in the country, and you waited for years for a line. Then, we got one when I was . . ." Fiona tried to remember but couldn't pinpoint it. "I forget. About eight or nine, maybe? But anyway, to get back to the subject at hand, I've had no time to make calls since getting back from Ireland. I've been working away furiously on these reviews."

Pam looked surprised. "But I thought it was almost finished when you left. You said you were nearly done."

Fiona plunked her coffee cup onto the desk, collapsed back down into her chair and leaned towards Pam.

"That's the trouble—I was. It was. But when I got back, I don't know, I just couldn't settle, couldn't . . ." She struggled with how she could possibly explain to Pam. Would she sound crazy? Maybe Declan was right and she was a bit odd and would end up in the proverbial garret.

"Fiona." She heard Pam as if she were at one end of a long tunnel, her voice rich and soothing. "Your Dad just passed away; it's been very traumatic. Hmm—maybe this film assignment really would be good for you right now. A complete break."

This pushed a panic button in Fiona, and she leapt up again, agitated.

"I don't see what I could contribute. I mean, I know nothing about that medium, that world, and . . . I need to keep writing." The thought of not being able to write terrified her.

"You look flushed, girl. Do you have a temperature?"

Fiona realized that she was fiddling with the dead leaves on the climbing ivy.

She took a deep breath, plucked off two faded leaves and let them fall into the waste-paper basket. "Don't mind me. It's that old fear of distraction, you know."

Pam leaned back in her chair, observing Fiona.

"You know, you're the only person I know that doesn't jump out of her skin at the prospect of working on a film—not to mention an adaptation of your own novel—but hey, zip!" Pam glided her thumb and index finger across her closed lips in the gesture of zipping them up and continued to talk through closed mouth. "My lips are sealed." She repeated the gesture and continued through pursed lips. "I promise I won't bring it up again—for at least another week!"

Fiona burst out laughing. "Thanks a lot! You're such a clown! Anyway, maybe this *New Yorker* story will be it, the big breakthrough." She started to do a little improvised dance around the room and executed a graceful pirouette. "Can you imagine Pam? Just being able to write all day? Heaven!"

Pam reclined languorously in her chair and stretched out her arms, her intertwined hands supporting the back of her neck. "Yeah! Raking in the bucks. French Riviera, Caribbean, Ocean Cruises."

"You can have your ocean cruises—dinner at the Captain's table? I just want to be solvent and to write like a dream!"

Pam guffawed. "Fiona, you're such an old Puritan—for a Catholic that is! What? No vacations? Nights on the town?"

Fiona continued her swirling and twisted her body in a graceful curve in imitation of a South Seas dance. "Oh, maybe some exotic locales to stimulate the muse. Tahiti . . . my laptop (if I had one) at the beach house, a few painting lessons." She stopped her dance abruptly and swung to face Pam.

"Pam. What if I mess it up?"

"Fiona, it's right up your alley. You could write this story in your sleep, and you know it."

No, Fiona didn't know it. But she did know that she had to write, so she would tackle this. She summoned a bolt of energy, flung the doubts from her mind and catapulted herself into the chair opposite Pam, straightened her shoulders, and got down to business.

"Okay. Let's go over it. What do they want, and how long do I have?"

EYE OF THE STORM

Excerpt from a novel by Fiona Clarke

I was beginning to deeply regret having begged Mam and Dad to let me come to this stupid dance. Here I was, like a wallflower, holding up a pillar on the sidelines. I thought my dress was all right until I walked in the door and saw all the other girls had minis creeping up to their bottoms. I had already been asked to dance by a few right eejits. I couldn't believe the first fellow actually said, "Do ya come here often?" And another one kept pulling me into him during a slow dance and I kept pushing him back—felt more like a wrestling match, for God's sake! If no one asked me again by the next number, I had decided to ring Dad and ask him to pick me up. If I left it go too long, he'd be in bed, and I'd have to stick it out and wait for a lift from someone else. It was at this point of desperation that I saw Peter Rawlings walking in my direction.

Peter stood out from everyone else by dint of his confident bearing. His tailoring was several cuts above the others, too, simple, yet elegant.

"Would you like to dance?" he asked, in his lovely precise manner.

I had a monstrous attack of shyness. "I can't really dance very well." Stupid thing to say, Sheila!

"Neither can I," he said with a confidence that belied his words. "But we can give it a try?"

I swear I felt a jolt of electricity when he took my hand. It was a fast dance, and in disco you could do what you felt like, really. We did as well as anybody else. I couldn't, for the life of me, focus on the song or the words, so just tried to keep moving and, every once in a while, sneaked a look at Peter. Sure, I knew who he was, of course, and he would have known who I was, by family anyway. The Rawlings were Protestants and lived on a big estate on the opposite side of the village from our farm. One of only three Protestant families in the neighborhood.

He asked me to stay on for the next dance. It was a slow one, and the lights were lowered in the hall. Peter held me gently but firmly in his arms. I could feel the imprint of his hand against the small of my back and the crispness of his light blue shirt when my chin brushed his shoulder. He was actually a great dancer—I knew he would be. I felt like I was floating, my feet barely skimming across the wooden boards. The nice thing about a slow dance was that you could talk, and Peter and I certainly did.

"You're at St. Killian's boarding school, aren't you?"

"Yeah, and you? You're at boarding school, too?"

"I went to Kilabban. Just finished up my Leaving and waiting for results."

Kilabban was a very good boys' boarding school in a town fifteen miles away.

"I'm hoping for Trinity," he continued. "I want to study medicine. I think I have the marks."

He was quietly confident, not boastful. We Catholics are always apologizing for ourselves, find it impossible to think or say we're good at something.

"What about you?" Peter asked.

"I've one more year to go—going into Sixth. But I want to go to Trinity, too. If I get the honors. I need honors in Latin and also in English, as I think that's what I'm applying for. My Science teachers want me to go for Biology!"

Peter laughed. "An 'All-rounder'! You should do what you want, though. I remember now that you won several national writing competitions."

Well, that threw me for a loop.

"Read it in the Nationalist. I read the paper cover to cover. You don't see Ballyduff showing up much, so it stuck in my mind—local fame!"

I blushed to the gills. "It's just a bit of a shock. I'm surprised my parents didn't mention it. Or maybe they're afraid it will strengthen my resolve to be a writer if they draw attention to it!"

"They don't approve? Surely, it's a very honorable profession in this country of ours? You might put this place on the map. The latest literary prodigy from the environs of the village of Ballyduff!"

This made me laugh. "It's not very practical, though. They don't see it as a solid anything. How do you get a job as a writer? I don't want you to think they're ogres or anything, 'cause they're not. Just worried, I suppose, concerned."

"Most parents around here are like that, Sheila. They mean well. I know from talking to the chaps at school. Though I suppose there are different pressures on girls than on boys."

"There's a double standard. But boys are expected to get a good job so they can support their families, and girls are supposed to just be able to work until they get married and have children. All expectations heaped on them from outside. They don't think that maybe we want to do things differently from them."

"That's true." Peter mused. "I think my parents expected me to be a doctor or a lawyer. It's lucky for me that I passionately want to be a doctor, so I didn't have to get into any fights!"

When it was clear that neither of us had any intention of dancing with anyone else for the rest of the night, the gossip began. Mostly, it was obvious by dint of looks and gestures, but I picked up snippets of conversations that made me wish the ground would open up and swallow me. Peter and I chatted away, never for a minute stuck for something to say. On the last dance, a very romantic piece, "Je t'aime," I distinctly heard the unstoppable Nora Green whisper, "I wonder what it's like to kiss a Protestant? Do you think it's a sin?" My heart was beating to the mounting rhythm of the song, the French words adding to the charm, and I was sure he must be able to hear my heart beating. It didn't bother me at all though, because I could hear his, too.

Peter drove me home in his dark green Ford, not a new or fancy model, but nice. We parked outside the gate leading into our front yard. The car had one long front seat, so it was easy for Peter to slide over and put his arm around me. We talked a bit, which only prolonged the delicious anticipation. The talk got quieter. There were more pauses, and then Peter moved towards me. Our lips met and tasted and savored and grew hungrier and tasted again, and we shifted our bodies closer and I could feel the tips of my breasts brush against his chest and the pounding of his heart. Then his lips were on my neck and cheeks and the tip of my ear, and he explored the outline of my face with his fingertips as if he were blind and trying to memorize my features. I looked into his hazel eyes and circled his beautiful lips with my fingertip, outlining the place I would kiss again and again.

When I closed the front door behind me that night and slipped off my shoes, I stifled the impulse to burst into song. It would have been opera, if I had been able to sing (which I can't for the life of me.) But it was one o'clock in the morning, so I decided it wasn't a great idea and shimmered up the stairs feeling not in the least bit constrained by gravity, imagining the whole summer spread out before me like a glorious gift.

Our lovely romance was not to last.

CHAPTER FIVE

UNFORGETTABLE

"What we play is life."
LOUIS ARMSTRONG

The wind tangled her copper hair and pried it loose from its carefully constructed knot as Fiona stood on the outer deck of the Staten Island ferry and watched the Statue of Liberty draw closer. She was hoping for inspiration, trying to clear her brain and generate some ideas for her new writing assignment. She thought of the millions of Irish ancestors who must have held out hopes of freedom and a decent living as they came to these shores on rotting ships—the lucky ones who survived the crossing. They fled from famine, from corpses piled up by the roadside, from cartloads of dead trucked to the mass graves while the fields were fat with grain destined for the absentee landlords living high on the hog in London. The black potato rotted in the soil, and the Irish starved to death in their native land amidst bounty.

Fiona didn't leave under such bleak circumstances. She didn't flee from poverty or political oppression, just from its legacy—the ingrained fear of failure, the smallness, the tightness, the walls closing in, the not being good enough, the birthright of the colonized. America was big and vast, a place you could lose yourself in, a place where you could become someone. A place where you could be free.

Fiona recalled her successes. Getting her first story published, then the collection. The long wait before getting an agent. The novel. Some individual short stories and many reviews and articles. It was a dream come true—to write for a living. Even if she couldn't fully support herself from it yet. Or did she write for her life? Fiona knew that she was most alive while writing, most comfortable packed away alone, weaving her words. It was a private existence, and she depended on it to go on.

In the haze of the horizon, viewed from the ferry, she saw the figures floating. A bent woman in dark wool cape and long skirt. A man in tweeds and Donegal cap with a blackthorn stick. Two small children, a boy and a girl, wide-eyed, clasping hands. The wind brought a wisp of Irish air and a hint of a sweet bygone melody. As Fiona gazed, wondering who they might be, reaching back to see if they had ever lived in her memory, she felt the salt tears biting her cheek and forming a tiny rivulet in the corners of her mouth. A sadness for something lost, or something yearned for. Then the figures faded.

She looked around to see if anyone noticed her, but the passengers were all involved in their own worlds. Children looked over the sides at the water or begged their parents for ice-cream. People read newspapers or paperback romances. Friends chattered. Tourists pointed. She glanced back at the misty horizon, then turned to the food-vendor and ordered a hot dog with everything. She didn't really like hot dogs and found it funny that something that tasted as strange and bitter as sauerkraut could be called relish. But maybe, just maybe, it would make her feel more American.

■ ■ ■

Fiona spent the rest of the afternoon in a darkened movie theatre watching Fellini's *8 ½*. Almost alone in the blackened space, she followed the procession of people across the screen and entered into the dreams of the filmmaker. He, too, was examining his life, unsure of where to go next— revisiting, creating fantasy scenarios, blending the fantasy and reality so that the dividing lines between them were blurred, creating a dream world. Maybe she could hold on to the dream until she got home, and it would inspire and ease her into the flow of her own writing.

■ ■ ■

Fiona finished the Chinese takeout and poured herself a glass of robust Burgundy in her favorite big-bowled glass. She breathed in the oak scented bouquet and took a sip, enjoying the dry tingle on her tongue and the gentle heady rush. She felt relaxed and mellow, full of impressions of the ferry and Fellini, as she moved over to her workspace. She had been building up to this moment all day, giving herself a breather, creating a space where she could write away to her heart's content as in the past. She pulled out her chair and sat down and stood up again. She would put on some music first. Hold the spell. Billie Holiday, played softly, would help.

Fiona sat herself down at the computer. She cradled the chalice-like glass in the palm of her hand, breathed in and savored, took a sip and laid down the glass.

"Blue moon, you leave me standing alone . . ." She stared at the screen. "Without a dream in my heart . . ." Her own reflected image looked back at her. Despondent.

■ ■ ■

She went to her favorite Jazz and Blues club that night in an effort to relax and unwind, and hoped that by visiting the closest thing she had to a "haunt," she could get her life and her writing back on track. She was in a tizzy about the *New Yorker* assignment. This could be a breakthrough, and she badly wanted to make it work. *The Blue Angel* was a small low-light space in Greenwich Village where the wooden fixtures and the small circular tables, each with a single lit candle, lent it the air of a Parisian bistro in the shadow of Montmartre. As Fiona ordered a glass of Pinot Noir at the bar from the reed thin woman in the black dress who she knew by sight, she glanced around at the posters of Blues singers that graced the walls. Billie Holiday, Marlene Dietrich, Duke Ellington, Edith Piaf. Marlene was blonde and glimmering against a black frame, with her pursed lips and white feather boa. Billie was smiling sadly, dressed in black, embracing a tiny white dog. Ellington, with bemused, upturned eyes, sported a tiny mustache and dapper bowler hat. Piaf looked sorrowful, her right hand reaching over to touch her left cheek, her other hand supporting her right wrist. Piaf, with her sad and soulful melodies, was her favorite.

The bartender could have passed for a very young Piaf; she wore a perpetually pained expression, and she hardly ever spoke. This suited Fiona fine and was one of the reasons she liked this spot. It was the antithesis of an Irish bar—and New York was awash with Irish bars. They were loud and boisterous, and the bartenders were always gregarious, full of quick talk and witty conversations and bursts of songs and jokes and heated discussions on politics and literature and sports and religion and everything under the sun. Fiona wondered if she missed out on that Irish gene. The bar gene. She much preferred this soft, dimly lit, relatively smoke-free hideaway.

She headed for her favorite spot, a secluded corner table in the shadow of Piaf. The place was quiet as it was mid week, but she recognized one or two of the regulars she knew by sight. She spotted Anton, wearing his signature leather jacket, sitting at a table with a man she didn't recognize. She nodded hello and escaped to her table. Out of the corner of her eye, she could see Anton making his way over.

"Hiya. Did you come to hear Sonya?"

"I just came to sit and relax, really. Is she the new vocalist?"

Anton nodded. "She's really good. I've heard her a few times. My brother-in-law," and he indicated the man at his table, "is overnighting on business, so showing him my hang-outs!"

"Is he from New Orleans, too?"

"Yep. So far I'm the only deserter! After six months in New York, I'm now the official tour guide."

Fiona liked his slight southern lilt and wry humor. She knew what was coming next.

"Care to join us?"

"Thanks, Anton, but, I need a bit of quiet time tonight."

"Sure." He started to leave and then turned back and leveled his earnest green eyes at her. "Any point in me asking again? Dinner, movie, concert?"

Fiona smiled. "You're nothing if not persistent, Anton. I'm sorry, but thanks."

He nodded, disappointed. Then he resumed his jovial manner. "Catch you later!" and was gone.

The band was setting up after a break, and Fiona recognized the bass and drum players but not the piano player. The violinist, Ernie, was the same one who had taken over for Phil when he moved on eighteen months ago.

Fiona had been cradling a glass of Merlot in this very bar over three years before when she first set eyes on Philip. She had heard his music first, the clear melodic strains that struck her as plaintive and personal. As she looked up to see from whence they emanated, she saw the tousled sandy fringe thrown forward with the intensity of his playing, eyes shut, concentrated, completely wrapped up in the emotion. He was pale, slight build. His face was lively and expressive and allowed the ebb and flow of the notes to play over it, to register, to animate. At the same time, she intuited a shy streak about him, and this she found attractive.

It was her third weekend coming in and exchanging small talk during the breaks when Philip asked if she'd like to meet for coffee. Two days later, they sat in the corner of a bustling coffee shop, sipping lattes, surrounded by the buzz of late morning comings and goings, looking out at the early autumn city.

"Reminds me a little bit of Dublin." Fiona mused, as she watched the people in their mufflers and boots and scarves, keeping warm in the face of the bite in the air.

"Did you go to coffee shops a lot there?" Phil asked.

"The flats I was in were always so poky that I needed to get out. So I'd escape with a book, or notebook. You could sit in Bewley's for hours, fire blazing, nursing a cup of coffee."

Philip laughed. He had a gentle musical laugh, like an extension of his playing.

"Is it a big café?"

"Yes, they're a Dublin institution. Bewley's Oriental Cafés. All the décor is Eastern, lots of red plush, beautiful fireplaces in some of the rooms. I loved sitting by the fire in the cold weather. Watching people. They'd come with their *Irish Times* and cups of tea or coffee or soup, alone or with friends. You could spend the whole day there, if you wanted to."

Philip nodded. "Reminds me of San Francisco. It's a great café town. You can ensconce yourself with your book and grab a coffee, and you don't have to budge until you're ready to leave."

They talked easily. About their work, their lives in San Francisco and Dublin. Music. Books. Their hopes and dreams. Until it was time for Phil to go and teach.

Over the next few months, the two spent a great deal of time together and gradually became lovers. They went to movies and concerts and clubs and sat in cafes and talked. They hung out at Fiona's apartment and at Philip's. They got Indian or Chinese take-out and a bottle of wine, and she read poetry to him, and he played the violin for her. Seamus Heaney, Brendan Kennelly,

Nuala Ní Dhomhnaill; Beethoven, Sibelius, Stephane Grappelli. She hoped that eventually she would get better at killing that old sexual anxiety. Her lover was patience personified, but it was Fiona who judged herself harshly. She wished she could relax and let go of what she assumed were religion-induced irrational fears. Ingrained shame. In spite of this, she and Philip grew closer.

Phil invited her to visit his family at Christmas, and she got on famously with them. The trip solidified their relationship, and, back in New York, they spent more and more time together. Fiona was slow to talk about her family, but little by little, in tiny increments, she revealed pieces of her past. Philip seemed to have infinite patience and never rushed her or tried to pry. He was fascinated by her dolls. There was one of Orla, of Aunt Rita, of her school friend Sinead, of President Kennedy. There was one of her grandfather on her mother's side whom she had never met but had made from a photograph at her mother's request.

"It's like a gallery, but instead of photos there are dolls." Philip remarked one night they were spending at Fiona's apartment.

"I suppose. Maybe they're my photo substitutes."

Philip was impressed. "I'm sure you've been told these are good enough to sell. Not these particular ones, of course, as they're yours, but the work."

Fiona nodded. "I've often thought that I'd be better off trying to parlay this into a little side business than washing other people's toilets! And I actually enjoy the work. The physical part of working with my hands, choosing the colors, designing the shapes, the challenge of getting the likeness right. All that."

"So? Why not? You'd be good at designing your advertising copy. I'm sure there's a market for handmade dolls. They wouldn't have to be of real people but that too maybe. A lot of folks would get a kick out of a doll made in the likeness of people they know."

Fiona was quiet. She picked up a piece of fabric and fingered it. She pulled out another shape that she had begun. A blank model, like a blueprint. Without any identity yet.

"I'd be afraid," she almost whispered. "I'd be afraid to make one of someone living, unless it's someone I'm a hundred percent sure I won't see again." Philip waited. He let her continue. "I'd be afraid I'd jinx them."

"You mean like a hex?"

"It's just that the dolls I've made are almost all of people who are dead or absent in some way."

"But you made them after they died. And anyway, even if you hadn't . . ."

"I know it's not rational. I'm just afraid to chance it. I'm too embroiled in it all, Philip."

"In what?"

"Death. Compared to most people I know, I've had an inordinate number of deaths in my family. Three people very close to me within a few months when I was nine years old. And my mother's going away was like a death at the time."

Philip encircled her with his arm and hugged her close. "You were unlucky, Fiona. That was a lot of suffering to bear. But it's not your fault. None of it is your fault."

She wasn't so sure.

The very next morning there was a phone call from Fiona's father to say that her mother had a heart attack. Fiona was still in her dressing-gown (the word "robe" was another she couldn't get used to) and starting to brew the coffee when the phone rang. She nearly dropped the receiver when she heard her father's voice. He had never rung her before, not even when she lived in Dublin.

"She asked for you and Declan, Fiona. She's very poorly."

Fiona was aware of Philip stirring in the bed in the loft. He had heard the phone and was beginning to emerge. She couldn't speak.

"Fiona?" her Dad's troubled voice pierced through her grief.

It felt like a century passed before she could drudge up a small voice. "Dad. Oh God! I'll see what flights I can get."

"Good girl." He sounded bereft, like a lost child. He hung up.

Philip was behind her. As she turned towards him, her face was set, closing. She was going on automatic. Her voice when she spoke was monotonal. "I need to get the first flight out to Ireland. My mother . . ."

"Is she . . . ?"

"No. But it sounds bad. Heart attack." She dragged out the telephone directory and called the travel agent.

"I'll come to the airport with you."

"No, you don't need to."

"I'd like to."

"Phil, I have so much to do. I need to pack and call Pam and arrange about work . . ."

"Will you let me do some of those things for you? I could call and get a substitute."

"No. I don't want you disrupting your life. It's my mother. I need to handle it"

"Fiona. This IS part of my life. YOU are part of my life."

"But I'm fine. I need space, and I'm used to . . . used to . . ."

"If it was my mother, wouldn't you want to help?"

"Of course. But that's completely different. Your mother brought you up; she loved you."

"And yours didn't? Fiona. It wasn't her fault she was ill, that her daughter died and she was lost in grief."

"But did they have to cut off their living children?" Fiona was angry. "Myself and Declan? We were still alive. Why didn't they protect us, protect me? Why?"

"Protect you from what? I can see the neglect part. What do you mean about protection?"

Fiona stared at him. She had never told Phil, or anyone, about her uncle's sexual abuse. "I didn't feel safe. Maybe it's the same as not feeling loved. But I felt betrayed." Fiona looked into Philip's trusting eyes. "Phil. My mother is dying, and I never knew her. She's sixty-one. Maybe I thought I had time. That at some point we'd work it out. That I could feel something. It's unnatural not to love your mother."

"I'm sure you do love her, Fiona. Otherwise you wouldn't be suffering like this."

Fiona sat in her big armchair and curled up.

"I saw her once in the sanitarium. We weren't allowed to visit her in her room as T.B. was contagious, so they let us stand outside and look up at her window. We stood in the knee-high grass. It was damp, and I could feel my socks getting wet. Declan was behind me, and I was holding Orla in my arms. Three children in the middle of a field, staring up at this huge, gray, brick building, trying to find the right window. Then we saw her, far away, a frail figure who was a shadow of our mother, a nurse holding up her arm so she could wave at us. I don't think we believed it was really her. I thought that Dad was making it up to keep us hoping. That she was already dead but he couldn't bring himself to tell us the truth. At that moment I decided she was dead so I wouldn't have to face it again. Better to get it over with. That's what I decided at the age of seven."

"But she wasn't dead. She recovered."

Fiona nodded. "She came back. But I'm not sure I accepted her back. I thought I had done a good job of being a mother to Orla. And Orla's illness and all the deaths—they all came in quick succession. All the same year she came back. She brought death back with her."

Fiona retreated into herself. This had happened before with Phil, but most of the time she slowly came back around and started to open up again. This time her armor was tightly sealed up.

"Fiona. Please."

She looked at him as if seeing him from a great distance. Her heart was breaking, and she had to protect herself. She realized in this moment how much she loved this man, and at the same time she felt she did not deserve him, that she couldn't love in the way someone like Philip deserved to be loved. She had an image of her mother dying, and knew she would not be alive when she arrived in Ireland. Her gallery of death was increasing.

When Fiona returned from her mother's funeral two weeks later, she had grown another protective coat. The ritual from house to graveyard, the gaping hole, the earth swallowing up the coffin. It had all happened already. She kept Phil at a distance and made their eventual breakup an inevitability. Fiona knew that they might well have made it if it wasn't for her. She knew deep down that she wasn't prepared to meet him or anyone else face to face on a deep emotional level, that if anyone had been able to get through to her, surely it would have been this talented, lovely, man who made magic on the violin. When he played to her it seared her soul. It was so intermingled with old pain and pleasure that she wasn't able to accept the gift, to take it in. So she let it go.

Yet another death, that of her father, had widened the chasm between Fiona and the possibility of intimacy. She didn't believe in fate, but she did believe that our futures are formed out of our past. "Time present and time past, Are both perhaps present in time future." She sipped the dry oaky wine. It was over two years since she and Phil broke up, and she hadn't been out with anyone since, despite repeated offers from both Saul and, more recently, from Anton. As the opening notes of "Unforgettable" on the violin soared through the air, Fiona felt the need to escape before she unleashed her pent up tears.

The strains of the song were still dancing in her head as she climbed the stairs to her studio. "Unforgettable, that's just what you are." The vocalist had delivered her songs in the jazzy, soulful style of Aretha Franklin. "You're unforgettable, near to me or far . . ." She tried to get the song out of her head. "You're unforgettable, in every way. And forever more, that's how you'll stay." She tried to push back the loneliness, to dispel the yearning. "That's why, darling, it's so incredible, that someone so unforgettable, thinks that I'm unforgettable, too."

EYE OF THE STORM

Excerpt from a novel by Fiona Clarke

The summer flew by in a flash. Picnics, walks, films, dances. Before I knew it, I was beside Peter in his car and on my way to meet his parents for the first time. I was a nervous wreck. I was wearing my favorite summer frock, light blue with tiny lemon flowers, I had my hair swept back and tied with a blue satin ribbon, and if I say so myself, I thought I looked really nice.

Peter looked smashing as usual, and the turquoise shirt made his blond curls look even brighter. He squeezed my hand. "Don't worry. You'll like them; they're not so bad."

"It's not me liking them I'm worried about, Peter!"

"What? They'll be crazy about you. How could they not?"

We approached the Rawlings' property up a long tree-lined entranceway—massive, and impressive despite some subtle signs of disrepair. As we stepped into the drawing room, Peter's parents, Josephine and Clayton, came forward, and he did the honors. Josephine was about forty-two or -three, robust and healthy with strongly etched features and a fashionably short hairstyle. Clayton, around the same age, had a slight build and a strong sensitive face. I thought that they managed to be both thoroughly modern and yet retain a whiff of late Edwardian grandeur.

"Peter tells me that you're a talented writer, Sheila," Mrs. Rawlings proclaimed in her strong sure voice.

I blushed, though not as furiously as I was wont to do in the past.

"He exaggerates!" I started to protest, but Peter jumped in.

"She's already won some of the most prestigious prizes for her age group," he told his parents.

"Are you intending to go to University, Sheila?" Mr. Rawlings asked.

"Yes. I'm going to apply to all of them," I said. "But I really hope I get in to Trinity."

"Clayton and I are both Trinity graduates," Mrs. Rawlings boomed.

I knew already because Peter had told me, and it had always been the Protestant university.

"In fact, we met at a Law Society party," Mrs. Rawlings added.

"I believe it was at a Society Debate, my dear," Mr. Rawlings interjected. "We were on opposing teams."

"No, no, Clayton," Mrs. Rawlings insisted. "I distinctly remember—in fact, I . . . " and she was poised to continue, but at that moment Moira entered the room, dressed in a proper maid's black and white starched uniform.

"Excuse me, Ma'am," Moira interposed with the slightest of bows. "Tea is served on the veranda." Her accent had the strong country flavor of the region. A Catholic accent.

Mrs. Rawlings nodded. "Very good Moira." And Moira did another little bow and left.

Mrs. Rawlings turned to her son. "Peter, my dear, would you take Sheila out? We'll follow directly."

On the sunny veranda, which overlooked what seemed like acres of rose gardens, a very elegant afternoon tea had been laid out on crisp white linen. There was a warmer for the pot of tea, scones and jam, cucumber sandwiches, strawberries and clotted cream. Peter offered me a seat on a white wrought iron chair with a pale pink cushion. Ashes of roses to complement the garden.

"I'm glad Moira came in, in the middle of that discussion." He

plunked down beside me. "They can never remember where they met!"

"But it's a safe bet that it wasn't at an Irish country dance!"

"I very much doubt it! I think their dancing was confined exclusively to the yacht and golf clubs." He glanced around to see if anyone was coming and then stole a quick kiss.

"Peter!" I was terrified. "They'll come out!"

Peter just laughed. "I'm glad I went to that Irish country dance." He kissed me again quickly. "Of course, I could have met you at Trinity—but I would have had to wait a whole year."

"I haven't been accepted yet." I reminded him. "I mightn't get in."

"Of course you'll get in." Peter declared confidently. "This time next year you'll receive your offer, and you'll set off for Dublin, and a few months later you'll be a prominent member of the Literary Society. By the time you graduate and we get married . . . "

"Shh! Peter—for God's sake, they'll hear you!"

Peter consented to lower his voice to a whisper. "All right. We don't want to give them a heart attack yet!"

"We'll wait 'til you're a prominent physician and can handle such medical emergencies!" I said sotto voce, and we both laughed.

Peter plucked two red ripe strawberries from the table spread, plopped one in my mouth and another in his own.

"This would be a nice place for you to write, wouldn't it?"

I looked around at the grounds, the rambling roses, the labyrinthine pathways.

"Perfect! Absolute heaven!" We kissed. Long and slow and sweet like honey. Heaven.

CHAPTER SIX

WOUNDEDNESS

"I learn by going where I have to go."
THEODORE ROETHKE

By late afternoon the following day, Fiona was still enfolded in her Kelly green velour bathrobe. Her breakfast and lunch dishes were stacked up in the sink—the cereal bowl with its traces of Cheerios and milk, plates with crumbs from bread and scones, the coffee pot which had been put into service several times since morning, several rows of mismatched mugs. An empty Chinese takeout carton with a happy Buddha face sat across from her on the kitchen counter, and the smiling face made her even more despondent. Out of the corner of her eye she saw the answering machine blink. Blink, blink, blink, blink, blink. Her computer screen radiated blankness in blinding white, and the thrum was deafening in the silence of her defeat.

■ ■ ■

She was hardly aware of her movement along the street and vaguely registered the muggy day. Her book bag was empty. Her bloodshot eyes were shielded by the dark shades and wide-brimmed straw hat as she ducked down into the subway on her way to Pam. She registered only shapes and colors—large and small, gray and black and some bright splashes of red and blue and yellow. She caught glimpses of the edges of newspapers and books and fingers and heard voices and grunts and the whirring sound of the train, the whish when the doors opened and the sucking in when they closed. She blindly found her way to Pam and mounted the stairs.

Pam looked brisk and fresh as ever in a crisp, red, sleeveless summer dress, and this only served to further Fiona's feeling of wretchedness.

"Nothing—not even a glimmer?" Pam busied herself watering the plants as she glanced over at the defeated Fiona.

"I might as well be paralyzed—I'm frozen up." Fiona slumped even further into her chair. The effort to keep her body erect felt super-human. "I'm sorry."

"I can explain about your father and Ireland—I'm sure they'll understand."

"God! First decent chance, and I ruin it—for both of us." Her self recrimination stirred her.

"Give yourself a break girl! Your Dad just died—it'll take a while for you to get back in your stride."

"He always wanted to be a writer, Pam. Imagine!" Fiona was more alert now, fueled by her profound sense of failure. "And I never knew that. I don't know much, do I?"

Pam finished her watering and poured two fresh mugs of coffee. She fixed her own cream and sugar, sat herself down and slid a mug of black coffee across the desk towards Fiona. They sat in silence for a while, the hum and occasional roar of city traffic playing in the background. Then Pam broke the silence, gently, with caution.

"Fiona, I don't want to push—but this might be the perfect time for you to think about the film."

Fiona slowly started to spin her mug in a circle.

"It seems pretty certain it'll be a go." Pam went on. "There are a few script hurdles they want to tackle, but there wouldn't be any pressure on you to write—I get the impression he wants your expertise, a sort of cultural attaché."

Fiona slammed down the mug with unintentional ferocity.

"Why would I want to delve back into that whole mess again?" She looked Pam straight in the eye, accusatory, and the remaining color drained from her face. "I had no idea . . . You led me to believe . . ."

"What?"

"That it was a good source of income, the option money. That the film would never really get made."

"What I probably said was that the odds were against it—I didn't want you to have false hope."

"I was sure it'd never happen—it was, I don't know—a Hollywood thing."

"But you must have realized that it was a possibility."

"No. I'm telling you I didn't. I honestly didn't. I . . . can't do it." Fiona shot up again, agitated, unsure where to turn.

After a long moment, Pam's voice cut through the silence. "Fiona, sit down, please."

Fiona was struck by the firmness, the business edge. She turned and sat back down.

"Fiona," Pam took a deep breath. "This is hard for me, I'm your friend as well as your agent. But I'm putting on my agent cap here."

Fiona took a punishing mouthful of bitter coffee.

"I can deal with the *New Yorker*. It's a big let-down, but they will understand your bereavement. However, we can't let this film deal slip away. Not if you want to continue as a writer, or at least . . . working with me."

Fiona stared at her, trying to take this in.

"It's been over two years since *Eye of the Storm* was published. I've been placating the publisher, but they want to take the book out of print.

"Because of sales?" Fiona hardly recognized her own voice it was so shaky.

"Yes, as you know they've reached a plateau."

"And they want to know where novel number two is." Her voice was dead.

Pam nodded. "They really believe in you, Fiona, as do I. But honestly, that second novel is crucial . . . I tried to spare you this. I thought maybe the *New Yorker* story could get us over the proverbial hump . . ."

Pam's soothing voice continued.

"This film is your chance. Sean Collins really wants you working on it. The publisher would be thrilled with that, and I'm sure they'd give us a reprieve . . ."

Fiona flashed on her last few days and the failed effort to write. She knew she was hugely stuck. And on top of that she was in danger of losing Pam, and no other agent would have the patience to take her on. She felt like a deer caught in headlights. Frozen, panicked. All of the memories from the past week came crashing down on her, and she felt that she would go mad if she had to revisit that territory in depth with the filmmaker. She shot up and spilled her coffee. She grabbed her bag and started towards the door. Pam sprung up and bounded round the desk to face her. "Where are you going?"

Fiona turned away not wanting Pam to see that she was on the brink of tears.

Pam reached out and touched her shoulder. "Please don't leave like this."

Fiona brushed off her hand and swallowed before trusting herself to speak. Her voice came out low and husky. "I can't do it, Pam." She was out the door and gone. Pam let out a deep sigh and slumped back into her chair.

The onslaught of street sounds assaulted Fiona as she ejected herself into the bright daylight from Pam's office. A group of bronzed Italian men holding Styrofoam cups of espresso, engaged in a heated, fast-paced, discussion in heavily accented Brooklyn-ese. An old Armenian woman with a multicolored shawl thrown round her shoulders sold vibrant scarves and shawls from her street-side stand. Two Asian business men in almost identical navy suits and striped ties were deep in discussion of a business transaction. Fiona registered the rhythms and cadences of the sounds. Sirens roared, horns honked, brakes screeched and ghetto blasters blared out pounding rhythms as they echoed her mounting terror.

As Fiona approached her apartment, the sky darkened, and she looked up quizzically at the gathering storm clouds. Once inside, she turned on the radio to get the weather report, and the somber and mysterious opening of Stravinsky's "The Rite of Spring" with bassoons, horns and clarinet swelled to fill the space. The fragmentary music suggested dark gropings and crawling life, and Fiona stealthily began to circle, like a cat when a storm is impending. She could not be still. She was afraid to stay in one spot. Her entire career was in jeopardy, and she felt as if she were losing her mind. She turned up the volume on the radio, but she knew what it would say. Unseasonable storm; barometric pressure rapidly dropping. She continued to circle as the horns intruded on the repeated string cords and the wood-wind shrieked. A lightning flash blazed by her window and she counted the seconds, *a haon, a dó, a trí, a ceathair* ... until a violent thunderclap rent the air. Powerful beats from the drums, then from the whole orchestra, a break in the pattern of the music as if some mighty convulsion of nature was taking place. The rain burst through the storm clouds in blinding sheets and smashed the city pavements. Fiona caught a glimpse of Orla's doll out of the corner of her eye—the same doll of their mother that Fiona had made for her little sister, and that seemed to taunt her in that bygone storm. She picked up speed. Thunder continued to roll, and a volley of hailstones pelted the tiled roof as the symphony gained in intensity. She pumped the volume up even higher as she tried to drown out nature's sounds and the mounting explosion inside her head. She grew more and more agitated. She circled with increasing speed like an animal trapped in a cage, her terror magnifying as the storm raged and the music waxed. She worked herself into a mad craze and then set to attacking the shelves as she swept all the books and papers to the floor. The music became increasingly frenzied, with rushing scale passages from the strings, but even Stravinsky, with all his passionate potency could not obliterate the sounds of the mounting storm. Fiona pushed and pulled and flung ferociously, the music pulsated with its bizarre forcefulness, she slashed out in every direction, and the drums and orchestra pounded out their threatening arrhythmic beat. Fiona thought she must be going mad, she experienced the storm inside, outside and all around her. She felt that both the symphony and the storm were playing themselves out in her head. She had lost any sense of boundaries, of safety, of protection. She disgorged a terrifying scream as she launched a final violent attack on all the papers and notes on her desk—her failed inspiration—as nature outside and the symphony inside responded with spasmodic fervor. The combination of sights, sounds and shapes, both internal and external, finally threw her into overload, and she wrenched the radio plug from its socket, grabbed a blanket, slung it over her and collapsed in a crouch into a dark corner. Folded up. Spent.

Her sleep was black. She did not dream.

■ ■ ■

Awakened by the dawn light, Fiona found herself wrapped in the blanket, her books strewn all over, her apartment a shambles. It looked, for all the world, like the aftermath of a bomb blast. She lay there for a time without moving and stared in horror at the destruction she had wrought. Then slowly, painstakingly, she extricated herself from her blanket and cautiously stretched her aching limbs. She dragged herself into the little kitchen, located her kettle and filled it with water. She lit the gas stove and watched the flame lick the bottom of the kettle and heard the hiss as it found a globule of water. She tore her eyes away from the mesmeric flame and found her tea caddy and her mug and her mother's embroidered tea cozy. Then she returned her gaze to the flame until the water screamed to be let out, and she made herself a good strong pot of Earl Grey. She left it to brew in its warm jacket as she traversed the living room, climbed into her favorite old armchair and curled up in a ball.

As she inhaled the aroma of the bergamot, Fiona remembered inscriptions she had read on tea bags about the quiet precious moments spent calmly sipping magical tea. She tried to regain her composure. She could do with a magic formula right now to stop the throbbing inside her temple. She crossed to her answering machine and pressed replay. "Ms. Clarke, this is Sean Collins. Your agent, Pamela Long, may have mentioned I was in town. I'm the director who optioned your novel for a movie . . ." She stopped the machine. As she poured the milk into the bottom of her cup and then the hot tea through the strainer, her right hand shook so violently that she had to brace it to prevent the boiling infusion from scalding her. Time slowed down. She watched the golden tea as it metamorphosed into a creamy brown as it blended with the milk in the cup below. She listened to the crunch of sugar as she slowly stirred until one by one each of the grains had dissolved. She pressed the message button again. " . . . I'm the director who optioned your novel for a movie about eighteen months ago. I'm in New York until Sunday and would love to meet with you, if possible . . ." The voice calmed her. She cradled her sweet, comforting drink and carried it carefully back to her chair.

Fiona reached into the wicker basket behind her and pulled out a doll. It was a doll in the making, an off-white color, fashioned from heavy cotton fabric. As of yet, this one had no identity. She had made the generic body and left it there until such time as she decided to make it into a recognizable entity. There were a few other shapes of varying dimensions in the casket along with cloth, thread, ribbons, buttons and the accoutrément of doll making. Fiona pulled these out on to the rug along with her sewing box. Unconsciously, her fingers worked as they turned the shape over and up and down and sifted through the bits and pieces of fabric on the floor and in the basket. Was she going to make a doll in the likeness of her father? She knew she had remnants of one of his old tweed suits in here—a few squares that Mam had given her for her collection. And an old tie. But she wasn't ready yet to create a likeness.

As she sipped and sewed, Fiona could see the shambles in her peripheral vision. She had had a mad fit, no doubt about it. She had gone berserk. Had lost her head and lost control of her hands and body. She had felt propelled to destroy her safety net, her books, her work, her cocoon. She felt as if she were being visited by spirits from her past, ghosts of the memories she had tried to ignore. They were coming back to her in the present and invading her psyche and making it impossible for her to continue with her normal and creative life. It had started in Ireland, back in her family home. She felt them in the bedroom, in the portraits, in the house itself, but also outside and most especially in the hideout.

Then they had followed her back to America where she thought she was at a safe remove. They began to inhabit her work, putting her entire career in jeopardy and taking away her ability to create her own stories.

■ ■ ■

Fiona luxuriated in the shower to the sounds of Pam puttering about, trying to restore some semblance of order to her shambles of a studio. She had practically forced Fiona into the shower and ordered her to take a long time. As she soaped and shampooed and allowed the warm water to caress her, Fiona realized that she knew when she rang Pam she would be there for her. Looking back, Fiona wondered if she herself had put limits on the friendship. When Fiona was dating Phil, Pam once suggested that they go on a double date with her beau at the time, a six-foot six Sicilian sculptor named Umberto. It hadn't come to pass and Fiona couldn't remember why. Maybe she had felt private about her relationship with Phil and not ready to open it up. Pam didn't ask again after that. For the past eighteen months, Pam had been dating Sammy, and they were now living together. Fiona had met him on a couple of occasions at the office, and the three of them had gone out for a glass of wine from time to time. He was a slim, handsome, bright-faced man who seemed like a good match for Pam—intelligent, energetic and enthusiastic. His parents were immigrants from Hong Kong and, once they had gotten over the initial disappointment that Pam wasn't Asian, seemed to have embraced her wholeheartedly. The romance was going well.

When Fiona emerged from the bathroom, glistening from her shower, Pam had undone much of the damage. Fiona folded the caressing robe around her still fragile body and curled up in her chair as Pam poured them tea and sat down.

"You're sure you don't need a doctor?"

Fiona shook her head.

"What's with the new doll? Is it you?"

Fiona stared at the doll-in-the-making and realized with a flash of horror that it did resemble her.

"What's wrong? Are you okay?"

"I've never made a doll of a living person before—unless it was someone I knew was lost to me."

"Well, you are very much alive so don't worry about it! Maybe that's an old you."

"You're so practical, Pam!" Fiona couldn't help laughing. "Maybe you're right."

"Pam," Fiona continued after a pause, "I'm really sorry about earlier—at the office."

"It's okay—no sweat. I know you were strung out. Mind you, I didn't know how badly or I would definitely have tried to keep you off the streets. I didn't know you were going to turn into a maniac!"

Fiona smiled. They both sat in silence and enjoyed the tea and the calm. Fiona fingered the partly made doll.

"I've decided to do it, Pam—the film."

Pam spluttered on a mouthful of tea. "Okay. When did you decide this? In the shower?"

Fiona laughed. "No, that's really why I called you—and of course because I needed help."

"Mr. Collins will be pleased. He was very disappointed you weren't interested in working on the project."

"I still don't know what good I'll be to him."

"I'm sure he'll figure it out—he sounds very competent."

Fiona recalled the voice on her machine. He had sounded quietly confident. Trustworthy—was the word that came to her mind. Maybe that had in some unconscious way fueled her decision to take this step, even though she didn't feel at all assured of the outcome. That, and the very conscious knowledge that she had no choice if she wanted a writing career.

Fiona fiddled with her cup, turning it slowly in a circle.

"I do know that you gave me an ultimatum, back at the office. I know this will buy me some time, at best."

Pam reached over for the doll Fiona had started. "And it will make the publisher happy. Keep him at bay for a while."

Fiona nodded.

"I'll fix up all the legal issues for you. I'll stipulate 'consultant'—no writing, if that's what you want?"

"Thanks, for now anyway." She looked over at Pam who was examining the new doll. "I feel like I'm going into the jungle."

Pam laughed. "More like leaving it I'd say! You mean L.A.? You might need a few new wardrobe items!"

"No, I mean the past! And L.A. too—Declan's there. What do you mean by 'wardrobe items', may I ask? Is this a hint?"

"Well, you might want to show off a bit more flesh! Flaunt that lovely figure!"

Fiona grabbed back the doll from Pam. Pam threw her hands in the air in mock capitulation. "I'm just sayin'."

"Oh, Pam! I'm comfortable in these kind of clothes."

"Yeah. I'm sure the caterpillar is very comfortable too in his old skin—for a while."

Fiona laughed. "Are you suggesting that I am emerging? Need to shed my old skin?"

"I bet you can find a butterfly store in L.A.!"

"Called 'Metamorphosis'?"

They both laughed, and Pam gave Fiona a tight hug.

"Hey, girl, I'm going to miss all this silliness! More tea?"

Fiona warmed her hands with the cup as Pam poured. "Ironic, isn't it, Pam? Here's someone willing to pay me to write for the next few months, and I can't do it. I want to be a nice safe hands-off consultant."

"Maybe it'll rub off—just by being there. Then, when the movie's a hit, you can quit your glamorous night job beautifying offices and lead a perfect life!"

"Writing away to my heart's content. Right! Now, if I had one of those laptops you're always talking about, I could bring it along just in case—but I'm not going to Tahiti, am I?"

Pam returned to her chair and raised her cup as if in a toast. "Dream on girl. Dream on!"

PART II

NEW FRONTIERS

CHAPTER SEVEN

ARRIVAL

> "One does not discover new lands without
> consenting to lose sight of the shore
> for a very long time."
>
> ANDRÉ GIDE

Fiona was enveloped by white light as she stepped off the plane. It was stark and blinding, and for a brief, wavering moment she wondered where exactly the plane had been headed. Was she in some outer zone, some no-man's land, or was she alive at all?

She began to detect flecks of moving color amongst the white. Her vision focused on swarms of people milling around in shorts, pastel t-shirts, caps and sneakers. She was struck by the intensity of the light. In Ireland and other parts of Europe, the light was noticeably different, more diffuse. The rays reflecting on the architecture and foliage and faces helped to sculpt and create the flavor of a country. Fiona hadn't expected such a radical difference in Southern California—maybe it really was another planet out here.

She felt distinctly out of place in her trademark cover-up. Despite Pam's not-so-subtle hints, Fiona hadn't changed anything about her wardrobe, but as she looked around at the bare tanned flesh, sun-bleached hair, and gym-shaped muscles, she got an inkling of what Pam meant. The easy voices and friendly gestures complimented the sunny good looks, and she didn't know whether to laugh or cry, whether she liked it or didn't. She plunked down on her carry-on bag and looked around—no sign of Declan.

Fiona was nervous. She had not wanted her brother to meet her at the airport and hoped to sneak in as unobtrusively as possible. It was Julie, her sister-in-law, who had answered the phone when Fiona rang to give the news about the novel and her impending trip to Los Angeles, and it was Julie who insisted they greet her upon arrival. Fiona scanned the entire area, hoping that she wasn't missing her—she remembered her as petite with shoulder length brunette hair and olive skin. As she stood up resolutely and headed for the baggage claim area a little girl's voice resounded through the open space and startled her.

"Aunt Fiona! Aunt Fiona!" Though she knew who it must be she still felt the shock of non-recognition. The designation of Aunt, and what it implied—a belonging, a family—were alien to her now. But there was affection in the call that Fiona couldn't resist, and she felt an involuntary tug. She hadn't earned a real claim to aunt-hood but got it anyway, by default.

She looked around and saw a perky seven-year-old straining on Declan's hand. In his other hand her brother held the half-completed *New York Times'* crossword puzzle. Una was pulling away from her father, trying to hurry him along, and Declan was holding her back with a firm grip. Julie, barely visibly pregnant, walked beside them, and Fiona realized she would have recognized her. She was just as she recalled except her hair was short now and close cropped which accentuated her youthful energy. She gave Fiona a warm hug.

"Welcome, Fiona. It's good to see you again."

"Thanks, Julie, good to see you too." And it was.

Declan reached out and shook Fiona's hand. Neither of them was totally comfortable with the American way of hugging when you met people. To Fiona it seemed a bit profligate and indiscriminate. If you hugged everyone you met it lost all significance. Despite all this she was grateful for Julie's warm welcome as she knew it was genuine. Fiona envied her the ease of natural expression. Why did everything have to be so bloody complicated? Why did a hug or lack of require major analysis? She was as bad as her brother!

Una jumped up to kiss Fiona. "Hi, Aunt Fiona. I'm Una."

Fiona bent down to greet her and was charmed by the dancing eyes. "Oh, I know you are! Last time I saw a photo of you, you were just an itty bitty baby."

"I'm seven and a half now." Una informed her proudly. Fiona gave her a big hug. She looked like the Clarkes, Fiona thought, like Declan. Her hair was reddish-blonde and her eyes a gray blue, but her complexion was darker, more like Julie's. From first glance Fiona felt that she had her mother's disposition and was glad for her. She thought that her niece wasn't so much pretty as handsome and that she had an evenness in her glance which defied her years, though she was very much a child. She looked right at you, no evasion. Lucky girl!

"I didn't expect you all to come and meet me." They were walking towards the baggage claim area.

"Una is so excited about having a real, live aunt, we couldn't keep her at home," Julie replied.

"And she's crazy about planes," Declan added, a little too hastily.

"I'm going to be a pilot when I grow up!" Una chimed.

"I thought you were going to be a writer," her Mom said. Una thought about this for a few seconds. "Hmm. Maybe I'll be both! Can I be both, Mom? Dad?"

"Don't see why not, love," said Declan.

"You could write about your flying adventures!" Julie added.

"Are you staying with us?" Una asked Fiona, now that her future was settled. Fiona hardly got a chance to open her mouth when Declan answered for her.

"Aunt Fiona has her own place to stay—a hotel."

When they reached the baggage claim, the conveyor belt was just starting up. For what seemed like an interminable interval the same three pieces of luggage went round and round, and no one claimed them.

"Who do these suitcases belong to?" Una asked.

"Somebody on the same plane as Fiona." Julie replied.

"I sometimes wonder," Fiona smiled, "if every airport puts a few dummy pieces of luggage on the carousel so that all the passengers will think the process has started and they won't get too despondent."

"Is that true?" Una asked wide-eyed.

"I'm only making it up, Una." Fiona replied laughingly. "But can you imagine a scenario in which passengers hire their own detectives to go from airport to airport, seize those first fake pieces of luggage and unveil them before the eyes of the horrified staff and tired angry travelers?"

"Just like in a detective story." Una offered.

"Exactly." Fiona agreed.

"And it could happen at lots of airports—all over the country." Una continued.

"Yes." Fiona agreed. "Maybe there would be a fleet of detectives, all poised to descend at the same moment at airports all over the country."

"And all over the whole world." Una went on, getting caught up in the game.

"Yes—the whole entire world. The Airline Sting!" Fiona announced, in her best melodramatic voice. "Then the passengers would riot and tie up the airline staff responsible and put them on the carousels . . ."

" . . . so they'd have to go round and round instead of the luggage." Una added, laughing.

"For hours and hours and hours," Fiona finished up, "so they could get a right taste of their own medicine. The end!"

"That's funny." Una clapped her hands delightedly. "Are you coming over to visit us, Aunt Fiona? When are you coming over?" Una said all in one breath.

"I was hoping you'd come for dinner tomorrow night, Fiona." Julie asked.

Declan had remained doggedly silent during this whole interchange and continued to work on *The Times'* puzzle. Now, he broke in and asked her if she had the address of her hotel. Fiona searched in her purse and found the piece of paper where Pam had written down the address.

"Can you come?" Una asked Fiona pleadingly.

Fiona was conflicted. She really liked her niece and her sister-in-law, too, but dreaded being with her brother again as soon as the following night. The tension between them was palpable, and Fiona was hoping to postpone the inevitable as long as possible.

"Santa Monica," he said looking at it. "This is a nice little hotel, right on the beach, if it's the one I'm thinking of."

Fiona had a longing to be alone. "Do you mind dropping me off there today?" she asked them. "The flight really wiped me out."

"No problem." Declan was somewhat more pleasant, maybe relieved. "In fact it's only about twenty minutes from our house. Do you want me to pick you up tomorrow?"

Fiona was surprised by his implicit approval of the dinner invitation and that nudged her to agree to come after all.

"Thanks. Don't bother driving though—I can easily get a cab, if it's only twenty minutes away. I'll just make sure I have your address."

Declan wrote down some directions as Fiona turned her attention back to the baggage and saw hers coming, her new blue wonder. She had assigned the old brown suitcase to the rubbish heap and bought a lovely blue one with polished leather and sparkling straps and buckles. She pointed it out to Una as it sailed towards them.

"There's my luggage. Call off those detectives!" She gave her niece a conspiratorial wink.

"Okay." Una laughed. "For now!"

They headed out through the glass doors into the blinding light of the Los Angeles afternoon.

Fiona understood right away what people meant when they talked about the traffic in Los Angeles. The freeways were ubiquitous, long sprawling fingers of metal and concrete, underpasses and overpasses, spanning the greater metropolitan area. The immediate environs of the airport were particularly congested, but as soon as they got on the section heading to Santa Monica, the traffic sailed along smoothly. Declan kept his attention on his driving. Julie and Fiona sat in the back with Una who was writing notes in a big loose hand on a scrapbook. She was working on getting information for her class project on family trees.

"What is Grandma Kingston's name again, Mom? I forget."

"Adele." Julie answered. "And Grandpa Kingston's is . . . do you remember?"

"I think it's . . . Roger."

"Good memory." Julie laughed. She turned to Fiona. "Poor Una has lots of space to fill up and not too many family members. She's decided to put photographs of everyone in the scrapbook, too, so you'll probably be solicited!"

"I don't have any photos . . ." Fiona began and then remembered the album. "Well, no recent ones anyway."

"We can take a photo of Fiona, can we, Mom, please?"

"Of course we can, honey. We'll get some film for the camera—you can take it yourself, if you like."

Una jumped up and down at this prospect. "But I might ask you to help me in case I shake the camera like the last time when I took a picture. Remember?" and she laughed. "It was a blurry one of you and Dad."

"We'll make sure you get good ones, don't worry." Julie assured her.

"Oh, yes." Una spoke rapidly and excitedly. "And I'm going to get pictures of everyone when they were babies, or small children, so we see how much they grew. So far I just have one of me, but I'll get more."

"The grandparents are a bit of a challenge." Julie told Fiona. "Declan thinks he has some of when they were young stashed away somewhere."

"I have an old album with me." Fiona offered. "I'll look through it when I get a chance and see what's there."

"Here we are." Declan announced as he pulled in to a small resident hotel. It was close to the beach and was tastefully designed in a Mediterranean style, duck-egg blue walls, red tile features. It consisted of a series of small houses arranged around an inner courtyard.

"It's lovely!" Fiona exclaimed, pleasantly surprised. "I think I was expecting an ugly motel."

"And it has a pool around the back—look!" Una pointed out excitedly. "You can go swimming, Aunt Fiona."

"Oh, if only I could, Una. I can't swim."

"Daddy! You told me you used to go to the beach when you were small." Una shouted to Declan, who was opening his car door. "You said you went swimming."

"Well, we did. I thought you swam too, Fiona?"

"Never." Fiona started to bundle out of the car. "I've always been terrified of the water."

"You can learn here, Aunt Fiona. You could start in the shallow end—it's not so hard!"

Fiona laughed happily. "We'll see, Una. I can cool off my toes, anyway! And I like this place."

"Your producer has good taste." Julie added. "Bodes well for the film!"

"I'll get your case from the boot." Declan went around to the back of the car as Una squealed with delight. "The boot! Daddy, you haven't said "boot" forever. And you said it with an Irish accent!"

Una was still giggling and waving furiously as they pulled away.

■ ■ ■

The baggage clerk, a young tanned teenager in shorts and a name tag that said "Freddy," carried her bag to her quarters.

"The café is open from 6 a.m. 'til midnight," he informed her. "And you can order room service, too, during those hours. Sorry about the phone not being connected yet. We get a new service for each customer, and we had an unexpected delay in getting the hook-up, but if you have any messages, we'll walk them over to you. Or if you need to call out, you may use the office phone. Your line should be all set within twenty-four hours."

Fiona thanked him as they approached her suite, number eight, on the side near the beach.

"The gentleman specifically requested beach side and luckily we got a cancellation." Freddy told her. "I'd prefer the beach, too, if it was me."

■ ■ ■

Fiona stood in the entryway and looked around. It was a mini suite, designed by an architect, tasteful though not luxurious. It was painted a restful but cheery peach, and Fiona fancied she could smell the fresh, succulent summer fruit. There was a good sized bedroom area with a queen bed, a nightstand, a comfortable looking armchair and a bathroom off the bedroom area. There was also a little kitchenette and a lounge. The whole place felt light and airy.

Fiona strolled into the lounge which was furnished with a table and two chairs and a writing desk with the requisite hotel stationary. On the desk sat a small computer with a note attached. She slit open the envelope and quickly scanned the note. "Fiona—my treat—sorry the laptops are still out of my range. Maybe by the end of summer they'll have dropped in price and we'll get you one in case you head off to Tahiti and are already working on your next novel! Good luck with everything! Pam."

Fiona smiled at the thought of Pam choosing this for her. She also felt slightly under pressure, as if she now should really try and produce something on it. She glanced over at the small table, swept off the cotton apricot tablecloth and draped it ceremoniously over the computer. That way she wouldn't have to see it all the time but knew it was there if she got inspired.

Next to the computer lay a copy of Sean's script, *Eye of the Storm, a screenplay by Sean Collins, based on the novel by Fiona Clarke*. Fiona had never seen a screenplay before. She picked it up with trepidation. Part of her life was contained between these covers. She thumbed through it—118 pages—shorter by necessity than a novel. She fished in her book bag and checked the exact number of pages of her novel—288. What had been kept in the screenplay, what left out and what had been added? She could read it in one evening.

Still clutching the script tightly, Fiona opened up the French doors and stepped out onto a little patio with its view of the beach. A small group of children played in the fading light, and their excited shouts rang through the warm air. She stood and gazed out on the ebbing tide, allowing the motion to lull her into a dreamy relaxed state.

She recalled their family visits to the seaside every summer. There was that first delicious pot of tea, which Mam said tasted so good because of the different water. There were the towels spread out on the warm sand, the banana sandwiches on fresh crusty white bread, the salt sea smell and the crash of the waves against the rocks as Fiona lay on her stomach and read her books. There was Mam in the summers when she was well—relaxed, eyes half closed, a faint smile on her lips, hair glowing in the warm sun. And Dad, contentedly reading. And at night, the drifting off to sleep to the ebb and flow of the tide.

Her Dad had tried to teach her to swim several summers in a row, but she screamed in terror every time her face touched the water. She was convinced she was going to drown, and no amount of breathing talk helped, so her Da finally left well enough alone. Fiona sometimes walked down to the edge of the water, stood on the wet sand, and let the waves rush in and splash up against her ankles and calves, over and over again. She stood there and watched Declan and the other holiday-makers as they swam and cavorted like dolphins in the sea. She herself never ventured any further than the shore.

CHAPTER EIGHT

IMAGININGS

> "Why, sometimes, I've believed as many as
> six impossible things before breakfast."
>
> LEWIS CARROLL—*Alice in Wonderland*

The morning after her arrival, Fiona had a ten o'clock meeting with Sean Collins by the pool of her hotel. She took a little longer than usual getting ready. She reasoned that it was because she had more time on her hands since she wasn't writing, and it felt like she was on her holidays by virtue of just being in Southern California and that it had nothing really to do with the fact that it was her first meeting with Sean Collins of the soft voice and easy sounding ways. She had spoken to him just a few times on the telephone and despite her initial antipathy towards any intrusion had gotten to like how he sounded. She felt somewhat shell-shocked from having read through a version of her life story, albeit in disguise, the previous evening. She had not been able to formulate any clear responses to the script yet, but she had a strange and uneasy sensation of her past floating just above her head in a misty cloud.

She sat under an umbrella by the deep blue pool and poured herself a mug of morning coffee from the café. She felt a bit overdressed in her beige cotton pants and pale blue long-sleeved shirt, and Pam's hint about her clothing choices nagged at her. She leafed through Sean's script from time to time but found it hard to focus, as her mind kept wandering to the anticipated meeting with this person who apparently admired her work and had enough trust in her novel to want to film it. She was nervous.

Sean arrived on schedule, wearing khaki shorts, a pale green cotton shirt and leather sandals. He seemed to be about thirty-four or five, was dark blond, fresh-faced and freckled and had an easy, confident manner that matched his telephone voice. He carried a slim black leather briefcase and a bag of fresh muffins. Fiona got up to shake hands.

"I assume you're Sean," she smiled.

"Must be the muffins that gave me away," he grinned as he shook her hand with a firm grip.

"Is this the best-dressed L.A. director ensemble?" Fiona teased as they both sat down. "Shorts and briefcase?"

"Only on weekends—and pool meetings!" Sean laughed and offered her a muffin. "How is the place—okay?"

Fiona poured coffee for them both. "It's grand, thanks."

"Sorry about the phone." Sean munched his blueberry muffin, "I think it'll be hooked up by tomorrow." He sipped his coffee appreciatively. "And an answering machine, too, of course."

"I don't mind," Fiona replied. "I don't really care about the telephone. Answering machines, on the other hand, I have great respect for—they save me from the phone!"

"Okay." He munched his muffin. "We'll try to keep calls to a minimum!"

"Are you a native of Los Angeles?" Fiona asked him.

"No—San Francisco Bay Area, Berkeley," he replied. "My parents still live up there."

"I visited San Francisco a few years back." Fiona recalled her visit to Phil's family. "I liked it. It's so open compared to New York."

"The architecture? Or the people?"

"Both, maybe. I think of it as a kind of polymorphous organism, where all of these disparate worlds exist side by side without regard to the others, and, ironically, this seems to offer an inordinate degree of privacy."

"And is that very different from, say, here, or Ireland?" Sean queried, between bites of his muffin.

"My first impressions of the West Coast are of an openness and friendliness. In Ireland, especially the Ireland of the past, everyone knew everyone else and made it their business to know your business. As Nellie, my father's cousin, would say, they'd live in your ear, if you let them!"

Sean had an open infectious laugh. "Well, you might say the same for some aspects of L.A."

"I think New York is the antithesis of that. There, you could dart around in a mad rage, tearing your hair out, and everyone would think it was normal!"

"And you like that?" Sean asked.

Fiona thought she detected a mischievous note in his question. Was she challenging Sean in order to ward off probing into her own private world? She answered him honestly and frankly.

"It's easier to get lost that way. Easier to be invisible."

Sean smiled but didn't comment—he let her remark stand.

They continued to eat and sip until they had finished their muffins, and then Sean pulled out his copy of the film script and of her novel.

"Well, what do you think?" he queried. "Any first impressions?"

Fiona thought about it for a minute and then launched in.

"It's strange and a bit eerie for me, really. It's as if I partly recognize the characters, like they were ghosts." Ghosts again.

"Do they seem like your characters, though?" Sean asked. "I know they're what drew me to the book initially."

Fiona paused and took a deep breath. "The main character, Sheila, she seems—very sympathetic in your script," she ventured.

"How do you mean?" Sean inquired.

"Well, she's careless, negligent, she's to blame for her little sister's death."

"Actually I didn't think that." Sean countered.

"But she's older," Fiona cut in, "so when they're out in the storm and their hide-out is caving in, she should have acted sooner."

"Yes, but still she's only a child, too. It's not fair to expect . . ."

"Of course, it's fair." Fiona was getting adamant. "Her parents had trusted her, she prided herself on being responsible, so . . ."

"But none of this makes her a villain," Sean countered.

"But I think it does!" Fiona ventured.

Sean laughed easily. "Well, it must be some Irish Catholic guilt thing that I don't understand," he said lightly. "But I'd like to." He reached into his briefcase and took out a portfolio cover.

"Here. Maybe it'd be easier to start with place and get back to the characters later."

A diplomat, Fiona smiled to herself.

"I have location shots here of various places in the U.S. which could work for the Irish landscape." He opened up the large covers and began to lay out beautiful photos. Rich green landscapes, rolling hills, charming valleys and lush vegetation. Fiona looked at them all and appreciated their beauty, but they did not resonate at all with her experience of her own rural Irish landscape.

"Sean, I know these are not actual photos of Ireland, but they don't seem real to me in the context of the Ireland I grew up in. And it relates to something it's hard to put a finger on about images of Ireland in American films. There seems to be a haze, a gloss, a kind of veil that makes everything look vague and mysterious but plays into some kind of nostalgia. Maybe these images could pass for a 'generic' Ireland—but they don't feel right, exactly."

"So, in film terms, do you mean that the image should be grainier, and we shoot (literally!) for more definition and detail?"

Fiona nodded affirmation. "I don't know much about the technicalities of film, but yes, I think so."

"Okay. Thanks. I think we're on the right track. I want to understand the world of your novel as much as I can. Try to cut through the layers. This is rural Ireland in the 60's and 70's. It wasn't in Technicolor, was it?"

Fiona laughed. "Definitely not. Not in my experience anyway, or Sheila's. But I do remember that I'd sometimes change scenarios in my head—after we got T.V. and I watched some of those American sitcoms. When my Dad came in, worn and weary from working in the fields since early morning, in my mind's eye he would metamorphose into a clean, perfectly groomed businessman. The kitchen would be transformed from its basic sensible farmhouse quality to a bright, sparkling model room, where all the appliances glistened with blinding intensity. You could practically see the silver polished stars glinting like you do in commercials! Mam was perky and neatly dressed in a checkered apron, with a tidy trim hairstyle. Dad breezed in, packed his briefcase away neatly, carefully hung up his pressed jacket, and kissed his model wife on the forehead. Just like *Donna Reed*!"

"So you had your fantasy of the 'perfect' home?" Sean chuckled. "A lot of city kids romanticize the country—especially farm life."

"Right." Fiona agreed. "I always thought city people and their homes were spotless, spic and span. Never a dust mite in sight! Then I'd be sick with guilt after, because it was like I was betraying my parents."

"You mean you felt guilty for just thinking about it?" Sean asked, incredulous.

Fiona laughed. "I can see you're definitely going to need some lessons on guilt—sins of the mind!" she chuckled. "But didn't you have notions like that too?"

"I'd put on plays with my friends—and I was usually the director. I suppose that was fantasy, wish fulfillment."

"Well, it came true," Fiona remarked. "Here you are—a director!"

"And here you are! You escaped!"

Fiona thought about this a second. The notion of escape.

"I left," she said then. "I came thousands of miles, but I'm not sure I escaped."

In a moment she began to leaf through the photographs again. "These photos are ideal landscapes," she said to Sean. "It all depends on the kind of film you want to make—a realistic, honest-to-God portrait—or a picture of a quaint romantic Ireland."

"You know I'm Irish too," Sean began. "My . . ."

"But you've never set foot in Ireland, have you?" Fiona cut in. "I bet even your parents have never been there?"

"No, but my grandparents . . ." Sean countered.

"It's so often portrayed as this perfectly charming little place, with perfectly charming little people," Fiona continued.

"Look," Sean answered reasonably. "I'm not in competition with you about being Irish. A lot of my sense of what it is to be from there, to grow up there, comes from films and from books like yours."

"And what image do you get from my book?"

"It's confused," Sean replied honestly. "I know you're very adamant about truth versus fantasy, but I think there are some of both in your book."

"Do you now?" Fiona wasn't sure how to respond. Sean was calling her on what she had already begun to intuit from re-reading her novel and her Dad's diaries. That there was a confusion, a contradiction, between the essence of her past story as she remembered it, as she had fictionalized it, and the way her father experienced it. She already knew that Declan was at odds with her version of events. And here now was Sean, a stranger, with no source but her own novel, interpreting it differently also.

"But you were hired as an expert on this film," Sean continued disarmingly, "so here's your chance to set us straight!"

Fiona considered this challenge—or invitation—for a second. She took a breath, and relaxed. "Okay. It's a deal!"

Sean smiled, then glanced through his notes and started to put them away.

"I've got a lunch meeting so better take off." It was approaching noon, and the L.A. sun was getting high in the sky. "I'll sort through my notes and work through some of the other main characters with you, the brother especially I have questions about. And we'll work on the location when I chat with the producers."

Fiona nodded, holding her breath. As she shook hands with Sean and watched him walk away, she flashed on the Irish myth of Fionn mac Cumhaill and the Salmon of Knowledge. Once Fionn had tasted, merely by licking his thumb, the transfer of knowledge was irreversible. Despite her own fears, Fiona had opened the door to Sean, offered him a taste of the truth of her past, and knew there could be no going back.

EYE OF THE STORM

Excerpt from a novel by Fiona Clarke

Our house was beautifully decorated and lit up for the holidays. The living room was festooned with colorful decorations, spiraling constructions of red and green and gold silvery material. In the corner, a tall live tree rose from a green pot, and the branches glimmered with angels and bells and gold and silver orbs. The carefully wrapped presents nestled under its branches. Mam had bathed myself and Conor and put on our night clothes so we could listen to letters from Santy on the radio. We sat in front of the crackling fire sipping hot cocoa. Mam sat on one side of the fire, knitting, and Dad on the other, doing a crossword puzzle. I was mesmerized by the voice of Santa Claus who was reading letters he had picked out from the hundreds of children who had written to him. My heart nearly stopped when I heard my own name, and all four of us stayed still like statues, breath held, rapt, as we leaned in towards the radio to catch every word.

"Dear Santy,

Please bring me a doll and a coloring book and crayons for Christmas. I'd also like a new baby sister. Please bring my brother whatever he asks for, too—he will write you a letter of his own, separately.

Love, Sheila

P.S. My Dada will leave out a bottle of Guinness and a slice of Christmas cake like he does every year for when you come to our house."

I let out a squeal of delight and nearly burst with the excitement. Now I really believed in magic. Mam was smiling broadly at me, and then suddenly she stiffened, glanced over at Dad, stood up quickly and left the room. Dad gave myself and Conor a friendly tousle on the head, and out he went after her. We cuddled up, warm and toasty, and listened in to the rest of the Christmas letters.

The next thing I remember, I was being lifted out of the chair, carried up the stairs and tucked into bed. I dreamed of snow and new born lambs and reindeer. It seemed like no time at all until Conor came in and tugged on the sleeve of my nightdress. The house whispered with a sweet and mysterious excitement, and, bleary-eyed, I rolled out from under the warm blankets and let my brother lead my by the hand down the stairs.

My feet hardly touched the steps as I sailed down. I could hear the crackle of the fire and smell the turf as Conor and I stood a moment in the open doorway. The Christmas lights on the tree and the fire in the fireplace were the only illumination, and, to me, it seemed like fairyland. I saw Dada in his chair beside the fire and raced over to jump up in his lap. Then I turned around to go to the tree and saw Mama sitting in semi-darkness in her chair on the other side of the fire. She wore a pale lemon fluffy dressing gown and cradled a white bundle in her arms. She was still and calm and sleepy. I climbed down slowly from Dad's lap and cautiously approached the bundle. Mam opened the blanket, and there lay the most beautiful sight I had ever seen. She was a golden child with deep amber eyes, luminescent skin and a glowing face framed with fiery tendrils. I was mesmerized, transfixed. I couldn't pry my eyes away.

"Well, Sheila, you got your little sister." Mama's voice seemed to come from far away.

I continued to gaze at her, half afraid I was dreaming and would wake up in my bed. "Can I touch her?"

"Gently, yes."

And I reached out and placed my finger in the tiny curled up hand and felt the smooth flesh and ever so gently touched the silky cheek, soft and pliant like butter. "Oh, Mama! She is so beautiful. She must be the beautifulest of things in the whole wide world!" They all laughed. Then Mama closed over the blanket to keep her new baby warm.

"Did Santa bring her?" I asked. "I think I heard the reindeer bells."

"She's a Christmas present all right." Dad said. "A special little bundle."

Conor had closed the door to keep out the draught and then walked slowly over to the other chair where he stood silently as I examined and admired my new sister. He tried to interest me in the tree. "Sheila, don't you want to see what Santa brought?" he asked. But I was riveted to the spot beside the baby girl. I couldn't take my eyes off her.

I did open my presents later, and I saw the empty plate with the crumbs from the Christmas cake that Santa had polished off. He made short work of the bottle of Guinness, too; it was all gone, down to the very last drop. But, though I liked my presents and played with Conor and enjoyed all the special foods and treats, my life was changed forever the moment I laid eyes on my new sister who later was given the name of Aoife. I was drawn to her like a magnet, overwhelmed by her beauty, lost in admiration. She became the centre of my life for the next five years.

CHAPTER NINE

BIRTH

"The center that I cannot find
is known to my unconscious mind."

W.H. AUDEN

The evening after her Los Angeles arrival, Fiona visited her brother's house for the first time and surprised herself by liking it. It was the polar opposite of her little New York studio—Declan's home was spacious and airy with expanses of wood and glass and wonderful light. The walls were mostly white and decorated with contemporary abstract paintings which complemented the newness and freshness of the space. And it managed to convey a sense of lived-in-ness—it wasn't just a showcase.

Fiona, Declan, Julie and Una sat around the cedar dining room table eating dinner. They had sweet strong cantaloupe for starters and had just begun to savor a wonderful Gorgonzola pasta.

"This is delicious, Julie."

"It's your brother that deserves the praise—I made the salad, but the rest is his creation."

Fiona tried not to register her surprise at the mere fact that her brother could cook at all, let alone cook this well. Yet another tidy notion she needed to retire.

"Daddy's a great cook," Una piped up as if reading her thoughts. "Are you, Fiona?"

"Afraid not, I have to admit. My culinary skills mostly extend to ordering Chinese take-out and opening cans of soup!"

Una continued with the line of questioning. "Do you make films?" she asked between bites of pasta.

Fiona laughed. "No. I'm a writer," she told her. "Sometimes. Right now I'm just helping out on a film here."

"You're being modest," Julie turned to Fiona. "Fiona is working on a film that is being made from her own novel." She told Una.

"What's it about? What's the story?" Una chimed in.

Fiona hesitated before responding. "Well, it's set in Ireland . . ." she began.

"And it's our family history," her brother interjected.

"It's a fictional acc—" Fiona defended.

And Una jumped in to ask what fictional meant.

"It's made up," Fiona started to tell her. "It's based on . . ."

And again Declan cut in. "Actual events, thinly disguised!"

Una was trying to figure this out. She started to ask what disguised meant but skipped it to get to the meat of the story. "Are you in the story, Dad?" she asked Declan. "Are you, Fiona? Are there other brothers and sisters, too?" There was a pause as Una looked from Declan to Fiona to get an answer.

Declan began to explain. "Una, do you remember I told you that Fiona and I had a little sister . . ."

Una turned to Fiona in her breathless excitement.

"I'm going to have a little sister, too, or it could be a boy." Then she turned back to her Dad. "What was her name, I forgot her name, your little sister?"

Julie interjected. "Maybe we can talk about that later, Una. We had a late dinner, and it's close to your bedtime."

Fiona breathed a sigh of relief.

"Fiona's going to be visiting for a while, so there'll be plenty of time to talk."

"Can Fiona read me a bedtime story?" Una pleaded, not quite ready to give up her new-found aunt yet. Fiona was about to say fine when Declan interrupted.

"Una, it's time for you to run up and brush your teeth."

Una protested. "But, Daddy, I'm not tired." Declan insisted. "But I'm not even a little bit sleepy. Can't I stay up longer? Can't Aunt Fiona please read to me? Can you play to me on the violin?"

Declan laughed. "I don't think my violin playing would put you asleep yet—more likely keep you awake all night, sweetheart!"

Julie came up with a compromise. "How about Fiona will read you a story the next time she comes over? And I'm sure Daddy will play to you when he has some tunes worked out. But you have school tomorrow, and we need to hustle now and get ready for bed." This worked like a charm. Una jumped up and said good-night to Fiona, and gave her a big hug.

"Are you coming up to say good-night, Daddy?"

"Yes, I promise. I'll come up to kiss you good-night when you have your teeth brushed and are in bed, love. And maybe there'll be time for a very, very short story." Una gave a little squeak of delight and bounded up the stairs, followed by Julie.

Fiona and Declan were left alone, and an awkward silence

descended. She started to clear away the dishes and bring them into the kitchen. Declan put on water for tea. She tried to break the ice. "You've started to play the violin?"

"Just playing around—fiddling around a bit! You remember I took lessons?"

"Now that you mention it, I have a vague recollection."

"I used to play with Dad a bit. Then I took it up again in third year or so—you were away in boarding school."

"I don't remember you practicing." They continued to clear away the dishes.

"I didn't much during the holidays. And later on Dad didn't want to play—so I dropped it, eventually."

"And you're interested in taking it up again?" Fiona asked

"I think Dad used to think I had some talent, though he never really said that. Then, at the wake, one of the fiddlers remembered me playing as a teenager, said that Dad wished I had kept it up."

Fiona flashed on Mrs. Connelly's remarks about her Dad's pride in her writing. "There was a lot left unsaid, wasn't there?"

Declan nodded. "Oh, yes! So, since he left me his violin, I'm starting to try it out again. Might take some lessons to get back in my stride—it's been a good few years!"

"That's great, Declan. Dad never played again after Orla died, did he?"

"I gather he occasionally joined in a few sessions locally from time to time, but he never played at home. He lost the heart for it, I think."

Lost the heart, is right, Fiona silently concurred.

They worked in silence for a while. Fiona noticed a photograph of Una on the sideboard. "She's the image of Orla, isn't she?"

"Una?" He nodded and helped Fiona clear more dishes from the table. "There's a definite resemblance—the curls I suppose. She definitely takes after my side."

"The good-looking side," Fiona added, a bit deviously, remembering "The Old Maid in the Garrett."

Declan was quick to jump in. "I meant, as opposed to Julie's."

Fiona laughed. "I know what you meant. And I didn't really mean just looks, but personality. It's almost uncanny." She loaded up the dishwasher.

When Declan had the tea brewing he pulled out the big folder from his desk and placed it on the table. "You sure you want to start on this tonight?"

Fiona nodded affirmation. She really wanted to try to work out some agreement. They sat down opposite each other. Declan took a deep breath, and Fiona wondered if he was more nervous than he looked. He cleared his throat. "It seems like Dad was hoping we could—get on."

"Do you mean like some kind of test?"

"Maybe. Fiona, we're family. Julie and Una are my family now, too, and it's important to me to be able to bring them to Ireland, to our old home."

"And how do we reconcile that with my wanting to say goodbye to it all, to leave it behind?"

"I honestly don't know. I'm hoping we can talk it through. There must be a way we can both get what we want."

"But if I don't want anything to do with it . . . ?"

"Why should it bother you that I still have ownership?"

"But it's about the ties, the connections to the past."

Declan paused before responding. "You say you don't want to

hold on to those memories, but your work on the novel, and now the film, belies that."

Fiona felt herself losing her grip on the barely controlled emotions. "Why are you so threatened by my novel?"

"Your view of our childhood is so skewed."

"I could understand that you would be in denial about the past—you were such a bully and liar."

"See. That's exactly what I'm talking about," Declan was red in the face now and his voice had lost its cool command. "I can't let you portray me that way. I know it's not really me, but, as I'm your brother . . . " He stood up abruptly and went to the kitchen to pour the tea. He took the teacups from the cabinet and filled up the milk jug.

Fiona wondered for the millionth time if Declan knew about the sexual abuse and knew that was why Frank would side with her and break the tie on the will, if it came to that. She measured her words carefully.

"You know, I exaggerated and changed some real life incidents when I was writing the novel. If you think the brother is that unsympathetic, maybe you have a guilty conscience over things I don't even know about."

"What are you implying, Fiona?" Declan fumed. "What would I have a guilty conscience about?"

She hazarded a reply. She tried to keep her voice even.

"Uncle Frank. He used to hurt me. After Orla died and Aunt Rita, of course, was already dead." Fiona glanced sideways at Declan to try and gauge his reaction.

"What do you mean, hurt you? How? When?"

"I remember him sticking his fingers into my shoulders, maybe he was trying to reassure, you know the way people do, but he always did it too tight, like he was prying his fingers between my bones. And it always hurt for a long time afterwards."

Declan seemed puzzled. "But when; were we there? Maybe he was just giving you a hug or something and he pressed too hard."

"I remember in the bedroom once, Orla's and mine, when she was sick, and we were all standing around in the dark. Then lots of places—when we said the rosary at night, remember? He'd be behind me and had this habit of pressing my shoulder. But you and Dad and Mam were there, so I didn't know why you didn't stop him. From hurting me. I thought you would try to stop him."

"But how could we know if you didn't say? He couldn't have meant to hurt you. Not deliberately. He was a bit distracted then, wasn't he, a bit strange?" Declan's voice was agitated.

Fiona nodded affirmation. "Weren't we all?"

She then looked directly into her brother's eyes. "I thought that you were the only one who was sane, normal. Who could see things clearly. I was a bit afraid of all of them. So I thought you might stop him. I hated those rosaries. Do you remember?"

Declan nodded. "Oh, yes! 'Thou, O Lord, wilt open my lips . . .' et cetera. Then the launch into, 'Glory be to the Father, the Son and the Holy Ghost, as it was in the beginning is now and ever shall be, world without end, Amen.'"

"And the five mysteries—Joyful, Sorrowful or Glorious."

"And then Dad always continued with a litany of other prayers, 'Hail Holy Queen, Mother of Mercy. Hail our life, our sweetness and our hope.'"

"I liked 'our sweetness and our hope'" Fiona interjected. "I liked those words. But the whole thing went on so long, and my knees were always sore, and then there was Uncle Frank."

There was a long silence before Declan added, "Me, too, I hated them too."

He shifted his attention back to the pot. "This tea is probably turned to porter by now!" They smiled, and Fiona sunk into the chair, drained. It seemed as if her brother didn't know about Frank.

As Declan re-emerged with the tea, Una's twinkling voice called out from her upstairs bedroom. "Daddy, Daddy! I'm ready for my very, very short story!"

He handed Fiona her cup of tea. "I'd better attend to the little empress."

And he called up to Una, "I'll be right there pumpkin."

Fiona watched his disappearing back, shifted to an armchair and took a deep sip of her tea. It was going to be a long haul.

■ ■ ■

"Will I pour you a cup?" Fiona offered when Julie came downstairs

"No thanks." Julie laughed. "I'll fix myself an herbal one. I haven't picked up the Irish habit of drinking tea late. I tried it a few times and was awake half the night."

Fiona had last met Julie at her mother's funeral in 1988, and, once or twice, their visits to Ireland had briefly overlapped. Fiona always found her easy to get on with. Julie and Declan had been married over ten years now. They got married in a small civil wedding in Los Angeles, and none of the family had been invited. His parents wouldn't have traveled anyway—neither of them liked to budge beyond their own environs, and Fiona wouldn't have been inclined to come either, so it was probably just as well.

"You must be excited about the new baby. Declan was saying it's due around Christmas."

"Yes. December 23rd—a winter baby."

"Orla was born on December 24th, Christmas Eve. I always thought she was a Christmas present, because she was born at home—she just appeared."

"That's interesting. I recall Declan saying something very similar about you once. You were born around Easter?"

Fiona nodded. "I was actually born the day before but came home from the hospital on Easter Sunday."

"He said he thought you were an Easter present. What age was he, about three?"

"Right. He would have been about three and a half. Maybe he thought I came from a golden egg!"

Julie laughed. "Was that an Irish tradition?"

"No. But in our family it was the Golden Hen who came at Easter when we were small. And we believed she laid the chocolate eggs!"

"And does the name Fiona have a connection to Easter?"

"Not particularly. It means white or pale."

"Well, that fits your lovely skin." Julie flashed a smile, and Fiona blushed. She didn't mention that Fiona also meant "fair."

"And now your baby is arriving as a holiday present, too. For years I thought babies came from Santa. I bet Una doesn't think that!"

Julie laughed. "No, she knows this baby is in my womb. She hasn't asked for too many details yet, but I bet it's around the corner. Sometimes I think she's seven going on seventeen."

"And she's probably old enough not to be jealous, do you think? Or are they ever?"

Julie laughed. "I suspect she'll be happy to have a sibling of either gender to boss around. I know I would have loved a brother or sister myself growing up—you always romanticize what you don't get."

"I suppose I never thought about it much with the three of us, though we were a tiny family in Ireland at the time. Everyone around us had six or eight or ten or more. Once, when I went to the hospital with Orla and was waiting outside because I was too young to go in, I met a Dublin girl who came from a family of twenty-two. Can you imagine?"

Julie groaned and held her expanding belly. "No! I can't imagine or don't even want to! Poor woman. She must have spent half of her life pregnant. Not that I mind it, but twenty times, I would!"

"Declan mentioned in Ireland that you were having a hard time?"

"Was as sick as a dog for the first couple of months. Swore I'd never go through it again. But it seems to have miraculously cleared up. I feel great now."

"Would you want another child, then?" Fiona asked. "Were you planning on more?"

"I'm not sure. Declan would have been happy with just Una. But I really wanted her to have company."

"Maybe Declan felt it would be less complicated with one." Fiona thought of their convoluted relationship. "But then you were lonely on your own. Will we ever get it right?"

Declan appeared down the stairs at that moment and joined them in the living room.

"How is she?" Julie asked.

"Grand. Out like a light. She was worn out."

"It was a big day for her." Julie smiled at Fiona. "Her entire family expanded by a quarter! Since she started the school project on family and ancestors I think she feels rather impoverished. Even though she only met your mother and father once, she says she remembers them. We all visited before your mom died in '88, so Una was five. She added deceased signs to the chart when they died."

Fiona felt a wave of loss for the little girl. "What about your parents, Julie? Are they still alive?"

"They're very much alive and well. They're only in their mid-60's. Same ages as your parents, come to think of it."

"But they're not inclined to visit." Declan added.

Fiona thought that he appeared somewhat agitated as he headed to the wine rack and browsed through the selection.

"Would you like some wine, Fiona?"

"Yes, sure. Red if you have it."

"I have a good rich Pinot here, local—well northern California. Julie, would you like a juice or anything?"

Julie shook her head. "I'm fine with my tea, thanks." And she continued to Fiona. "My parents have developed a kind of mania for travel. They never went anywhere until about ten years ago, and now, I never know where they are. They've retired to Florida, but they're always taking some trip to Europe or Costa Rica or an African Safari or Bermuda."

"Los Angeles doesn't seem to be on their itinerary." Declan threw in sardonically as he uncorked the wine.

Julie sighed. "They've only seen Una twice, once when we flew out there to visit them and once on a brief stopover here when they were on their way to some place else—New Zealand, maybe, or Hawaii." She shook her head. "They don't seem to be interested."

Fiona felt bad for them and guilty. She hadn't made any effort herself to get to know her niece because of her unspoken feud with Declan. She also felt the weight of the responsibility of being the only remaining candidate for a family relation. But she couldn't be sure Declan had any interest in her filling that role, either. She genuinely liked Julie and Una, and now her head was beginning to fill with yet another new version of her past reality—Julie's perceived version of Declan's childhood. She couldn't get the idea of Declan remembering her as a gift out of her mind as she sipped the wine and chatted easily to her brother and new-found sister-in-law.

■ ■ ■

In the shower later that evening, Fiona allowed the warm water to gently lull her. Maybe the film would be the clincher and get her career back on track—and maybe it would also reactivate the muse. She had escaped from the meshes of her existence in Ireland ten years before and ensconced herself in the safety of her East Coast refuge. As she recalled her beloved nest, she reflected on how it had cradled her. She had woven her way in there and she was part of the fabric of the wood, of the walls, and the bookcases and the old oak desk, just as years back she had bound up her existence and her breathing and her thinking with the oak of the treehouse cocoon. But, as she luxuriated in the shower in the light of the West Coast evening, she thought of her chosen home and wondered if it might have also stifled her. She had now headed west, to the sun. She had put the whole mass of the United States between herself and New York. She had left the Atlantic Ocean, shared between Ireland and the East Coast, for the new and foreign Pacific. Half way round the world, she was still running headlong into her past.

CHAPTER TEN

REVISITINGS

> "If you bring out what is within you,
> it will save you.
> If you do not bring out what is within
> you, it will destroy you."
>
> GNOSTIC GOSPELS

The next morning, Fiona was awakened from a deep sleep by the sound of the telephone. At first she was disoriented as she looked around at the unfamiliar room. She started to recall the bits she had read from her Dad's diary before drifting off to sleep and the sense of love and loss that pervaded them. She had a panicked thought that the underlying truth of her novel was all wrong and that she had to let Sean know so that it could be adjusted. Then she roused herself and made her way to the ringing phone, which sat on the desk in the lounge. "Hello?" She always expected bad news if the telephone rang early in the morning or late at night.

"Fiona, is that you, Fiona?"

She froze. How did Uncle Frank know where she was?

"Hello?"

"Yes, yes, I'm here, Uncle Frank . . . where are you?" She fought back the irrational thought that he was in the U.S.A.

"I'm here at home, of course. Mr. Stanley is keeping track of your whereabouts due to his responsibility over the timing of the will, you know."

She began to breathe again. Tried to steady her voice.

"You're the first one to ring." She knew that sounded lame. "I just got the phone connected."

"And you're in Los Angeles with Declan. That's grand, that is. Have you two talked yet?"

"Yes, I mean, no. We haven't come to any agreement yet. I'm out here working . . ."

"On the story, yes. The same one you wrote?"

Did he think she would change it? Add more details? Shame herself by writing about such unspeakable happenings.

"Yes, it's the same."

There was a silence on the other end. Fiona wondered if she imagined that he breathed a sigh of relief. Then back to his jovial self.

"The clock is ticking, you know. Don't leave it too long."

"Well, we have 'til the end of the summer, don't we? We have some time."

"But time has a way of getting past you. And you know that you don't have to worry. You have me on your side no matter what. You don't have to worry."

Fiona felt sickened. Her violator was offering her protection twenty-seven years after the fact. She needed to get it over with. To remove him from her life forever.

"I'll work with Declan. And if we can't work it out, as you said . . ."

"I have the tie-breaker."

He sounded triumphant. Fiona hated giving him the satisfaction of knowing he had the upper hand.

"We'll let you know."

"Good then. So long. I have your number now, and you know where to reach me."

Fiona pounced on the answering machine the second Frank hung up, and she began to lay down a message.

■ ■ ■

Sean had scheduled a mid-morning meeting with the film producers and invited Fiona to come. She thought for a brief moment about canceling, and then decided against it. Sean had a way of breaking through her defenses without even trying. There was an ease of presence, a sense of him being there and not preoccupied, a feeling that she didn't have to make small talk but could go directly to whatever needed to be said. And a relaxation. This last was the most refreshing for Fiona who was anything but relaxed in her own body and mind. She would have to talk to him about a possible change of direction in the script anyway.

When Sean arrived by cab at 9:30, Fiona was still reeling from the phone call from Uncle Frank. She grabbed her bag, now heavy with his script of her story, and jumped in beside him. The driver was a woman in her mid-twenties, tall and tanned and blonde and wearing a fuchsia halter-neck t-shirt and khaki shorts. She sported a peaked cap which matched her shirt. Her long shapely legs seemed to dance suggestively as she drove. It turned out she was an actress and had figured out Sean was a director, so she was doing all she could to impress him with her acting abilities.

Fiona felt overdressed in her long sleeves and modest cotton skirt, especially in contrast to the *chauffeuse*. She sank into her seat and let the driver babble away, half listening to the drone of voices as she looked out the window at the Los Angeles skyline. They were whisked away from the beach with its clusters of houses, hotels and condominiums, and soon approached the downtown area with its interwoven tapestry of freeways and an endless stream of cars. The buildings were shiny and modern and seemed the opposite of New York because of their newness. Even though New York had a multitude of new buildings, the prevailing sense was of oldness and history. To Fiona, Los Angeles seemed all about novelty, and it was typified by this perky cab driver who was seriously hustling for a job. Most of the New York cabbies were not American-born, were covered up, perpetually hassled, and gave off an aura of having been cabbies all their lives. This would-be movie star was the epitome of youth and health and freshness and seemed bound and determined to not stay a cab driver for a second longer than she could help it. As they pulled up to the studio, she extracted a head-shot and résumé from a portfolio cover on the passenger seat and handed it to Sean. He accepted gracefully as they disembarked.

"Sorry about that." He grinned. "Par for the course!"

"I kind of enjoyed it." Fiona admitted. "Part of the culture!"

"Are you okay?" Sean looked concerned.

Fiona thought she had managed to cover her upset. She nodded.

"Are you sure? Ready for this?"

She assured him she was fine.

Fiona absorbed the impression of light, wood, glass and piles and piles of scripts as the two producers, Leonard Shaw and Les Graves, greeted them at the door. The office was spacious and filled with mid-morning Southern California sunshine. Leonard was tall, gangly and lightly tanned and spoke with a relaxed California accent. His partner was short, stocky and very pale and spoke with a heavy Boston accent. They seemed to be identically dressed in a smart casual manner, immaculate tan trousers and light blue, perfectly pressed, short-sleeved shirts. They both wore ties which admittedly were not identical. Leonard's was a slightly deeper shade of blue than his shirt and decorated with tiny film cameras. Les's was brown with a blue speckled pattern. They greeted Sean warmly and Fiona with a less gushing but still friendly reception.

"Ms. Clarke, it's a real pleasure." Leonard shook her hand vigorously.

"A pleasure." Les echoed and motioned them both to sit down.

Fiona and Sean sat on one side of a very long table filled with neat piles of documents. The two producers sat side by side opposite them. They had a copy of the screenplay that they shuffled back and forth between them. Leonard led off.

"Ms. Clarke—may I call you, Fiona?"

"Please." Fiona was relieved.

"And please address us as Leonard and Les."

Fiona nodded, amused by the formality of the invitation to informality.

"First, I want to let you know how pleased we are that Sean here is going to helm this project." Leonard paused and fingered the script.

Les reached out and pulled the script towards him and added, "Based on your most interesting story."

"Most interesting." Leonard nodded. And he continued. "The timing is perfect for an Irish script. There's a resurgence of interest in all things Irish—in music . . ."

"U2, Celtic Music in general. In dance . . ." Les interjected.

"Irish dancing—it's a phenomenon here; everyone loves it . . ." Leonard continued.

"Irish theatre is big on Broadway—lots of young playwrights, . . ."

"It's a Renaissance . . ." Leonard continued.

"A Celtic Renaissance . . ." Les added.

"And the perfect time for a lovely script with a rural angle." Leonard began to conclude.

"For your script, Fiona. Sean." Les looked at them.

"For your script." Leonard finished.

Fiona experienced both déjà vu and unreality. Maybe it's a flashback to *Alice in Wonderland,* she thought—this scene did have the semblance of a Mad Hatter Tea Party! She smiled her thanks for the compliments to the two men. They smiled back and continued.

"Good. Well. Location. We need to pin that down, Sean, as soon as possible." And he and Les together attacked one of the piles and began to lay out photos, similar to the ones Sean had shown Fiona at their first meeting. Green rolling hills, flat lush landscapes, perfectly manicured farmyards. Fiona glanced at Sean, but, before he could speak, Leonard launched into an enthusiastic appraisal of the proposed locations.

"These are all available to us. Our scouts have sussed them out and several of them could work, in our opinion."

"These ones here," chimed in Les, "of Montana, are perhaps the most perfect, don't you think?" But he didn't look up to see if they did.

"The lush greenness, lots of rain." Leonard pointed out.

"Almost forty shades, don't you think?" he remarked, again, without checking.

"Just look at those hills, adorable, picture perfect." And then as if on cue, they both swiveled the photos around so that Sean and Fiona could see them better. Fiona wondered if they actually rehearsed these speeches, or were they just so in tune that they knew when the other was finished? She politely glanced at the photos and waited for Sean to speak.

"I had a discussion with Fiona earlier in the week," Sean began, "and she had a question regarding authenticity." You could hear a pin drop. Sean continued. "She felt, and still does," he looked at her for assurance, "that these don't convey the gritty sense of Irish country life, especially rural life, in the 1960's and 1970's. That they are missing—reality." Again he checked with Fiona. She nodded agreement.

Les and Leonard had recovered from their shock and found their voices again.

"But," as always Leonard led off, "are we talking location here or cinematography? You know that light is magic Sean. With a good D.P., Director of Photography," he added for Fiona's benefit, "with a good D.P . . ."

"And Ryan is the best . . ." added Les.

"The very best . . ." agreed Leonard.

"With a good, knowledgeable D.P. like Ryan, you can achieve whatever look you want. He can give you authenticity."

"But . . ." Fiona summoned up the courage. "Is there really any substitute for the real thing? The actual place, the soil, the light, the colors? I wonder if you can really capture that, no matter how skilled the crew is."

"Of course you can, of course you can." Leonard again. "That's our business; it's what we do. We deal in illusion, but we convince you it's real."

"And these pictures," Les indicated them, "these pictures are perfect." He placed his palm on one of them and continued emphatically. "This is Ireland. I'm from Boston, for God's sake. I know Irish when I see it."

Fiona swallowed. She didn't dare make eye contact with Sean. She was afraid she might either laugh or cry. Leonard went on.

"We have to remember our audience here, Sean, Fiona. With all due respect, most of them won't be able to tell Montana from County Kerry or Cork or whatever."

"But surely," Fiona continued, "surely, you don't want to feed them images that make them think Montana is the same as Cork or Kerry or any Irish county. Sean told me that he gets a lot of his information about places like Ireland from books and films. If you keep shooting Irish films in Montana or a place where the landscape vaguely resembles Ireland, then they really won't be able to tell the difference—but can you want that? For it to be fake? For people to never see the authentic landscape? For it to become this generalized lovely green pasture like every other green countryside place? I know I'm not a filmmaker and don't know the ins and outs of creating mood and texture and the feel of a place with light and angles and so on, but I think there's no substitute for being in the actual place itself, if you're trying to capture the quiddity, the real nature of a thing, it's essence."

There was a long pause. No one spoke. Les and Leonard had their eyes fixed on her, but she had no notion what they were thinking. Sean was still and present. It was too late to retreat so she pushed to the finish. "I know it's a lot more money, maybe it's not in the budget, but I believe that this film will be stronger and richer and more believable if you shoot it in Ireland."

The team of two unlocked their eyes at the same time and then re-focused them on Sean.

Leonard spoke. "Are you in agreement with this, Sean? You said you discussed it."

"Yes, I am. Fiona has convinced me. Maybe we could work out some economical ways to get the footage. The exterior scenes at least."

"Hmm," Leonard demurred and looked longingly at the photographs. Les echoed his "hmm" and he, too, glanced sadly at the photos, as if trying to understand how they could lack the essence of Ireland.

"This wasn't budgeted for, as you said, Sean. This is not a big budget film, as you know I'm sure, Fiona. There aren't any car chases or explosions, so we're not appealing to a mass audience here. We can't expect a big return. We'd have to think it over."

"Talk it over. Check with our backers." Les added.

"But we can't promise. It's a bit of a surprise, frankly. It may not happen—so don't get your hopes up. Either way . . ."

"Either way, we're sure we can produce a fine film." Les concluded. He looked at Leonard, and they nodded as if to agree that this topic had been dealt with.

The meeting continued on as the men discussed details of the crew, logistics and time lines. Fiona let herself sit back and listen to the timbre of the voices: Leonard's elongated vowels and flowing sentences, Les's more syncopated rhythm and harsher sounds uttered in shorter phrases, Sean's cool and assured but slightly urgent speech. The sun rose in the sky, the shadows shifted in their lazy progress across the room, and Fiona basked in its luminosity. As she drifted in and out of awareness of the conversations around her she reflected on her passionate call for a film that reflected reality. She had surprised herself and experienced a tug-of-war between aspects of herself, her desire to alternately conceal and reveal. She also had no desire to go back to Ireland herself but was advocating strongly for authenticity. Her drive towards the truth was asserting itself through this story.

Sean touched her shoulder. The meeting was over. Les and Leonard shook hands and thanked them, and she and Sean left the sunny air-conditioned room and emerged into the mid-afternoon heat.

■ ■ ■

"Are you okay?" Sean asked.

She nodded. "Yes. I'm fine. Maybe a bit overwhelmed."

Sean proposed a bike ride.

"I hope I remember how!" Fiona joked. "I haven't been on a bike since I was about seventeen."

She realized that it would be good to get some exercise and that she wouldn't need to talk unless she wanted to. It was Sean's way of letting her have room to breathe and to think.

They rented bikes and went cycling on a bicycle path along the beach front from Santa Monica to the Marina del Rey. Along the way, they passed joggers and walkers and skaters and other cyclists. Fiona and Sean rode at a leisurely pace. It was a glorious morning, and, though initially a wee bit shaky, Fiona quickly regained her poise. She revelled in the sheer physical pleasure of pedaling and sailing along. They rode in tandem for a while, and then Sean pulled up beside her.

"I think the meeting went very well. I'm pleased overall with the progress we made."

Fiona nearly swerved into him. "Really? You considered that progress? I thought it was disastrous!"

"But we did make progress," he insisted. "Although the idea of shooting in Ireland was a bit of a shock!"

Fiona put on a fake authoritative voice and her version of a West Coast accent as she mimicked Leonard Shaw. "We have to remember our audience here, Sean." She began with a slight shake of the head. "Most of them won't be able to tell Montana from County Kerry or Cork or wherever!"

Sean got into the spirit and played along, imitating Les Graves in a passable Boston accent. "I mean, these pictures are perfect. This is Ireland. I'm from Boston, I know Irish when I see it!"

Both Sean and Fiona nearly toppled off the bikes, they were laughing so hard, but they steadied themselves and rode along slowly, enjoying the bit of fun. Fiona was getting in her stride.

"Is it that hard to at least shoot exteriors in Ireland?" It just dawned on her that she might have inadvertently jeopardized the film by inserting this new request. "There is so much farmland, I imagine lots of people would give permission to shoot."

"Les and Leonard will look into it. They must have some contacts. It's probably mostly a budget issue, and it may involve some union issues, too, with crew."

"They're great, the two of them—like a comedy duo!"

Sean laughed. "They're not the worst. They have their blind spots for sure—but I do have them to thank for giving a new kid on the block a chance to direct."

Fiona glanced over at him as she pulled in to let two other cyclists pass. She and Sean paused to take a breather. "But you're not that new, are you?" she asked.

"I've done a lot of shorter work," Sean answered, "some TV and a low, low budget feature. But this is different. This is my first shot with a half decent budget."

"So why do you need me on the project? I think I'm more of a hindrance than a help." Fiona laughed.

"But you have a take on these characters . . ." Sean started to say.

"That you don't agree with!" Fiona topped him.

"But that's it," he jumped in. "You have a different spin on this story, which is obviously very close to you."

There was a deadening silence. "What do you mean, close to me?"

Sean faltered just a little. "Well," he paused, "the situation is really similar to your background—brought up on the farm, you said you went to boarding school, so I just assumed that some portion . . ." he broke off.

"Well, don't assume!" She remounted her bicycle and sped off.

Sean hesitated, got back on his own bike, started to try to catch up with her, obviously thought better of it and let her ride on.

Fiona kept her advantage for a while, aware of Sean holding back but following not too far behind. She felt the pull to the personal and resisted it. At the same time she felt bad for shouting at Sean—he was only trying to do his job after all, get some clarity on her story. She slowed down and let him catch up so they were riding abreast again. She looked sideways at him, his freckles seemed darker and his cheeks brighter.

"I don't have any great insights, you know," she ventured as a sort of peace offering.

"But I like your work," he insisted. "Your short stories and articles as well as your novel. And you've done well," he continued. "You're published, have an agent."

"I just got lucky with Pam," she said quietly.

"But you've got well reviewed, and . . ."

Fiona cut in. "It's all a fluke, is what it is," she said, no trace of self pity in her voice. Then, almost under her breath, "One of these days they'll find out."

"Find out what?" he asked.

She paused before completing her thought. "That I'm a fraud." It was barely audible. Sean had no idea how to follow this up and decided wisely not to even try right at this moment. They continued to ride along the beach in silence as the noontime sun achieved its zenith.

CHAPTER ELEVEN

DOWN THE RABBIT-HOLE

> "In another moment down went Alice after it, never once considering how in the world she was to get out again."
>
> LEWIS CARROLL—*Alice in Wonderland*

"Mum, does 'novelist' have a small 'n' or a capital 'n?'"

Julie smiled. "Small 'n,' sweetheart,' and then she whispered to Fiona. "She's writing her school essay about 'My Aunt, the novelist'!"

Fiona was pleased and unexpectedly shy. She really liked Una, and the child seemed to take to her as well. "I'm impressed she's able to write so well. She's seven . . . so finishing up second grade?" she asked Julie, as she moved in and out of the kitchen area where Declan was helping clean up.

Julie laughed and tousled her daughter's hair. "She's a clever one all right. Yes—she's going into third grade in the fall."

"Mo . . . . . . m!" Una squealed. "I'm trying to write! There!" and she put the final period to her assignment. "Now I just need a photo of Fiona." She had her camera in her hand. "Ready? Say cheese!" and she snapped off a photo. "I don't think I moved my hand. I think that's a good photo. You're pretty!" Then Una turned her dancing blue eyes up to Fiona. "Can you read me a story tonight, Fiona?"

Before Fiona could answer Declan butted in. "Una, Fiona is tired from working hard all day . . ."

"You promised!" Una cut him off. "You said next time, and that was last time!"

Julie intervened. "Do you want to, Fiona?"

"Yes, I'd love to," Fiona said, and Una started to jump up and down with excitement.

"Mom, what can we read, what can we read?"

"What about *Alice in Wonderland?*" Fiona ventured. "I read that when I was about your age."

"I'm not sure we have it . . ." Julie began, and Fiona said she had a copy in her bag.

Declan walked into the room, and there was a distinct chill in his voice.

"You mean you just happen to have a copy of *Alice in Wonderland* lying around in your purse?"

"I brought it with me, because of the script," Fiona explained. "It's the one I got from Aunt Rita when I was about seven or eight."

Una was getting all excited now. "What's it about?" she asked. "Does it have pictures?"

"It's about a girl who goes on great adventures," Fiona told her. "And it has lots of pictures."

Julie helped Una put away her homework. "Fiona, if you want to finish drying the pots, I'll take Una up and get her ready for bed."

Una hopped up. "I'll call you when I'm ready for the story!" she announced to Fiona and started up the stairs two at a time with Julie following.

Fiona was very conscious of Declan's silence as they worked side by side in the kitchen, she drying and putting away the pots, he loading the dishwasher.

"I'm not going to kidnap her, you know!"

Declan slowly and methodically loaded the wine glasses on the top rung of the dishwasher. Then he spoke quietly and evenly as if trying to stay calm. "I remember you reading *Alice in Wonderland* to Orla. You were always holed up with her." He didn't manage to keep a note of resentment out of his voice.

"And what's that got to do with Una?" Fiona asked. "Orla is an entirely different case, as you well know. She was sick, she needed to be taken care of . . ."

"But not to be possessed," Declan blurted, "not to be idolized."

"She needed to be watched and loved," Fiona retorted, "to be kept well."

Declan all but banged shut the door to the dishwasher. "She wasn't a thing, Fiona. She was a little girl . . ."

"She wasn't just a little girl, any little girl." Fiona restrained herself from smashing the pot down on the counter top. "She was beautiful and delicate and perfect. Even Mam always said she was an angel, a little angel."

"That's because you were a child." Declan said a trifle gentler. "And Mam believed it, too. She thought she must have been meant to go to heaven. But Orla was still just a little girl, an ordinary . . ."

"There was nothing ordinary about Orla, and you know it!" Fiona was almost shouting now and close to tears. She suspended the pan in midair. "She was extraordinary in every way. She was gorgeous, she shone at everything she did. She was my little sister and . . ."

"You seem to forget that she was my little sister, too," Declan replied, his voice edgy as he wiped the wooden salad bowl, "just like you were before Orla came along!"

Fiona stared at him, unable to speak for a second. "Oh God!" she finally blurted out. "You're jealous!" And with that thought she lost all desire to cry. She was amazed and astounded—it had never occurred to her that Declan cared enough to be jealous of anyone. Then she had a memory flash of the magical Christmas morning when Orla had appeared, miraculously, and Fiona had been drawn to her as if by magnetic force. She had a vague memory of a boy, her brother, in the background, trying to entice her away, trying to get her back to playing and presents, back to their life before. It gave her a grudging respect for him that he cared enough, seemingly about both her and Orla, to experience jealousy at the loss of their company. It might help to explain why he acted like such a jackass most of the time when they were children.

Just then they heard the tinkling innocent voice of Una from upstairs. "Fiona, Fiona. I'm ready!"

It broke the spell. Declan placed the bowl in the cabinet, and Fiona slipped the last pot into the cupboard.

Una's bedroom was small and cozy, the wallpaper covered in Minnie Mouse cartoons, the pine shelves packed with books and toys. A small pink tape-player stood on one of the shelves. The bed had a fat pink comforter and fluffy pillows with clown pattern pillow-slips. Una was sunk into the pillows, eyes wide open, listening to Fiona who sat on the edge of the bed, reading aloud from *Alice in Wonderland*. She had gotten past the first few pages, and Una was rapt as Alice followed the pink rabbit down the rabbit hole.

"In another moment, down went Alice after it, never once considering how in the world she was to get out again."

When Fiona paused in her reading, Una piped up. "Do you have this book a really long time?"

Fiona showed her the inscription, and Una read it aloud, trying to make out the words.

"Chri . . . Christmas 1962, Love to Fiona, From A . . . Auntie Rita and Un . . . Uncle Frank. Who were they? Did you like them? Did they live near you or far away like you do from me?"

Fiona paused. "Yes and yes. They were my only aunt and uncle, and I liked them a lot. They lived a short way from us. Uncle Frank was a baker in the village near where I grew up, near where Grandma Anna and Grandpa James lived."

"You're lucky to have them near you. I don't have any relatives near me. You're my only aunt, and you live far away."

"True. But I'm here for a good long visit now, aren't I? We'll have fun while I'm here."

"Are they dead, too, your aunt and uncle?"

Fiona considered lying, but realized Una would probably meet Frank if they came to Ireland at the end of the summer as planned in order to finalize the will.

"Our Uncle Frank is still alive."

Una looked at the inscription once more. "It's really old, this book! Can you read me more?"

Fiona laughed. "Sure! Ready?"

Una nodded and settled happily into her pillows.

"The rabbit hole went straight on like a tunnel for some way, and then dipped suddenly down, so suddenly that Alice had not a moment to think about stopping herself before she found herself falling down what seemed to be a very deep well."

When Fiona came back downstairs after Una had fallen asleep, Declan had retired to his study, and Julie sat in the living room reading the *Los Angeles Times*.

"Wine, Fiona?"

"Sure. Is Declan joining us?"

"He's behind on some of his work. He's got a foster care case tomorrow so has to finish up his prep." Julie seemed apologetic.

Fiona nodded. She had a moment of despair about ever connecting with her brother. Maybe there was too much water under the bridge for them ever to manage to reach a rapprochement.

"He may join us in a while." Julie added.

"Does he work much at night, at home?"

"Not usually. He mostly manages to take care of everything during work hours—but with an especially difficult case he's sometimes under the wire. I think this one is either a foster care or adoption case; the mother was or is a heroin addict."

"So, she's in danger of losing her child?"

"Her son has already been taken away, temporarily, more than once. This is her last chance, I think."

"And Declan is working with her?"

"Yes. He doesn't discuss details, of course. But, he puts a lot into his clients."

"I'm sure he's really good."

Fiona thought that Julie seemed embarrassed.

"Julie. It's okay, really. Declan and I have never been the best of friends."

She seemed disturbed. "He doesn't talk about it, you know. His past. Hardly at all. Strange for a psychologist, I suppose. I know about Orla of course. And he told me about you, your birth. But later stuff he doesn't mention."

Fiona nodded.

"And he seems to avoid all things Irish."

At this Fiona laughed. "Well, maybe he and I do have some things in common then!"

Julie looked puzzled. "But why? I have to say I didn't mind so much; I'm not that hugely into family trees and my family isn't terribly 'familial!' But we never ran headlong away from our roots—and I guess for Una's sake, I'm starting to feel that she's missing out."

"Have you asked Declan about it?"

"When we first met he talked about Boston. He did a residency there. He seemed to be put off by all of the Irish."

Fiona couldn't stop herself from laughing. "Julie, I'm sorry. It seems really rude, and silly, to avoid your own people. I don't think it's an insult to Irish people as much as a reflection on our family—and maybe the Ireland that Declan and I left around 1980."

"The economy wasn't very good then, was it?"

"No. But I know I left to get away, try and make a clean start. And like Declan in Boston, I ended up meeting all the Irish in New York! For some people that's exactly what they wanted, and needed. For me? I needed to be anonymous."

"So how did you manage, then? Did you consciously cut yourself off?"

Fiona took a sip of wine and swept Julie back to her first summer in New York.

"I got my first job as a hotel receptionist and cashier at the Waldorf Astoria. I'd been in New York for several months but hadn't found my feet yet, wasn't really sure what I was doing."

"Where were you living?" Julie asked.

"I'd found a room in a house in the Bronx, sharing with a bunch of people: two Italian-Americans, Mario and Isabella, an Irish-American woman named . . . Imelda, I think, and an Irish fellow Jack, from Galway, who had been in the country about two years. Jack and his girlfriend Mary were coming to a shindig at the Waldorf this night—it was a big Irish dinner dance, and he had joked with me about coming up stairs for a dance during my break. I had no notion at all of going to an Irish dance!"

Julie laughed. "So this was 1980?"

Fiona nodded. "Yes. It was the year of the Hunger Strikers. Not sure if you remember that? Some of the I.R.A. were conducting a hunger strike in the high-security prison Long Kesh to get political prisoner status."

"They were considered criminals, right?" Julie asked. Fiona nodded.

"I had an Irish-American uncle in New York," Julie recalled. "My aunt married him; he was very militant. I think he collected money for the I.R.A."

"A lot of the funding comes from the Irish-Americans in the States. My two Irish house mates were very pro-Nationalist. Brits Out! Down with the colonizers! Of course, we were all taught in school that the proper thing to want, the ideal, was a united Ireland."

"And what do people want?"

"It's gotten very complicated. There's a whole population in the North that consider themselves British and want to stay with England. How do you reconcile that with a united Ireland? And in the south, there are many mixed opinions. My Dad called the Protestants 'planters.' Well, their ancestors were planters. They were given the land four hundred years ago. These people's families have been there longer than the U.S. has been in existence."

"And there are extremists on both sides."

"Yeah. So that night I was handling this reservation. An American man, mid-forties, gray suit, heavy glasses, I remember him very clearly. It was early evening, about eight, and he seemed to be a little drunk. I still remember his name—Jonathan Fredericks. I was entering his credit card details in the computer—these were clunky pieces of equipment, but cutting edge at the time, CRTs—this man, he was staring at my name plate and suddenly started accusing me of supporting 'murderers'. For a minute, I wasn't sure he was talking to me. So I just said, 'Excuse me?'

'You heard me, your compatriots. Murder innocents and then try to get people to feel sorry for them.'

I couldn't let that go. 'Are you calling all Irish people murderers?' my gall was rising.

"He told me his nineteen-year-old nephew from England was stationed in the North. First tour of duty, and shot dead in cold blood by the I.R.A. I didn't want to get into an argument with a drunken guest, but I wasn't going to stand there and be insulted either, so I answered him back. Something along the lines of the Irish having helped build his country alongside the other immigrants like the Chinese.

"I bet he didn't like that!" Julie laughed.

"No! Said they didn't need terrorists and gombeen men! I was making a supreme effort at self-control, and noticed that the other receptionist had slipped away, most likely to get the manager. But Mr. Fredericks launched into a big tirade against Paddies, which eventually led up to Bobby Sands."

"He was the leader of the hunger-strikers?"

"Yes. He was a huge hero. Our guest started accusing him of being a fake, a bastard at home, beating his wife. At that point, I'd had enough. I walked resolutely to the end of the counter, raised the hatch, marched around to face him and gave him MY big speech about his having no clue as to the complexities of the historical situation that had led to this moment, when young men felt compelled to starve themselves to death for an ideal. I said it was tragic that so many, his nephew included, had died for this cause, but bloodshed and brutality had led to more bloodshed and brutality, and the situation would never end if met only with the kind of ignorance and bigotry he was displaying here tonight."

"Wow! How did he respond?"

"Well, the manager appeared midway through my speech and signaled to the bellhop to get his luggage. I think Mr. Fredericks was so drunk he was stunned and couldn't even contrive a rebuttal. He gave me a dirty look, mumbled something under his breath and disappeared."

"Wow. That took guts, Fiona." Julie was impressed.

"And got me into deep trouble! The manager said I was rude to a guest."

"Surely he was the rude one. He attacked you and insulted all Irish people!"

"That's what I said. But I got the speech about being in the service industry and the customer being always right et cetera, et cetera, to which I replied that I was giving in my notice as I didn't want to work in a place where employees were abused and the manger didn't have the backbone to stand up for them!"

"God!" Julie gasped, "What did he say to that?"

"He actually switched to being very nice, and he suggested I take a break and sit in on the Irish dance upstairs—the one Jack and Mary were at."

"I don't think I've ever been to an Irish dance. What was it like?"

"It was like a scene that might have taken place in an Irish dance hall in my grandparents' time. People of all ages, prancing around, some dressed in kilts, and performing jigs and reels and kicking up their heels, spinning like dervishes. It was a throwback."

"I thought kilts were Scottish." Julie commented.

"They originated in Scotland and were only really adopted in Ireland around the turn of this century by Irish Nationalists. I'm sure it was connected with the Celtic Renaissance, a huge resurgence of pride in all things traditional."

"And are the patterns similar to the Scottish ones?" Julie asked.

"Some of the Irish kilts I've seen are plain, all one color. But I think that companies have started to manufacture tartans for the Irish-American market, for specific families. But, I saw more kilts at that Irish dinner-dance than I'd seen in my entire life!"

"And the dancing was not what you were used to at home?" Julie asked

"Not by a long shot. In competitions, yes, but not for recreation.

Then, I remember Jack and Mary forced me to dance *The Walls of Limerick* or something. I protested, but they would brook no resistance!"

"You got more of an Irish experience than you bargained for." Julie chuckled.

"Much more! It made me think afterwards about why I had come to America, and I knew instinctively that I didn't want that 'More-Irish-than-the-Irish-themselves culture.' Within a month, I had quit the hotel, found a low profile office job, which I later on replaced with my glamorous night cleaning one! I found my cozy little hideaway, began to write short stories and pile them up in my drawer. And now, here I am."

"You certainly showed gumption, Fiona. You fought your corner."

"Thanks." Fiona looked at Julie, sitting across from her. They were getting to know each other. Chatting, like sisters. Interesting that Julie should pick up on her ability to defend herself, to fight when attacked. She herself had remembered that whole experience vividly because it was the catalyst for her escape after she came to America. She saw it as running away, tunneling in. Julie chose to highlight her courage rather than her cowardice. Did she still have that strength and pride? Here she was, ten years later, in Los Angeles, feeling she had managed to escape the hyper-Irishness of the expatriate population of her adoptive city and pushed her own Irishness to a safer remove. And yet, she was again delving back into her past, heading back to the source, wondering if she had missed out on something, and hoping that this time round the journey back in time would both save her sinking career, and finally give her some peace.

EYE OF THE STORM

Excerpt from a novel by Fiona Clarke

I could picture all the girls on folding chairs in St. Killian's assembly hall. The nuns always sat near the front, and now Mother Assumpta was on the stage behind a lectern in the middle of delivering a speech.

"I'm very pleased that this year two of our St. Killian's girls have won prizes in the National Student Writer's 1971 Competition." She rustled her notes.

"In the category of Best Non-Fiction, the first prize among all the secondary schools in the country goes to Siobhán McHugh. There's a monetary prize of twenty pounds and a certificate—so Siobhán—could you come up please to the podium?"

There was a huge outburst of applause and congratulations as Siobhán wound her way through the chairs and up the aisle to accept her prize. I knew that Mother Assumpta was shaking her hand and handing her the envelope and the certificate and that Siobhán was beaming. She had a lovely smile. All the girls in her class, 6A, were particularly loud and happy.

"And next, in the category of Best Fiction, the first prize goes to—Sheila Flaherty."

There was another great round of applause from the gathering and the beginnings of a murmuring. Mother Assumpta continued. "There is a certificate and, again, a money prize of twenty pounds," she announced. "Sheila, you may come up and accept your prize."

The murmuring grew in intensity as everyone looked around for me. Then a voice piped up, it was Anna Smith at the back. "I think she's sick, Mother," she ventured. The Reverend Mother was clearly taken aback. "Gracious, she couldn't be sick," she exclaimed. "I spoke to her just this morning to make sure . . . " And she had. Very nicely, on the Q.T., she told me I'd won the award and that she looked forward to presenting it to me. I was letting her down, too. "Well . . . " She recovered. "We'll give this to her later, but let's have a big round of applause for Sheila in her absence."

The cheers and applause traveled through the assembly hall and down the corridor to the bathroom where my sixteen-year-old self knelt on the tiles of the bathroom floor, having just thrown up. I had heard Mother Assumpta's speech over the microphone and was mortified I wasn't there. My face was drained of all color, and I thought my stomach was about to explode. I knew by now that my stomach problem didn't really have anything to do with food or digestion, unless it involved trying to swallow praise I never felt I deserved. I heard the wave of applause die out and another spasm caused me to lean over the toilet bowl with dry heave. I curled up in a ball on the tiled floor, eyes wide open, and lay there, feeling the cold hard stone pressed against my cheek.

CHAPTER TWELVE

PRIDE

"In a dark time, the eye begins to see."
THEODORE ROETHKE

Fiona and Sean sat by her pool under a large umbrella. It had become their regular meeting place.

"Are you enjoying the pool?"

"I love it, sitting by it. I can't swim, though."

"What?" Sean seemed surprised—as if he thought everybody knew how to swim. "Well, if you wanted to, here's your chance to learn. A pool in your very own backyard."

"I think it's too late," Fiona added, as she picked up her sun hat.

"I'm a great teacher, by the way," he replied, coaxing.

"I'm not sure I could learn, honestly." Fiona told him. "I'm dead afraid of the water."

"Well, if you change your mind . . ." Sean added. And he left it open.

Sean turned to the script and his notes.

"I'm trying to get a grasp on the boarding school sequences. I think they will be interesting to American audiences as we're just not that familiar. Was it the usual thing for boys and girls? Or did that depend on background? How usual was it for someone of Sheila's background to go away to school?"

"It wasn't that common, especially in rural Ireland. She was one of three girls in her class who went. She won a scholarship which paid her way—I think that even made her Dad a bit proud of her."

"Isn't it normal to be proud? I do have a big question mark here—pride? That seems to be a running theme."

"I suppose we were indoctrinated, and it's hard to cast that off. It wasn't okay to be proud, it was sinful. Our parents thought we would get a swelled head."

"And was it desirable to go away to boarding school? I get the impression that Sheila is conflicted? She wants to get away from her brother, from Conor. And from her family, to some extent. Yet, I think she misses them, and they miss her. I personally can't imagine going to live away from home at twelve or thirteen. And maybe that's a big cultural or maturity issue?"

"There were all sorts of reasons for going away to school. The most common reason parents sent their children was to develop good study habits and be more successful. Sheila suspects that her parents want to get her out of the house. That they favor Conor."

"And why didn't he go?"

"Conor? Well, because the local boys' school he went to was excellent, but the local girls' school had a poor academic record."

"So, Sheila's parents had her best interests in mind then. Wanting to give her a good education?"

"You could see it that way. I just think that her confidence was so eroded at that point that she imagined the worst—saw it as a kind of abandonment."

"Was it dreadful? Lonely? Did she mind it? And did she stay all through high school?

"Five years, yes, until the Leaving Certificate—high school graduation. And in terms of lonely—it was mixed. There was a certain freedom, friendships with girls, but then distance from family."

"I'm looking at the descriptions of the nuns here," Sean flicked through Fiona's novel, "and the costume designer would probably like to talk with you about specifics. If you had any photos, that would be great."

"I do, actually. I have some photos of when I went to school—they were still in full regalia then!"

Sean found the place he was searching for. "Here it is—'*A bevy of nuns walked two by two down the driveway, chatting to each other. They were covered head to toe in black and white, layers of flowing black skirts, stiff white chest plates like armor, and helmet-like head-dresses. The shiny black rosary beads attached to the belts jangled as they walked.*' I like the military connotation!" he laughed.

Fiona laughed too. "Yeah, and the black and white. Our favorite joke—'What's black and white, and black and white, and black and white?'

Sean chuckled, "I don't know . . . newspapers fluttering in the wind?"

Fiona exploded in laughter. "Good try. No, a nun falling down the stairs!"

"Ha! I'm sure you have quite a collection!"

"They're well buried by now, but that one popped in my mind!"

Neither of them spoke for a while, or mentioned the common threads between Fiona's experience and Sheila's. Sean continued, "I think that was one of the chapters where I felt the bond between Sheila and her mother in the novel."

Fiona looked at Sean, who scribbled a few notes from time to time, but mostly just listened. "You're reading very closely between the lines, Sean."

He smiled. "It's my job. I get an entrée into an amazing array of lives."

"And then you get to bring them to life on screen."

"Yep. As best I can." He paused a moment. "So, what about the other girls? Were they sad, lonely?"

"Oh, we had a right lot of moaners in my school! For the first few weeks every term half of the dorm would cry themselves to sleep every night. I don't think I wrote that in the novel, but it might make a good scene in a movie!"

"And did you see your parents often, did they come to visit? Were you homesick?"

"They didn't come too often. But I was fine with that. I enjoyed the feeling of independence."

"And did it live up to its reputation in terms of academic rigor?"

"It did, yes. At that time, late 1960's, it was not common for anyone I knew to go on to university. The sons of the teachers, maybe. Many farmers' sons would leave school early. Girls often got married right out of school or did a shorthand and typing course and looked for an office job. Nursing was a popular choice, or primary teaching, or the bank. They were considered good steady pensionable jobs."

"But you went to university, and, in the novel, Sheila does, too."

"I gave her the benefit of my experience! But, in truth, I probably wouldn't have gone if I hadn't gone to boarding school, so it really was a stepping stone."

"Right." Sean looked over his notes. "I'm still confused about Sheila's relationship with the parents. Maybe I'm grappling with the pride issue—but I think I understand that a bit better. The disconnect."

"Do you mean between Sheila and her parents or an internal thing?"

"Both, I think. I hear what you're saying about not being able to express pride. Yet, in Sheila's case, it seems implicit in the way her parents relate to her that they are actually proud but don't know how to articulate that."

"Really?" Fiona was fascinated. She remembered Mrs. Connelly's telling her at the wake that her father was proud of her, and it was clear, too, from his diary. "And you see that in my novel?"

Sean nodded. "Yeah, it's there. You wrote it!" he laughed.

"Do you have a background in therapy?" she asked, semi-seriously.

Sean laughed happily. "No, just in theatre! I was an actor and then a theatre director, before working in film. I've worked with playwrights on new scripts and surprised them by bringing up things they had written into their own work."

"The unconscious at work, I suppose. My brother would like that!"

"Brothers are another thorny issue in the script. Sheila's brother . . . but why don't we save that for another meeting. If it's okay with you, I wanted to look at the stomach thing that Sheila has. The recurring symptoms."

Fiona took a deep breath. More and more she felt like she was preparing to dive into a deep pool and she didn't know how to swim.

"She has these tests at school, but they don't reveal anything." Sean began.

Fiona nodded agreement. She remembered the medical exam very well. Sr. John's kind eyes peering through her horn-rimmed glasses. The birdlike nose and the ever-so-slight dark thin moustache on her upper lip. "All the tests came back negative."

"So, the nuns are puzzled." Sean added.

"Yes." Fiona continued. "She clearly has some problem, some recurring pain."

"And she's not the kind of girl to imagine things."

Fiona shook her head. "No, so the best they can surmise is that it's some sort of nerves—a nervous stomach. They advise her to eat slowly, digest her food well and to go easy on herself."

Fiona remembered her resolve to try to keep her stomach calm. Not to worry the nuns. And as she remembered this moment of her younger self, trying to hold her world in her center, the adult Fiona had a sudden stab of pain in her stomach. Sean's voice broke in on her recall.

"Are you all right? Fiona?"

She heard him as if through a long tunnel, and then she felt a shadow over her and a blow to her abdomen as if someone had punched a hole in her middle. On the screen in her mind, she saw the night face of Uncle Frank and fought, in vain, the urge to double over with the contraction. She pressed her hands to her stomach to try to relieve the pressure, as Sean sprung up and moved over to her. Was this the locus of her chronic stomach problems? The ones where tests revealed nothing because in fact there was nothing physical? Just psychic scars of violation?

Sean's arm was around her shoulder. His voice was worried, comforting. "Fiona. What is it? Can I get you something?"

Fiona pushed hard with her hands and crouched, bent over the edge of the chair until the pain had passed. Of course, Sean must know that there was an obvious connection between her own experiences and those of her fictional character Sheila. The novel, however, had no mention at all of abuse, and Fiona had no intention of bringing it up, as it was not necessary to elucidate the script. Sean gave her hand a comforting squeeze and returned to his own seat. Fiona felt herself tearing up at the tenderness of the gesture and struggled to regain her composure.

"Ghosts?" Sean asked simply.

She nodded. "They seem to be everywhere."

They sat in silence for a while, and Sean began to put away his notes.

"How about I take you to dinner tonight, and I talk about myself, and you can eat the best fresh crab on the coast and enjoy . . . say . . . a crisp Chardonnay? Not one word about the script!"

Fiona smiled. "Off the clock?"

"Most definitely off the clock!"

■ ■ ■

When she returned to her hotel room after her meeting with Sean, Fiona decided she would perform what for her was a radical act—initiating a phone call simply to talk. Friendship 101. Make a connection.

"Wow, what are you wearing?" Pam demanded.

"What do you mean, what am I wearing? It's just a dinner. He's the director, I'm a client."

"Baloney girl! Well, that may be true, but just in case. He IS pretty cute. Is he single?"

"I never asked him, Pam! You'd think I was thirteen!"

"Look. Sure, it may be just a business dinner, though as you said you are specifically not going to discuss business, so I guess it's NOT a business dinner!"

Fiona exploded with laughter and caught a glimpse of herself in the mirror.

"My hair really is a mess, and I don't have anything vaguely suitable for an L.A. dinner, whatever that is."

"Flesh, that's what it is. Sun and exposure and some nice flesh! You need to get out this afternoon and get a trim and something less frumpy to wear."

"What! You're saying I'm frumpy??"

"Now that I have your ear, and a safe three thousand miles between us, I can say yes, absolutely, you've been covering up that great body for far too long. Cregora chic is definitely out."

Fiona nearly choked on her laughter. "Don't blame Cregora. I'm sure there's lots of high fashion there. I lower their standards."

"Okay, now seriously. If I was there I'd haul you out—is there someone you could take shopping with you? Someone with good taste?"

"You really are pushing it! Okay, I suppose I could see if Julie is free, my sister-in-law. She's a smart dresser."

"Good, call her right away. And this is not for Mr. Collins, necessarily. Remember that. God, I wish I had found out if he was single. I know he'll have his pick of beach babes and screen-weight actresses—minimum ten pounds underweight, but, hey, you'll have something nice to wear for a real date when it comes!"

"Yes, Miss Manners. I'll get working on that right away."

"Don't forget to call me back—full report!"

■ ■ ■

Julie had a doctor's appointment, and picked Fiona up afterwards. She had Una with her.

"How did it go? Did you have the ultrasound?" Fiona asked when she was in the car.

"Dr. Michael gave me gummy bears and a puzzle book." Una piped up.

"She delivered Una. They're all excited about this new baby. I'm fine, thanks."

"Fiona. Auntie Fiona." Una tugged at her shoulder from the back seat. "I'm going to have a sister. A little sister!"

"Oh, my God!" Fiona looked at Julie for confirmation. "That's wonderful, fantastic."

Julie smiled, happy. "Yeah, we decided we'd like to know."

"Mom!" Una lost momentary interest in her puzzle. "We'll have to think up names now. Girl names. You can help us, Fiona! Did you learn to swim yet?"

Fiona laughed. "I'd love to help think up names. But no swimming—anyway I don't even have a bathing suit."

"But, but, we're going to the mall. You can get one—I'll help you pick one out."

"I bet you would!" Fiona chuckled. "But today we're just looking for a dress for me."

"You could always get a bathing suit, just to sit by the pool, get some sun." Julie said, as they pulled into the parking lot.

"It's a conspiracy, isn't it?" Fiona exclaimed in mock dismay. "You two are in cahoots!"

"Well, let's see what they have here." Julie said, as they bundled out into the balmy Los Angeles afternoon.

■ ■ ■

And so it transpired that the thirty-five year old Fiona, up until that point fairly disinterested in clothes, ended up in the mall on a shopping spree with her sister-in-law and her seven-and-a-half-year-old niece, and no doubt at all about who was in command of the proceedings. Una seemed to know her way around very well and led Fiona through the mall, pointing out the various stores and their specialties. Fiona was dressed in her usual cover-up, long sleeves and a calf-length cotton skirt. She did at least have the sleeves of her shirt rolled up to three-quarter length and the top button open at the neck. Una was looking very fashionable in a blue denim ensemble with matching cap. Julie looked equally fresh in a light summery cotton dress.

"What about this one?" Julie pointed to an olive-green linen sleeveless dress with elegant but simple lines.

"But it's completely sleeveless!" was Fiona's first reaction.

Julie laughed. "Why don't you try it on? And maybe this blue one, it has a little sleeve."

"What about this one, Mom?" Una had picked out a bright pink cotton dress with tiny straps.

"I don't know." Julie was amused. "What do you think, Fiona? Though it's more casual, good for everyday."

"You're joking!" Fiona exploded with laughter. "If you think you're going to get me to transition from complete cover to half naked in one second flat, you've another thought coming!"

"Daddy says that too, sometimes—'you've another thought coming!'"

"Okay." Fiona picked up the two dresses. "And maybe this creamy one?"

"Okay." Julie said cautiously.

"I have a sneaking suspicion that I'm being railroaded here. That I don't stand a chance with the two of you!"

'Try them on, and we'll see." Julie laughed.

When Fiona emerged from the dressing-room wearing the olive dress, Julie all but gasped. "You're a vision! It's gorgeous!"

"Oh, Julie! My arms. I'm not . . ."

"It's fabulous on you, and the fit is perfect."

"It's beautiful." Una chimed in. "You can see what you look like now!"

The sales assistant was equally ebullient. "It's very flattering. You're lucky with the lovely tall, slim figure."

Fiona couldn't speak. She had a lump in her throat. Then, out of the corner of her eye, she caught a glimpse of a young man eying her approvingly. He was waiting for his girlfriend who was in the dressing room. He gave her a quick smile—obviously he agreed with her female team that the dress was quite flattering.

Julie asked if she wanted to try on the others, and she nodded and disappeared in to the dressing room. Of course, she bought the olive wonder.

As they walked out, Una grabbed Fiona and hauled her over to another shop window. "Here are the bathing suits, Fiona. Mom, my bathing suit is all stretched out. One part, you can nearly see through."

"True." Julie conceded. "Let's see what they have."

They found a cute bikini for Una, and then they all began to look around for Fiona. At least, Julie and Una did. There was a range of styles from conservative to risqué. Fiona immediately thought of a more modest one, but Una fancied a sexy one in vibrant blue with a plunging back and high cut leg. The young saleslady was eager to find Fiona a flattering suit.

"Now I'm thinking you and Una have alerted everyone, and you are all involved in this effort to get me to show off some skin!" Fiona whispered in an aside to Julie.

All three of them agreed on and vetoed exactly the same ones, refusing to let Fiona get away with disguising her body completely.

"You've a lovely figure, you should show it off," the young woman said in that casual manner that shop assistants in underwear stores sometimes have. Fiona turned hot pink, which perfectly matched the bathing suit she was trying on at the time. All she saw was cleavage when she looked down. "I couldn't possible appear in this in public."

"The beach isn't public," said the young woman with absolute logic. "It's the beach!"

L.A., Fiona thought to herself, ruefully, and then laughed out loud at her own squeamishness. "All right," she said. "Maybe I'll try on the blue one again." She wasn't used to wearing such bright colors but had to admit it did look good on her. Of course, she wound up with it. What choice did she have?

"Your daughter's a little fashion tyrant." Fiona laughed, as they exited the store.

"Oh, I know," Julie agreed. "A seven-year-old tyrant with impeccable taste! Except for the hot pink fixation. Can't wait 'til she's a teenager! And—by then she'll have a seven-year-old sister to shop with."

EYE OF THE STORM

Excerpt from a novel by Fiona Clarke

Peggy helped me to get all dressed up in the lovely snow-white Communion dress and fixed the veil to my hair with the little tiara. She straightened my socks after I'd slipped them into the white patent leather shoes with tiny red roses on the front. Mam was still away so Peg had made my dress and come with me to buy the shoes, veil and tiara. Now she planted a kiss on my forehead.

"Your Mam would be very proud of you, Sheila. Come down when you're ready, pet, and we'll take some snaps to send to her."

When I was ready and sure I looked lovely, I clasped the white prayerbook tightly in my hands and raced down the stairs to show off my style to everyone. As I reached the last steps, I saw Auntie Maeve coming down the hall from the kitchen. Auntie Maeve was married to a brother of Auntie Rita. She had a big square face, and her hair was set in tiny curls close to her head. In honor of the First Communion, she wore a navy hat with netting around the edges and a navy blue suit with silver buttons. She stopped, looked at me appraisingly and put on a big broad smile.

"What a pretty dress, Sheila. Don't you look smashing!"

I glowed with the praise and smiled shyly at her. Then I waltzed off into the kitchen to look for Aoife, feeling every inch a princess. I caught a glimpse of myself in the little mirror in the kitchen, and since there was no one there, shyly examined myself and put some stray hairs back into place. It was at that exact moment that I heard the voice drift in from the adjoining parlor and guessed the other relations must be in there, too. The voice was Aunt Maeve's, and she was speaking in a loud whisper.

"Maura and John have such a lovely family. Conor is such a handsome boy—all those beautiful curls, and of course little Aoife is a picture." She paused and lowered her voice even more as she continued. "It's a pity poor Sheila is so P. L. A. I. N."

I froze at the kitchen mirror. I stared at myself. A minute ago I had thought I was lovely and saw now that I was only fooling myself and that Aunt Maeve had lied when she said I looked pretty—well, she said I looked smashing, that my frock was pretty. Burning tears began to well up behind my eyes. Now I knew it really was true what Conor always said—that I was ugly. I knew everyone thought he was gorgeous, and I loved Aoife's beauty and never got tired looking at her. But I didn't know the real truth about myself until now. I heard the symphony of voices from the parlor and assumed they all agreed with Aunt Maeve. I hated her for saying I was plain and for spelling it out. Was she afraid that I might possibly be within earshot? And did she really think that I wasn't able to spell a simple word like "plain?"

"Sheila! Where are you, dear?" Aunt Maeve chimed, as sweet as you like. "Come and get a picture taken with your brother and sister. Where are Conor and Aoife?" she asked in a somewhat quieter voice.

I didn't budge. I was still glued to the spot.

"Sheila! Sheila!" That false voice rang out again and unfroze me from my stuck position. "Sheila, where are you child?"

And I fled, as fast as my seven-year-old legs could carry me, taking my broken self straight out to the solace of the treehouse.

CHAPTER THIRTEEN

(FIRST) COMMUNION

> "The true mystery of the world is the visible, not the invisible."
>
> OSCAR WILDE

Fiona and Sean sat on the patio of the restaurant, and the waters of the bay lapped gently onto the shore.

"Angel. Is that her real name?" Fiona asked, between bites of succulent crab.

"Oh, yes! It's actually her given name, but perfect for a Berkeley hippie. Her parents were Iowa farmers, Irish father, German mother, I think they were hoping she would be more the angelic type."

"And is she not?" Fiona savored the promised crisp Chardonnay.

"Oh, she's wonderful. A real dynamo—just not at all religious, like her folks. She soaked up the Berkeley counter-culture of the 60's, Haight Ashbury, People's Park, the whole nine yards."

"And your Dad?"

"It's funny," Sean took a mouthful of crab, "my Dad was the one from Berkeley, and he met my Mom in his hippie stage, but then he became more conservative—well, more than her anyway!"

"Did they bring you up as hippie kids?"

Sean laughed. "Kind of. My sister, Adair and I were dragged to every peace march and rally—and we loved it. My parents divorced when we were teenagers—Adair is a year older than me—but my Dad just moved down the street, and they're still great friends, so we just got an extra house to go to!"

"That simple? Can it be that simple, really?"

"I'm not saying every second was perfect. But, yes, really. They explained to us how they had changed and that they still respected each other and so on, but weren't going to live together any more."

"So, you weren't traumatized?" Fiona noticed how the wine sparkled in the evening light. "You can see that I expect everything to be a trauma!"

"I think it's just the combination of the different personalities and cultures in our household, Fiona, and circumstances. My Mom got pregnant when she was eighteen—Adair's thirty-five now. Ten months later I was born, then they got married—all in that order! But she and Dad are still close friends. I know it might sound a bit crazy. And we did have friends whose parents divorced, and they were put through the ringer." Sean paused a minute. "I guess we were lucky." He took a few bites. "Do you like the crab?"

"Oh, it's amazing. Just melts in your mouth. Does this restaurant get it directly from the fishermen?"

"Yeah—just off the pier there. When we were growing up, my parents got crab fresh from the Berkeley pier for special occasions.

They had an Oscar party and a Tony party every year. They set up big tables, and we'd pick at crab, dip it in melted butter, eat artichokes and fresh fruits—and of course watch the awards."

"Is that how you got interested in film?"

"Probably." Sean savored a big piece of crab. "We went to the PFA—Pacific Film Archives—and all the art houses in Berkeley. But, I started in theatre, was very involved in drama at Berkeley High."

"It's like another world. An enchanted world full of light."

Sean laughed openly. "I love it—how it sounds to you! I hope I'm not talking too much? Our pact was that I do all the talking, but we don't have to stick to that."

Fiona laughed. She felt bubbly and clear like the wine. She usually drank red, but the white was cool and cleansing to the palette.

"No, I'm happy." And she was.

"By the way, you look wonderful. That dress really brings out the green in your eyes."

"Thanks." Fiona glowed.

"Did I tell you, Fiona, that I did a school project on Ireland when I was in middle school? It must have been . . . 1969, and a group of us did a class presentation on the civil rights march in Northern Ireland."

"You're not serious! Really? I did this big school journalism project on that at the time, too."

"The Troubles!"

"Characteristic Irish understatement, a bit of a euphemism, I'd say! It always made me think of 'sorry for your troubles!' What kind of project did you do?"

"I think this was social studies class, maybe international history—not sure. We divided up the research, trying to figure out the Protestant/ Loyalist versus Catholic/ Nationalist split. Do I have that right?"

Fiona nodded as she picked through her spinach salad.

"I remember we got newspaper clippings of the civil rights march. Was it the previous year, in 1968?"

"Yes, with Bernadette Devlin."

"So, was that big news in the south of Ireland at the time?" Sean asked.

"It was huge. There was enormous sympathy for the Catholic population. And my Dad was a fervent Nationalist, so he went crazy."

"Did you agree with him, with his view of things?"

"I did basically. I was just starting to think about politics then. I was about fourteen. The march was broken up very violently by the R.U.C.—the Royal Ulster Constabulary . . ."

"—which was the Northern Irish police force, right?"

"Right." Fiona confirmed. "Then later the British Army was called in, and the following year the I.R.A. began its bombing campaign . . . and the rest, as they say . . . is history."

Sean poured more wine.

"And still going on. Do you follow the Irish news over here?"

Fiona nodded. "It's tragic really—it's a game of reprisals. And people are continually fearful."

Sean nodded. "I always thought it had similarities with the Israeli-Palestinian situation."

"Definitely. The long history, simmering hatreds, differences ostensibly about religion but really about power. Then people get entrenched in their own views of course. Just like people do in personal conflicts."

"Yeah. We're a bit of a mess, aren't we!"

"The human race?" Fiona smiled. "We certainly are. I thought of pursuing journalism as a career for a while, but that didn't last."

"You know, I did too, briefly, but abandoned it in favor of fiction."

Fiona laughed. "I did too, I suppose. But I think it helped me see that history isn't a thing of the past—because I was living through it at the time. And I loved how I could journey back to the root cause of an event and trace its future progression out of that inchoate stage.

"I bet you would have made a great journalist." Sean extracted the last piece of crab. "I think I've exhausted all the possibilities with this fine fellow!"

Fiona laughed. "Me too. We didn't leave much!" And she took another sip of wine. "You know, I did work for a while as a journalist. It was my first job, after college. Oops, we're talking about me!"

"But a word about the novel has not crossed my lips! And Sheila doesn't have anything to do with journalism, does she?"

Fiona laughed. "No. So it's safe. My career was fairly brief anyway, and way too secure. My mother was terrified I'd end up in the North and get killed by a sniper, but mostly I did reviews, first of restaurants actually, then books and theatre."

"And how would you rate this restaurant?"

"So far, A plus! For food, service, and ambiance!"

"So far?"

"Well, we haven't had dessert yet!"

"Good point. Can't rush to conclusions. Let's rectify that immediately." And he looked around to catch the eye of the waiter.

■ ■ ■

The next morning Fiona laid the rest of the packages from her shopping spree on the bed and started to open them. Her new dress had been a great success, gave her a strong sense of being present in her own body. And Sean liked it.

But, as she looked at the other items, away from the encouragement of her female co-conspirators, she began to have doubts. She looked at the bathing suit skeptically. And weren't the shorts just a teensy, weensy bit too short? Well, she'd have a shower and try them on in the privacy of her room. If she didn't feel comfortable, she didn't have to wear them. You're such a wimp, Fiona! she told herself.

She spotted the old family album that she had brought back from Ireland. She put it on the bed with all of her new clothes and opened it up. She stopped at a picture of herself on the day of her First Communion—a sad little girl looking right at the camera. She wasn't able to avoid the camera that day, but she hadn't managed to smile.

When Fiona emerged from a long, languorous shower, she approached the new clothes spread out on the bed. After meeting her own approval in the satiny champagne bra and pants set, she selected a form fitting pair of mulberry cotton shorts. A crisp, nicely tailored short-sleeved shirt several shades lighter than the shorts completed the outfit. Fiona donned the new white leather sandals and then brushed her hair back and up, opening up her face. She fancied her hair was golden—maybe it had brightened up in the sunshine? She straightened her posture, let her spine float up and her tall frame seemed to stretch by a few inches. She went back to the bed, had another look at the photo of her First Communion day, and saw one on the next page of her Aunt Connie with navy netting over the tiny curls. Hmm, she's not much to write home about in the looks department, Fiona chuckled to herself, and closed the album shut. She had another peek in the mirror and gave herself the seal of approval. Just the thing for a script meeting with a handsome director.

■ ■ ■

A meeting was scheduled with the producers, Les and Leonard, in a week, so Sean wanted to tie up some loose ends and clarify some script issues.

"They seem in really good form, so maybe they are shifting on the location thing," Sean told Fiona. "Don't get your hopes up, but we'll know soon."

As Sean opened up his script and her novel, Fiona experienced a strange sensation of both floating and falling at the same time. The more she delved into the story, and the task of translating these words and actions into images, the more she fell, like Alice into the well of her childhood. She was continuously amazed at Sean's insight into events that she had written about, ideas he had extrapolated from her script but envisioned through a different lens. From their first meeting, it had been clear that Fiona judged her main character, her own alter ego, Sheila, very harshly. She also had a decidedly negative slant towards Conor, who was Declan in the novel. Sean had the ability to look at the same situations and come up with different conclusions. This, combined with her own personal insights, and the occasional glimpses into her father's diaries, nudged Fiona towards a shift in perception.

"Fiona, do you remember that day we took the bike ride?"

"Feeling like a fraud?"

"Yeah."

Fiona pondered a while before continuing. "Sean, did you know that George Bernard Shaw's wife left money in her will to teach the Irish the rudiments of social conduct?"

"What? Now you're pulling my leg!" Sean chuckled.

"I'm not. It's true. She left something like four hundred thousand pounds to help abolish from the lives of Irish people the social defects of shyness and some other things—inarticulate conversation, I think."

"Is this connected to thinking about Irish history?"

"I think so. It's the legacy—shyness, lack of confidence, inferiority—speaking for myself anyway. And, Sheila."

He nodded. He scribbled some notes.

It occurred to Fiona that she still didn't know if he had a girlfriend.

"I'm trying to grasp this connection between Sheila's personal life and the political and cultural currents in Ireland at the time, the 1960's and 70's. I'm getting to the Peter chapter."

Fiona nodded.

"And Les and Leonard are especially interested in this relationship—it's the love interest after all!"

"Of course!" Fiona smiled, but she was nervous.

Sean jumped up. I'll go get us a couple of ice cream cones first. Any preference?

"Anything with chocolate or nuts or caramel."

He flashed a smile and was gone.

Fiona knew that Sean was giving her a respite before launching into the Peter episode. She absent-mindedly slipped off her sandals, shifted over to the side of the pool, and dangled her toes in the cool blue water. She thought over their conversation about journalism and fiction, and reading to Una from *Alice in Wonderland* came into her head.

"Down, down, down. Would the fall never come to an end? I wonder how many miles I've fallen by this time? I must be getting somewhere near the center of the earth." She stared into the blue of the pool thinking of her own journey. "I wonder if I shall fall right through the earth?"

"Penny for your thoughts!" Sean's voice aroused her from her reverie. "Oh, but you're already being paid for those, aren't you?" he joked.

Fiona noticed his tanned, muscular legs, the khaki shorts and sky-blue t-shirt. His freckles seemed to get deeper each day. "Yes—under contract to share them!" She half joked back as she reached for her ice cream.

"Only the professional ones," Sean insisted, "if there is such a thing."

Fiona considered before responding quietly. "Not in this case, I don't think."

Sean slipped off his sandals and sat down beside her at the pool. He didn't comment on her admission. "Hope peanut butter and chocolate is okay?"

"Perfect!" She licked off the top peak which was already starting to melt. "Mmm, delicious."

"I was thinking of journalism and fiction—going back to roots, and of *Alice in Wonderland* and falling through the earth."

"And *Eye of the Storm?*" Sean took a big gulp of ice cream, saving it from slipping off the edge of the cone.

Fiona nodded. She dangled her feet. She made small circles with her toes as she used to do at the seaside when she was a child, standing in the wet sand at the edge of the water, never venturing in any further. She savored every bite of the ice cream cone, licked her lips, made a wider circle in the deep blue water, and then she spoke to Sean, almost inaudibly.

"I want to swim."

"Pardon?"

"I want to learn how to swim." Her voice was louder now, more certain. She looked right at him. "You offered to teach me."

Fiona hadn't planned this. She was going to override the fear. Maybe it was the memory of the lonely child at the seaside, not able to go in, listening to the squeals of laughter and delight of the other children in the ocean. Maybe it was the painful memory of the teenager crouched in the bathroom stall, unable to accept an award, feeling unworthy of being honored. Or, the girl who was afraid of making any new friends for fear of losing yet another person she loved. Now she was going to do something about it.

Sean seemed a bit taken aback, and a shyness came over him. "Sure. O.K. Just let me know when you're ready."

EYE OF THE STORM

Excerpt from a novel by Fiona Clarke

I had barely sat down to my breakfast that Sunday morning when Dad lowered his Sunday paper and started in on me. "You were out very late last night; I heard the car pull in."

It was a statement, didn't really call for a comment, and I was trying to decide if I should offer one when Mam came to the table carrying a pot of tea, nestled in the cozy.

"She'll only be young once, John."

I flashed her a big smile of thanks, cut myself a chunk of Mam's brown bread, lathered it with butter and strawberry jam and poured a cup of steaming tea. Dad raised his newspaper in front of his face and grunted a sort of disapproval. I had an awful feeling he wasn't finished, and boy, was I right! No sooner did I get the second bite of bread into my mouth than he resumed in the same solemn, admonishing tone.

"I don't recall, by the by, you telling me that your young man was a Protestant."

"You never asked me, Da," I offered by way of reply, trying to keep it light.

He lowered his paper ominously. "I'll have no lip from you, young lady! Now, back to this Protestant Englishman of yours."

"His name's Peter, and he's not English."

"I'm well aware of his name, and he might as well be English."

"His family has been here forever." I protested. "Hundreds of years."

"So have the boyos up in the North and look what they're doing to

our country. Joining the police force with the pretense of defending the people, and, behind it all, they're in cahoots with the British army."

"Surely you're not blaming Peter for the R.U.C.! It's not his fault."

"Not directly, maybe." His newspaper was strewn across his lap now. His face was red and he leaned forward in his chair. "But if he lived up there in the North, whose side do you think he'd be on? If he was in Derry a few months ago, who do you think he'd be rooting for?"

I was flabbergasted. It sounded like my father was blaming Peter and his family for Bloody Sunday. Even Mam couldn't let him get away with this.

"John. It's not fair to put something like that on the Rawlings. They're a very nice family. I can't imagine they'd countenance such a thing."

"They may appear to be nice but deep down people don't change their stripes. I don't care how long their forbears have been here in our country, they got their land and title over the suffering of the native Irish, and then they lord it over us. As if they were better than us."

"They don't think they're better than us." I protested. "You can't keep carrying on grudges forever, or we'll never get anywhere."

"Is that so?" Dad asked sarcastically. "And should we just forget all the injustice and carry on as if nothing had happened? And pretend that what's going on in the North has nothing to do with the British and their deep-down hatred of us. Should we just forget our history because the Rawlings are very 'nice' people?"

"That's not what I'm saying." I was frustrated. "But you can't lump everything together. Every English person, or every Irish Protestant whose ancestors were English, doesn't hate Ireland or even want to keep the North as part of Britain for that matter."

"Of course they do!" My father erupted. He had worked himself up into a state.

"They've spent hundreds of years trying to kill our language and our religion. They succeeded with the language, but we outfoxed them by practicing our religion in secret and making it stronger, and sending our sons to France to be trained as priests, and bringing them back in disguise. Now you want to go and dilute that religion which your ancestors have been fighting to defend for over 500 years—you want to go and weaken that by associating with a Protestant. Well, I won't have it."

"What?" I was struck by the hardness in his voice.

"I forbid you to see him again. You'll tell him he can't see you. I hope I make myself clear."

"What do you mean?" I started to choke on the bread.

"I mean precisely what I said. I forbid you to see him again."

"But, I love him." I blurted out. "We love each other! It makes no sense to blame Peter for all of our Irish misfortunes."

My father harrumphed. "Love, ha! It's little you know about love at your age. Wait 'til you have a couple of babies and he doesn't want them to be brought up in the proper Catholic faith. Then you'll have a problem on your hands."

I was devastated. "You knew from the get-go that he was a Protestant—you never said anything." I looked over pleadingly at Mam for support, but she wasn't siding with me now.

"I'm sorry, love," she said, and she did sound a bit sorry. "We thought it was a summer romance—that it would blow over. I'm sure you're very fond of him, but it's my duty to stand by your father, and I know he's only thinking of your own good."

"But I can't stop seeing Peter." I protested.

"You'll do what you're told while you're under this roof, lassie," my father barked.

"And you'll thank your father for it in later years, Sheila," Mam added, trying to attenuate the hurt. "It's hard enough to make a marriage work without starting off on the wrong foot with someone from a completely different background."

"Find yourself a good Catholic chap," Dad chimed in for good measure. "We don't need any Protestants in this family." And he gathered the sheets and raised his newspaper back in front of his face like a ship's sail floating up on its mast.

CHAPTER FOURTEEN

(FIRST) LOVE

"The words that enlighten the soul
are more precious than jewels."

HAZRAT INAYAT KHAN

Sean and Fiona sat by the poolside. They had taken to calling it their "office."

"I'll want you to talk to our production and costume designers about the dance hall scene, but I'd like to know now about the music that was played in Ireland at the time. That wasn't mentioned in the book."

"Let's see, I remember Rod Stewart was very popular—"*You wear it well*," Fiona started to sing, then Sean joined in with her. "*A little old fashioned, but that's all right*." They laughed.

"Speaking of 'wear it well,' Nellie, my Dad's cousin, made a lot of my clothes. I remember at one of my own dances, I had this lovely frock—dress, she made. It was a deep blue with a defined waistline and dark velvety trim around the neck, and it was a good few inches above the knee—as was the style in the 70's."

"Oh, I remember well! And hot pants, were they in, in Ireland?"

Fiona laughed. "Yeah! And all the rage, too. They were actually more comfortable than minis. Nellie made me a gorgeous lavender pair once, but my Dad wasn't too keen! You could pass that on to the costume department."

Sean took some notes. "Great! So, I guess we were listening to some of the same songs. What about 'American Pie?'"

"Yes! Don McLean." Fiona started to sing. "*Bye, bye, Miss American Pie . . . .Drove my Chevy to the levy but the levy was dry . . .* "

Sean joined with her. "*And good old boys were drinking whiskey and rye, singing this'll be the day that I die.*"

"Of course, I only know the first few lines or so of every song." Fiona laughed.

"Me too! What about Irish singers?"

"Well, there was Dicky Rock and Brendan Bowyer, they were big. In fact Brendan Bowyer might still play around the U.S. Maybe in Vegas?"

Sean nodded. "Yes, I've seen ads for him. Wasn't there a dance he created . . . ?"

"The Hucklebuck!" Fiona jumped up and started to do a version of the dance as she sang. "*Now, here's a dance you should know . . . baby when the lights are down . . . oh, hey . . . rock your baby in . . . et cetera, et cetera.*" She sat back down. "You get the idea!"

Sean laughed and clapped. "You'll have to teach me. And we'll have a designated singing night sometime, compare notes! Okay, to the tricky part—let me see if I can get a bit better understanding of the religion issue. Protestants and Catholics."

"The Great Divide!" Fiona added. "There was a big mystique

about Protestants. This was the early 1970's, nearly everyone was Catholic and we didn't mix. Protestants almost always lived on big estates, with hunting lodges and servants' quarters and gamekeepers."

"Sounds very posh." Sean was taking notes.

"Yes and no. A lot of structures were falling down, and the owners couldn't afford to keep them up. Masonry crumbling on pillars and window sills in need of paint—that kind of thing. But they were elegant eighteenth century stone mansions, built in the grand manner—with high ceilings and classical columns, bounded by acres of parkland, usually exquisitely landscaped."

"And these were the original homes of the Anglo-Irish?" Sean asked.

"Right. They were the remnants, really, of the landed gentry in Ireland, a testament to the time the English came and took away the land from the Irish and 'planted' it with their own. Of course, that was hundreds of years ago. The present owners, who inherited both the land and the system of land tenure it represented—to them it was probably ancient history."

"But not to Sheila's father?"

"No, definitely not to Sheila's father!"

"Before we get to that. What about Moira? In the novel, Sheila says her accent is 'Catholic?'"

Fiona nodded. "It's a bit tongue-in-cheek. Moira would have had a very strong country accent, whereas Sheila and Conor would have definitely an Irish accent but not as broad, and Peter and his parents would speak in a way that was considered more posh. More British. Does that make sense?"

"Yeah. I think so. It probably equates some to the Southern accent in the U.S., often associated with less cultured or educated—though of course it's not true."

"Same in Ireland. We'd jokingly call it a bog accent! We got elocution lessons in boarding school, and the nuns tried to get us to speak in a more 'refined' accent, tone down any strong regionalisms."

"Like Eliza Doolittle!"

"I suppose—something like that. I wonder if Shaw got the idea for *My Fair Lady* from his wife? Or, vice versa, if she got that notion of trying to wipe out the defects of inarticulate speech from the Irish, from his play?"

They laughed. Then Sean referred to his list. "Okay—back to location. Since we're hoping Les and Leonard will let us shoot in Ireland, I want to get a sense of where to scout. Do you have any preference regarding what area or county would work best for the story?"

"I think anywhere in the East or South—Leinster or Munster—you'd find the right kind of farm and village. The topography is quite different in the West of Ireland."

"Great. I think I have a good idea of the farm. But in this chapter with Peter, he and Sheila spend a good deal of time in and around the village that summer."

"Yes. They had their picnics on a grassy bank by a little stream that was easy cycling distance from the village. Spent a lot of time browsing in the local village bookstore. The village itself doesn't need to be much more than a long narrow street—book shop, a clothes shop, a haberdashery, bakery, a tea shop, a pub or two, school, chapel, dispensary. The kind of place where, if you blink when you're passing through, you could miss it!"

"And everyone would know everyone else's business?" Sean asked.

"Oh, most definitely. And a Catholic/Protestant romance was a big gossip item."

"Even in the South?"

"Even at such a remove from the sectarianism of the North, yes."

"Wow! Okay. So, this big confrontation scene here . . ." Sean opened her novel to the reference, "the show-down." He glanced over some parts. "Sheila comes downstairs on a Sunday morning, happy after a date with Peter, Dad's reading *The Sunday Independent,* Mam's at the sink cleaning up, the smell of bacon and sausages lingers in the air."

"Rashers and sausages!" Fiona corrected. "Rashers, sausages and puddings."

Sean laughed. "I await the pleasure! The rashers are bacon, the pudding—well, maybe I don't need to know all the details at this point of what goes into pudding."

"Better that you never find out!" Fiona joked.

"But, I bet it's delicious! Okay, now, wouldn't Sheila's father have known that Peter was a Protestant?"

Fiona nodded. "Of course, he would have known. But that was the way things happened in that household. Sheila and Peter would have dated all summer, and, he would have exchanged a few words with her parents when picking her up, but they just let it slide, until this particular day."

"And you talk earlier in the chapter about Trinity College. Would that have been a problem, too, for Sheila's father? That she wanted to go there?"

"Definitely. He didn't understand why she wouldn't just go to a Catholic Uni—in fact all of the other Irish universities in the South would have been Catholic."

"And there's a ban on Catholics going to Trinity?"

Fiona nodded. "There was a ban for years on Catholics going, but it was the Catholic Church that imposed the ban, not Trinity. They wanted to put the fear of God into Catholics who deigned to pass through those gates of iniquity!"

Sean laughed. "But Sheila wants to go there because of its reputation and the smaller classes?"

"Yes. And, of course, her father questions the whole idea of a girl going to university in the first place. In his book, a boy needs the education because he will be the breadwinner, but a girl was expected to get married, stay home and bring up the children."

"Her father refers here to Peter as her 'Protestant Englishman,' and then he connects him to the Troubles in the North?"

"Exactly!" Fiona jumped in. "It's the kind of skewed thinking that causes wars to last forever!"

"And this reference here is to Bloody Sunday—that was that year?"

"Yes. It was January 1972. British paratroopers shot into Catholic demonstrators during a civil rights march and killed fourteen people. But the whole thing is typical—not being able to let go of the past. And there's the whole Irish inferiority complex. We need to stop carrying grudges like that. Stop lumping everything together. Every English person, or every Irish Protestant whose ancestors were English, doesn't hate Ireland or even want to keep the North as part of Britain, for that matter."

"But her father can't see that, can he?" Sean asked. "And that's the crux of the argument."

"Yes." Fiona agreed. "And the end of the romance."

■ ■ ■

Later, they strolled along the marina, soaking up the sunshine and the buzz of people. Sean sipped his iced coffee. "As I look at the progression of Sheila's character in the story, it seems like Peter was one of the first people she started to open up to."

Fiona stole a glance, his intelligent, trusting face, his genuine interest in trying to get to the bottom of the fictionalized universe she had presented to him. She took a long cool drink of water. "Yes. He was the first." They walked a little further. "I think . . . I . . . had actually begun to develop some self confidence that summer. Nipped in the bud!"

Sean didn't look at her. He said nothing for a while. "Did . . . you ever see him again, in real life?" he asked quietly.

"After I broke it off we didn't try to meet—we couldn't have gotten away with it in such a small place if we'd tried to keep it secret." She kicked up the sand as she walked. "I was very depressed. I went in on myself. Imagine having to live with such ignorance! Such small-mindedness. Much good the so-called freedom had done for the south of Ireland if their minds were all locked up with prejudice. I felt I had finally begun to live that summer, to really grow and expand, and here were my parents reining me in, trying to confine me inside their world view, to keep me small."

"And then the boy, your boyfriend, did he go to Trinity?"

"Yep. Simon was his name. We corresponded for a while, then around Christmas time I got a letter from him telling me he'd met someone else. A Protestant girl of course!" Fiona sighed, and then she let out a little laugh. "Maybe it would have happened anyway. I'll never know. Saved my Dad worrying about having little black Protestants for grandchildren!"

Sean smiled with her. He spoke quietly. "So did you see him when you went to Trinity College?"

"I didn't go in the end. I elected not to go, went to the national university. I wasn't ready to bump into him. And maybe I felt guilty of buying into the colonial legacy—that I'd be selling out. So, maybe my father got to me on some level after all."

Sean pondered this. "Is religion still an issue in Ireland, in the South? Obviously it is in the North."

"I don't think you'd meet the same kind of resistance today. Things have opened up. But the North of Ireland is part of the equation. Our history book in school was called *March to Freedom* or was it *March to Nationhood*? Can't remember, but the idea is similar. So much of our history, going back hundreds of years, has been fighting for this thing called freedom. Freedom from something else—in this case from England."

"And the South is free now—politically free and independent?"

"Right. Since 1922. But that kind of legacy of war and unrest must leave its residue."

"You mean on the individual?"

"Yes, I mean, can you just wake one fine morning after hundreds of years of fighting and stretch out and say 'lovely morning, I'm free now, all my troubles are over?' Maybe all the troubles just start then."

"Because people have to look at their own lives, day to day."

"Exactly. And in Ireland's case, because of partition, there's still the North. There's a lot of energy going into fighting for freedom—and in the meantime lifetimes go by where generations have no experience at all of living freely, without fear. Imagine what that does to the psyche of a country, of its people."

"Like your father?"

"Yes. Like my Dad. His father and uncles were alive in 1916, some of them fought in the uprising. He wasn't able to shake the prejudices against England, against Protestants."

"And you were a casualty of the prejudice."

"True. And then I compounded the hurt by turning it in on myself. It was self-destructive. I see that now."

"Well, these family dramas don't resolve themselves overnight. In fact, most probably never do. People just live out their lives and let it all slide."

Fiona breathed in the fresh air from the marina, the caress of the sunshine, and noticed how much better she was feeling in her own body. She stole a glance at Sean.

"You know, Sean, for someone with such a seemingly calm and lovely upbringing, you have amazing insight into dysfunctional families and relationships!"

Sean laughed. Fiona loved the freedom in his laugh. "Maybe that's why. Because my family was, for the most part, so easy-going.

However, I've had my share of tumultuous relationships, too. I haven't just lived a charmed life."

"Romantic relationships?"

He nodded. "I wasn't immune to the attention I got when I hit L.A. It's amazing how attractive you become when you are directing, or even involved in film or T.V. or commercials."

"Were you beset by bevies of stars?" Fiona asked mischievously.

"Well, not exactly, but it was a sea change from Berkeley. I had just broken up with my college sweet-heart, Sacha. She headed for New York, and I headed south. So, I was lonely at first, a bit lost."

"And ripe for attention from the lovely would-be stars?"

Sean laughed. "I suppose I was innocent, too. I got hurt more than once."

"They were serious relationships, then?"

"Well, I thought they were serious at the time. I took them seriously. Until I realized what the game was."

"What game? Hollywood? Dating?"

"It's connected. Or was in the cases of the women I got involved with. I had to learn to distinguish between real and fake. I became a better judge of character."

"You don't sound bitter, though. You seem to have a great ability to bounce back."

Sean chuckled, "I probably have my hippie parents to thank for that! They really did give us some solid coping skills. At any rate, I was eventually able to take a step back."

"From relationships?"

"From the wrong ones." Sean smiled at her. "Just from the wrong ones."

Fiona had a massive urge to hug him. It was some quality that Sean had to connect without entangling, to be close without being cloying, to allow an infinite space to open up around him, and yet to create an assurance of being safe. To Fiona, at that moment, it felt unbelievably liberating, and she had a mad urge to fly. As if he could read her mind, Sean turned to her, smiling.

"If you'd still like that swimming lesson, we could fit one in before the water gets too cold."

Fiona thought about it for precisely four seconds. "Okay. Race you back!"

"You're on!"

They both turned on their heels and started to run, like little children, back in the direction they came from.

CHAPTER FIFTEEN

CONNECTION

> "Nothing has a stronger influence psychologically on their environment and especially on their children, than the unlived life of the parent."
>
> C.G. JUNG

In the realm of swimming, Fiona made rapid progress and improved both her stamina and technique. She had been having lessons with Sean almost every day before their script meetings, and, as her confidence increased, she perfected her strokes and soon traversed the width of the pool. One morning, feeling emboldened, she took the leap and swam all alone for the first time. Skimming through the water, she felt free and light and liberated, like a silver dolphin. As she emerged from the shower and dried off, the telephone rang, and she raced to pick it up.

"Mama mia!" Pam's laughing voice rang out. "I think that's the first time in living memory that you picked up a phone call from me on the first ring! What gives?"

Fiona laughed and sunk into an armchair in the lounge. "Maybe it's because I feel so exhilarated after swimming."

Pam had obviously taken a sip of coffee and almost choked. "Excuse me? Did I hear right the first time? You, Ms. Terrified of the Water, swimming?"

"Well, I used to dip my toes in . . . so I wasn't afraid of the water *per se* . . ."

"Right! Good one! That will get past the shrink. Hey . . . I hope you're not going to lose all your charming neuroses—we don't want you too perfect!"

Fiona laughed as she dried off her hair. "You'd love my bathing suit, Pam. Did I tell you that Sean is the one who taught me to swim?"

"Really? Would that be Mr. Sean Collins, 'he's the director and I'm just a client' Mr. Sean Collins?"

"Hold on now! It's a professional relationship, but we are developing a friendship too. It's strictly platonic."

"Except that he gets to see you half naked! Do you think I just came up the Liffey on a bicycle? To borrow one of your own fine expressions!"

Fiona giggled and wiggled to wrap her robe around her. "It's nothing like that, really. I do like him I admit, and I'm nearly certain he doesn't have a girlfriend from what he said yesterday. Anyway, we're making progress on the script, you'll be happy to know. I'm making . . . adjustments."

"Any word on locations yet?" Pam inquired.

"We have another meeting coming up with the producers, and we're hoping they'll agree to shooting in Ireland, at least the outside locations."

"Is your home, the farm, a possibility for that?"

"No way, Pam! Declan would have a conniption. We're doing better, I think, the two of us, but we're locked on the issue of selling or not selling. I wouldn't even want to be in the position of having to broach the topic."

"Well, there's no shortage of farms in Ireland! So hopefully it will work out. It sounds like it's been good for you, kiddo. This process."

"I wouldn't even know where to start. It still feels new and raw in some ways, but it will be great to get the film made, get past this chapter . . . " Fiona spotted the covered computer, "and hopefully get back on track."

"Well, the film will give you some mileage with our guys here for a while, so you're good."

"And with you?"

"My professional, agent me?"

"Yep, that one!"

"Yeah, you're good with her too. If films are successful they tend to have a long tail . . . multiple openings, videos, resurgence of interest in the original if it's an adaptation, et cetera, et cetera."

Fiona drew in a relieved breath. "Good. Well, let's hope. I'll ring you after the meeting. By the way, speaking of ringing, I had a flash on the phone thing."

"Your antipathy towards them, you mean?"

"Yeah. I told you that my Dad left me his diary? A big thick one. Well, I read a snippet last night about something I'd completely forgotten. The very first telephone call we ever got in our house was from the hospital to my mother, telling us that Orla had died."

"Oh, Fiona, that's horrendous. No wonder you can't stand them."

"It helps that I know, I think. Though I must have been getting better already. Witness today and your call! I don't think I could have processed it all overnight. I must tell Sean today as he probably thinks my telephone thing is wacky."

"Do you meet with him every day?"

"Not, but several times a week. Today we're having our meeting over a picnic on the beach."

Pam sputtered again. "My God! I can't safely drink a simple cup of coffee here! You meet on the beach?"

Fiona exploded with laughter. "No, we've never done this before. I think we're celebrating our progress."

"Sounds suspiciously like a date to me! Is there food involved? Drink? Bubbly?"

"Sean said he'd pick up something. Yes, there will be food. I doubt we'll be drinking, though. It's late afternoon."

"No rule against it that I know of! Hey, you're the Irish one, do I have to tell you that? I think I'll require a report before the meeting tomorrow! Hey—client here, gotta go. Don't do anything that I . . . you know."

■ ■ ■

Fiona's first ocean swim that afternoon was frightening at first, no boundaries. She and Sean had found a quiet cove where they laid out a rug and then went in for a swim. After a while, Fiona started to swim out away from the cove, further and further. She was aware of Sean's watchful gaze as she continued on. Then she waved to him, turned around and swam back. She was out of breath but exhilarated as they both dried off.

"That was daring," Sean pulled his sweat shirt over his mop of blond hair.

Fiona shivered and laughed. "I had to get out of my depth some time! Though I nearly drowned when I tried to wave!"

Sean uncovered a bottle of champagne, mixed it with orange juice and poured. "Mimosa?" he offered Fiona a glass. "I know it's a bit profligate, but it is a celebratory marker—and the OJ is to keep us on our toes for the meeting!"

"Is it really a celebration?" Fiona thought of the high stakes if the film fell through.

"We don't know what Les and Leonard will say yet, and their backers could put the kybosh on the idea."

Sean handed her a slab of brie on a crispy baguette. "My meetings with them have all been positive. They're happy with the direction the script is going in, and the speed. So, I'm hopeful."

"And celebrating in advance?"

Sean laughed and took a hearty bite of bread and cheese.

"Actually," Fiona joined in the laughter, "it's a good policy, I like it!"

They ate for a while in silence. Fiona savored the spicy salami and jet black Greek olives and listened to the ebb and flow of the waves.

"Has it really been worth it, Sean?" She asked eventually. "To bring me out here? Pay for me?"

"I couldn't even begin to measure, Fiona. I've got an immensely clearer picture of the characters and situations and a host of background details I couldn't possibly have come up with alone. And

I've really got a handle on most of the characters, an increased dimensionality, a softening."

Fiona smiled. "Me, too!"

"From the process? Looking at it from a different angle?"

"Yes. All of that, and you, your delicate touch." Fiona was embarrassed. She had meant it metaphorically. To cover she rushed on. "And my Dad's diary. Did I mention it?"

Sean shook his head. He filled a fresh glass for each of them.

"My Dad left me his diary. It's not that extensive. But I think it's lovely, and I've been reading through parts of it. As a matter of fact, he has a bit that I read a while back on the tape recording scene you were asking me about?"

Sean nodded. He lay back against a rock and closed his eyes. Fiona sipped her mimosa.

"His account really brought me back to that time when my Dad was recording on his old reel-to-reel player." Fiona went on. "It crystallized for me as a magic moment of connection between my parents. The thing is, Sean, reading my Dad's diary has brought home to me that your screenplay, which has distilled the story down to pictures and dialogue, has captured the essence of many of these moments. But I don't remember writing them into the novel."

Sean didn't respond, so she continued.

"I think now, from this perspective, that the novel formed in a frenzy, burgeoning out of control until it reached a bursting point. And then I expelled it without ceremony and left it to its own devices. Of course, I didn't know you were going to come along and get your hands on it!"

Sean opened his eyes—but he let her continue.

"As I read through your version of my story, what you have chosen to adapt for the screen, it's startling to see my dialogue extracted and streamlined, arranged in a more rarefied setting, somehow purer and fresher. In some cases, you haven't even changed the words, or the context, but their removal from the cushioned, protected world of the novel lays them bare, more open and vulnerable, somehow . . ."

Sean was listening intently.

"And when I re-read them in their new place, I find myself inserting in the interstices thoughts and emotions that I had long buried or maybe never even been aware of. That day that I spent recording songs with Dad and Orla, for example, was forever etched in my mind, though I have never heard the tapes since and have no notion if they even still exist. What I had not known or consciously remembered, was the secret connection between my parents, the invisible thread that bound them in sweet mystery and communion, the love they felt for each other. And yes, the way they loved us, me."

Fiona's voice was shaking by now, as she started to slip into grief over all the lost opportunities and connections.

"I have to recall these difficult connections, but I get the chance to remember the sweet ones too. Your script has helped me uncover the richness."

"Of the primal emotion that came from you?"

"Yes." Fiona's voice was breaking with emotion. "I had always thought of my novel as a catharsis of sorts, not as a therapy. It is first and foremost a work of fiction. But maybe I brought it to light prematurely, failed to explore too deeply that murky miasma, and filtered it through my own need to consolidate and reject. Now, through this process with you, I've had to re-immerse myself."

"Like a baptism?"

"Like a new baptism."

Fiona was sobbing gently now, in tune with the ocean. Releasing and starting to pour out her grief.

Sean moved closer and cradled her shoulders as she continued to cry. He reached for her hand. "Maybe with the film you can . . . maybe it will help?"

Through her sobs Fiona absorbed this. "Yes. Maybe. I think I may be ready now."

After a time, she started to breathe more naturally. She looked at Sean, grateful for his presence. He drew her closer and gently kissed her on the lips. She was surprised, even though she had wanted this, half expected it. She kissed him back. She laid her head on his shoulder, and they sat in sweet silence as the afternoon spread out before them in the secluded cove.

■ ■ ■

Fiona was feeling quite pleased with herself as she and Sean entered Les and Leonard's bright office for their meeting the following day. Sean's kiss still lingered. They were both aware of being in the midst of a delicate process and the need to take it easy, to keep the professional journey on track. At the same time, the spark had been ignited and was very much alive. Fiona also felt encircled by her father's love, even from beyond the grave, and was absorbing some of the emotions he hadn't been able to express while he was alive. That glowing confidence, enhanced by her pleasure in her freshly minted fashion, clung to her like a new-wrought skin.

Leonard's tan seemed to have deepened as the summer progressed, and Les, in contrast, was as pale as ever. They still were dressed within an inch of identical.

"Fiona," Leonard began in his ebullient manner. "A pleasure." And Les nodded as if silently echoing this salutation.

"I trust that your summer is going well?"

"And the script is progressing apace and to your liking?" Les finished.

Fiona smiled and looked over at Sean. "Yes. It feels like we are moving forward, working through some spots."

"And fulfilling well your position as adviser." Leonard added.

"As cultural attaché." Les concluded.

Fiona nodded thanks.

"I'm sure Sean has told you that we have taken into consideration . . ." Leonard began.

"Into serious consideration . . ." Les continued.

"Your passionate plea to shoot on location in Ireland."

"Yes." Fiona acknowledged. "He told me."

"Indeed." Leonard took a breath. "We have seriously considered it."

"And run the numbers," Les added.

"The budget numbers." Leonard clarified.

"And we've talked with our backers." Leonard began again.

"Our financial backers." Les echoed.

"And we've presented them with the very arguments you so eloquently presented to us in this very office, not so very long ago . . ." Leonard again.

"Clear, eloquent and very persuasive arguments," Les added.

"And have come to the conclusion that we will in fact shoot the film on location." Leonard.

"In Ireland." Les concluded.

"Gosh. That's wonderful!" Fiona gushed. "Thank you."

"Fantastic!" Sean added. "Thanks, guys." And he grinned over at Fiona.

"Have you scouted yet?" Sean asked. "Do you have some possibilities?"

Their eyes seemed to twinkle in unison. As always, Les deferred to Leonard to begin the new thought.

"We would like to shoot on your farm, Fiona."

"The very same farm you were brought up on." Les added.

"Based on the fact that this story came from you." Leonard.

"Your imagination." Les.

"And that your feel for the soil, the earth . . ." Leonard.

"The *terra firma* of Ireland, is second to none." Les.

"For the purposes of our particular story, we firmly believe." Leonard started again.

"As do all of our backers," Les continued.

"That this film will be shot on the very location." Leonard.

"The very farm . . ." Les emphasized.

"In Ireland." Leonard added.

"Where you were bred and nurtured." Les concluded.

Fiona was dumbstruck. She was in awe of their ability to actually converse this way, as if they shared a brain, and she was astounded by the unexpected information. "The farm, my father's . . . the farm is currently . . . my brother and I are co-owners."

Les and Leonard beamed.

"Great." Leonard.

"Wonderful." Les.

"Well, I'll need his permission of course."

"Of course!" they said in unison.

"I'm sure he'll be very impressed by your powers of persuasion." Leonard commented. "At this point the powers that be are astounded that we ever considered NOT shooting in Ireland," he continued.

"They are indeed astounded," Les added, "but pleased, nonetheless, that such a felicitous opportunity presented itself in the guise of the fair author who penned the original story."

"We got a little friendly rap on the knuckles." Leonard started

"Metaphorically speaking, a rap on the knuckles." Les clarified.

"But so long as we secure this situation." Leonard.

"Shooting on your farm, Fiona." Les.

"So long as we secure this situation, it's full steam ahead." Leonard.

"Green lights all the way." Les.

"Happily ever after." They concluded together.

Fiona looked over at Sean. She tried to shift her own brain from her sheer awe at their shared speech and at the weirdness of this duet being played out before her. And she didn't dare say anything about Declan for fear that it would jeopardize the entire project.

Sean caught her look, then turned back to his two producers.

"Great! Just so we're on the same page, and Fiona will get the all clear from her brother, the film has to be shot on their farm. Some other Irish farm isn't a possibility?"

"Oh, Sean." Leonard began. "You bring us in this talent," he indicated Fiona.

"And win us over." Les.

"Us and them." Leonard gestured vaguely in the air.

"Yes, yes, us and them." Les added.

"And they stipulate that it must be this farm." Leonard.

"Ms. Fiona Clarke's farm." Les.

"And no other." Leonard.

"No, no other will do." Les.

"Now, partly this is budget, our budget constraints." Leonard.

"Our budget constraints, yes," Les.

"But combined with our awakened sensibility to the value of capturing the essence . . ." Leonard.

"The quiddity, I believe was your felicitous expression, Fiona." Les.

"That combination, Fiona." Leonard.

"And Sean." Les.

"Fiona and Sean." Leonard.

"Have brought us to this particular moment."

Fiona tried to formulate a sentence. Despite her anxiety, she had a funny thought that maybe she could start with half and Sean might help her out and finish for her.

"Do you have a time frame? How soon . . . ?" She began.

"Well, you two seem to be making very good progress on script issues. Sean?" Leonard raised a quizzical eyebrow.

"Yes. I'm probably a draft away from finishing. We've covered many of the questions I had and you had. Are you really that close to getting crew and all organized?"

"We actually thought that by the end of the month we could have you both on a plane." Leonard began.

"To Ireland." Les finished.

"So you could scout, Sean." Leonard.

"Along with Fiona." Les.

"So you could scout along with Fiona, using her expertise and knowledge of the terrain." Leonard.

"And we would finalize the crew and try to get it all rolling about a month out from that." Les.

"Give or take." Leonard. "But taking advantage of the summer weather to try and get all exteriors."

"And hoping, too, that nature will send some summer storms." Les.

They paused. Fiona felt breathless, as if she were the one who had been carrying on both sides of this strange conversation. She also needed air. And it seemed as if the meeting was over.

"Okay." Sean found his tongue. "Great, well, thanks. Fiona and I will look at the logistics, look at the calendar?" He glanced at Fiona for confirmation.

"Yes." She found her voice. "Thanks, thank you both."

Les and Leonard were beaming again, standing up, extending hands.

"Next time in Ireland perhaps, Fiona?" She nodded.

"We'll set up a meeting soon, Sean, finalize details?"

Sean nodded. "Yes, I'll call to set it up. Thanks again."

And then Fiona and Sean were outside and stepped into the still air. Fiona waited until they had cleared the building to trust herself to speak.

"Sean, he'll say no."

Sean didn't speak right away. He hailed a taxi and bundled them in.

"But, you are getting on somewhat better?"

"I thought we were, but we seem to have regressed. I don't know why."

"He's probably scared of this, too. Have you told him about your shifts in perception?"

"In the portrayal of the brother? No. Of course, I've never actually admitted to him that it's based on him . . . but he knows."

Fiona was silent for a while. Sean reached over and squeezed her hand. "I'm sure Declan has his own insecurities, too."

Fiona laughed. "I would have denied that, right, left, and center, about a month ago, but I see that. He still pisses me off, though!"

The taxi was pulling up outside Fiona's hotel.

"Listen," Sean began. "I know we need to chat about the film and Declan. You're probably anxious to set up a meeting with him."

Fiona nodded.

"Let me know how it goes. Maybe you'll be able to talk with him tonight?"

Sean kissed her again, lightly. As if they were still at the stage of saying hello.

"Ring me anytime, this afternoon or late tonight, don't worry about the time, okay?"

Fiona felt nervous, as if her future was hanging in the balance. Sean squeezed her hand reassuringly. "And I'll see you tomorrow. Okay, later." And with a wave Sean was off in the taxi.

■ ■ ■

Fiona rang Declan at his clinic.

"No, absolutely not!" He was livid. "Why can't they find another farm? There are hundreds . . ."

"Well, budget for one, budget's a big factor . . ."

"I can't help you, Fiona. I feel very strongly about this." Fiona detected a waiver in his voice.

"But, it wouldn't inconvenience you. You don't have to be there."

"That's your argument for trying to persuade me to sell the farm. Saying it has too many associations. Well I don't want our family home imprinted on celluloid, especially with your story, your version . . . sorry, I need to go here. We can talk about it tonight."

Fiona's head was swimming. Her entire career was back in jeopardy again. It was already being kept afloat by virtue of her work on the film, but if that fell through, Pam could not be expected to keep her on. Friendship, or no friendship. And ironically, Fiona thought, the stakes were even higher now. In addition to her career being on the line, she had created a whole new family network, was weaving genuine relationships with Julie and Una, and that would all collapse if she broke irretrievably with Declan over the film. And then there was Sean. She knew she was falling in love with him. Acknowledged it now. Wanted it and dreaded it at the same time. Here she was starting to gain some semblance of self confidence, and it terrified her that she would be tested again in love and would fail. Fail again. Fiona recalled her reading to Una about the Cheshire Cat in *Alice*.

"'Cheshire Puss,' she began, rather timidly . . . 'Would you tell me, please, which way I ought to walk from here?' 'That depends a good deal on where you want to get to,' said the Cat. 'I don't care much where,' said Alice. 'Then it doesn't matter which way you walk,' said the Cat. 'So long as I get somewhere . . .' 'Oh, you're sure to do that,' said the Cat, 'if you only walk long enough.'"

EYE OF THE STORM

Excerpt from a novel by Fiona Clarke

We are all gathered round the open grave. The day is gray and gloomy, befitting a funeral, and the tiny white coffin is perched at the edge of the gaping pit.

"As angels hovered o'er the earth this blossom met their eyes.
So wondrous fair they marked it out,
As fit for paradise."

Mama starts to sob. Dada shuffles from one foot to another. Conor looks like he's crying but trying not to. I am wooden. I cannot cry. I feel like I am dead. I want to be.

The priest continues.
"O Lord, Thou gavest her to us to be our joy,
and now Thou hast taken her away from us.
We give her back to Thee without a murmur,
though our hearts are wrung with sorrow."

I open my mouth to scream, but no sound comes out. I want to say "No! We don't give her back!" I stand there, petrified, as the coffin is lowered into the ground and more prayers are said. Someone starts to shovel earth, and it falls like lead with a deafening thud. People move slowly towards us to offer condolences and then start to drift away. We stay.

Later, Dada makes a move to get us going. He takes my hand and draws me gently, but my feet have sprung roots down into the soil. They connect me to my dead sister.

CHAPTER SIXTEEN

RE-CONNECTIONS

"When the soul wishes to experience something she throws an image of the experience out before her and enters into her own image."

MEISTER ECKHART

At Declan's house that evening, Fiona found herself in a heated argument with her brother. The memory of Sean's kisses lingered as a balm and a fearsome memory trace. She was exultant and terrified. She had to first sort out her tangled family web, she had to finish this film and salvage her writing career. She had to banish Frank from her life and her mind forever.

There were papers strewn all across the dining room table and words flying about the room.

"Why should I agree to letting you shoot on the farm if you're going to libel me?" Declan almost shouted at her.

"I think you've been in this litigious society too long," Fiona shot back. "Everyone wants to sue everyone else."

"I don't want to sue you," Declan replied, trying to keep his voice even. "I want to try and sort out this mess."

Fiona was mollified by his tone and sensed his insecurity. She herself was developing an ever more labyrinthine notion of their past. She felt that things were being pushed up to the surface but hadn't yet gained the momentum to break through the barrier to some sort of clarity. She also didn't know whether she could trust her brother. Every time she felt she was beginning to understand more of the underlying tensions between them, she resented the fact that she might be prepared to give him the benefit of the doubt. She didn't understand her compulsion to needle him.

"You don't really know what you want to do either about the farm, do you?" she asked.

Declan pondered this. "I suppose I don't," he admitted. "On the one hand I want to keep it, take Una and Julie there to visit, and on the other—I just want to say goodbye, clean slate."

"So let's agree to sell it. Put it all behind us." Even as she said this, Fiona had a rush of panic over letting the farm go. "But not before we shoot the film; I have to shoot the film there."

"But why?" Declan asked. "Why can't it be somewhere else, some other similar location?"

"Well, I told you on the phone, budget for one. And authenticity." Fiona felt as if she was hanging desperately on to a lifeline. "The script has changed, Declan. The character of the brother is . . . well . . . not as harsh now. Can't you see your way to agreeing to let us shoot there?"

Declan hesitated. He didn't seem convinced.

Fiona continued. "Uncle Frank rang again. He's pushing us to settle the will, too. I said one of us would ring him before the end of the week."

Declan stiffened at the mention of Frank. He looked at Fiona suspiciously. "Why is he ringing you? Are you two in cahoots or something? He's supposed to be neutral in this. A mediator. He's not supposed to take sides."

Fiona panicked at the thought that Declan might guess her secret. The coupled shame of Orla's death and Frank's abuse. She worried that Frank's offer to side with her would be discovered, perhaps by a high-priced lawyer that Declan might hire, and that this would nullify the will; she would lose everything. Did the fact that she had listened to Frank and not stood up to him, not said that it was probably illegal, not to mention unethical, to take sides with her against Declan, did this jeopardize the whole process? Might she lose everything?

"If you let us shoot on the farm . . ." she faltered, "if you agree to this, I'll seriously consider . . . agreeing with you. Keeping the house."

Declan was dumbfounded. "I don't understand. There's some catch. Why are you giving in all of a sudden?"

"For my sanity. I need to move on." She didn't add that her entire career depended on it.

"Do you have a schedule yet, a projected schedule? I had thought I might visit home with Julie while she can still travel, and Una gets out of school next week."

"The producers are talking of moving fairly rapidly. They want me and Sean to go over as soon as possible to check out the locations. And they want to take advantage of the summer weather, while it lasts. I think the crew has been mostly lined up—they just hadn't planned on traveling to Ireland. And we could finish up our business with the will. Finalize it all. Move on."

Declan looked directly at her, as if trying to decipher what she was really thinking. "Are you sure about this, about the will? Yes, it's what I want, but you might change your mind again when we get to Ireland."

"I really do want to get rid of it," Fiona responded in a barely audible voice. She remembered Frank, the night visits, the shadows, Orla's fevered face on the pillow, her mother frozen in grief. "Shed it like a skin." Then memory flashes of the storm, her sister beating her with her little fists, reprimanding her for making her sick. Declan and Mam's icy stares of recrimination. "But I think the guilt wouldn't let me give it up anyway."

Declan seemed to falter. "Do you mean guilt about what Mam and Dad would think?" he asked. "That shouldn't be a factor in our decision. I don't think they would mind either way. If anything they were completely detached by the end. Even Frank said as much."

Fiona shook her head. She took a deep breath. "Not guilt over Mam and Dad." She didn't look at him. "Guilt over Orla." She lowered herself back into the chair. She felt weary. She was tired of keeping it all in.

"But why?" he asked.

And it was all Fiona could do to keep the sarcasm from her tone when she replied. "I thought that would be obvious, Declan."

"Well, sorry, you've lost me ... but it's not." Declan sounded genuinely puzzled.

Fiona was sure he had to be putting it on. "I was always certain that you had me pegged as a traumatic guilt sufferer or some such thing."

"Fiona, why on earth . . . ?" he began.

"Do I have to spell it out?" she challenged. "This is a ploy to get me to say it, isn't it?"

"Say what?"

"To admit my guilt, confess my sins."

"I have no idea what you mean. What sins are you guilty of?"

Declan looked at her. He waited.

Finally Fiona spoke. "The obvious and well-known one . . . that I hastened Orla's death, of course." There was a long pause. "I hope you're satisfied. You forced me to say it."

Declan was stunned.

Fiona felt as if he was playing with her and she was losing.

"Don't act innocent, Declan." She jumped up and began to pace the room. "I know you all thought it and knew it, and I knew it, too, but none of us could say it."

Declan's eyes followed her as she circled. "I think you're losing it, Fiona." He said quietly. "Orla died of leukemia, you know that."

"You don't have to lie to me," she lashed out at him. "Of course, I know she had leukemia, but she died as a direct result of that terrible cold she caught in the storm."

Declan stared at her. "Who told you that?"

"No one told me—that's the point! No one had to tell me. I knew. Just as surely as if it were imprinted on my brain."

"You knew wrong, Fiona." Declan was now the one making an effort to stay in control. "I swear to you. There was no connection between the two events."

"Don't lie to me." She stopped in her tracks. "It's all right, you know, I have to live with it and face up to it. You have your own conscience to live with."

Declan got up quickly and crossed over to his sister. He took a firm grip on both of her shoulders. "Fiona," he looked straight into her eyes. "Stop it! I am not lying to you—please believe me."

Fiona stared back, her eyes full of fear and mistrust. "And why the hell should I believe you now? You spent our entire childhood lying and blaming me for things you did."

Declan maintained his grip on her shoulders. "I admit I was no angel." He appeared conciliatory.

"Every second word out of your mouth was a lie!"

He released the tightness of his grip but kept his hands on her arms. "That's a slight exaggeration," he said, defending himself. "However, I'm not lying now. I had no idea you felt responsible . . ."

Fiona glared at him. "Don't you remember the storm? When she got drenched?"

Declan nodded. "I remember that, yes. But that was many weeks before Orla died. She caught a very bad cold—but that cleared up."

"I don't remember it ever clearing up. I remember it lasting forever, stretching out through that whole dreadful ruined summer, and then she went away to hospital again and never came back."

"But it did clear up," Declan assured her. "She was fine for a while. And then she got sick again. But Fiona, there certainly was no connection."

She was afraid to believe him. She searched to find her voice. "You say . . . there was no connection?"

Declan shook his head. "No, there was absolutely no connection. The two events are definitely unrelated."

Fiona stared at him, trying to comprehend: how two events that in her mind were inextricably bound together could turn out to not have any appreciable connection at all; how two incidents that seemed to form one cohesive conglomerate, could prove to be separate and unrelated; how two moments in time that in her world as a child had telescoped into a concomitant nucleus, a charged center of guilt and shame, could now exist independently from each other. She tried to contain this realization.

Declan let go of her shoulders.

They stood in silence.

For an eternal second Fiona was paralyzed. Declan's revelation had shattered her world more than any lie he had ever told. She was stunned and distraught and angry—all at the same time. That he had lied so much, and that this truth, had she known it as a child, could have changed her whole life. Every emotion she ever had seemed to converge at that moment, and when she thawed she lashed out at Declan and started to pound on his arms and chest, much as she had in the barn when they were children. He didn't resist. He just stood there and let her wear herself out.

"I know you're not to blame for what I didn't know." Her heart was opening up. "How could you be to blame for ideas and notions I had locked inside my head?" The sobs began. Great heaving sounds, laden with sorrow. She let the tears fall unabated.

When she had cried herself out, Declan put his arms around her and she buried her face in his chest. "You said I idolized her, Declan." Her voice was muffled. "It's true. Idolized and idealized."

"And probably even more so after you thought you were responsible for her death."

She nodded.

"It's not uncommon, Fiona. The linkage of events, the telescoping of a child's sense of time."

"Do you mean me thinking the storm and her death were practically the same, happening one right after the other?"

"Yes. It's our perception. Especially during a time of trauma."

Fiona was silent for a long while. "I really should have got some help, talked to someone . . ." Declan hugged her again. "I did think of her as an angel, as perfect. A golden child. And I didn't measure up to her in any way. I always came up short."

"Because you diminished yourself, Fiona. It's hard to live up to an image of a perfect angel."

"I felt a part of me died when she did. I always thought everything in my life was related to the loss of her, but the real tragedy was my own loss of self."

"That's right. You'd make a good shrink." Declan said it jokingly, but he wasn't smiling. He still held Fiona. "And yes, you may shoot on the farm. Get the film done."

She nodded her thanks. Declan hugged her tightly, and she felt his chest begin to heave. He started to sob. Fiona held him close, and she felt an answering sob in her own heart. They held each other for a lifetime. A lifetime past, during which they had never held each other at all.

■ ■ ■

That night, when Fiona returned to her hotel room, she lay down on the bed and stared up at the ceiling. The tears began again to stream silently down her face. She wondered how the body could hold so many tears. She let herself cry until she drifted into asleep.

Somewhere in the middle of the night she got up and took off her clothes and brushed her teeth. Then she curled back in the bed and cried until the tears dried up and she fell off to sleep again. Much of her life seemed clear to her now. A life of unshed tears and unexpressed grief turned back in on itself. The whole rhythm of the family had changed after Orla died, and Fiona knew now that her feelings as a child were right; she had lost both of her parents the same day she lost her little sister. It had all converged here in Los Angeles, City of Angels, where she had conjured up the spirits of her dead ones.

Although all this was clear to Fiona in this instant, it seemed as if her world stopped here. She couldn't see beyond this second in time. Had no concept of Time Future. She awoke in exactly the same position again and the tears were already streaking down her face. She just lay there. She had a meeting with Sean but didn't care.

When the phone rang early in the afternoon, she knew it must be Sean but didn't answer. She let it ring. The answering machine clicked on and played her message. She called later when she knew Sean was at another meeting and said she wasn't feeling well. She told him Declan had agreed to shoot on their family's farm and that he could go ahead and make arrangements for the filming. She gave him Declan's number.

The next day, she ordered room service and ate a few slices of toast. Food didn't interest her. She went back to lying on her bed, streaming out the torrents of unshed tears. There seemed to be no end. It was a slow deluge, steady like a mountain stream. The phone rang again. Fiona turned over on her side and curled up in the fetal position. The machine clicked on. It was Sean.

"Fiona, I hope you're all right. I realize you may want some time off—I know all of this has been hard. Please call me, though, just to let me know if you're all right, if you need anything."

Fiona never moved.

She knew now that she had fallen in love with Sean but that it was too late. She did not have the strength to venture into another disastrous love affair which would end in pain and failure. She rang him again later and left a message on his machine that she didn't want to work on this film anymore but that he had her full permission, per the contract, to continue. She wanted the film made, but Sean didn't need her, she thought. She was emotionally spent. She didn't know what she was going to do. She didn't even know how to get up out of bed.

Another message came in from Sean the next day. Fiona lay face down on the bed now and listened to his voice.

"Fiona . . . I got the message on my machine. I'm sorry you don't want to . . . that you want to . . . back out of the film deal . . . .as far as you working on it. Fiona, can I come over?"

He sounded sad. She was bereft but frozen. She couldn't afford to let him in.

That night, as the evening was folding in, Fiona left her room and set out alone for the almost deserted beach. She walked and walked and walked and walked. After a long time, she came to a playground, where a scattering of children frolicked in the fading summer light. She watched them play and laugh and swing and slide. Soon it got dark, and their parents took them home. When it was quiet and everyone was gone, Fiona sat on one of the children's swings and swayed herself back and forth and back and forth for a very long while.

Back in her room the answering machine blinked announcing its callers. She pressed the button and went out to the patio to watch the ocean while she listened to her messages. The ocean waves smashed loudly against the shore.

The first one was from Declan. "Fiona, we're all worried about you. I dropped by this evening but you were out. Una keeps asking. Sean told us about the plans for Ireland. I'll come, too, and we'll work out the business with the will. We can work it out. Please give us a ring."

Then, Sean. "Fiona." He hesitated. "I really hope that it's not . . . that you're not calling me because . . . Sorry—I really want to talk to you, not your machine. I came by but you weren't there. Please call me."

Fiona ordered a small fruit salad, and, when she had eaten about half of it, she threw on her sweatshirt and headed off into the night. She walked again along the beach near her hotel. A few stragglers were still out strolling and jogging.

Fiona kept walking. Soon it was dark, and she was the only person on the beach. The moon was full, and the stars were bright and clear. She walked and walked as if in a dream. She did not even consider her safety; she was considering nothing at all. She came to an area where there were no houses or lights. The only sound was that of the ebb and flow of the ocean waves.

Fiona stopped, as if on cue, and without looking around, she began to slip out of her clothes and walk into the ocean. Naked in the moonlight, she walked out further and further until the waves swept her up and she started to swim. She continued to swim out until she was only a speck in the ocean.

She slept like a baby that night and later into the morning. Her face in sleep started to drain of anxiety and she began to feel calm and peaceful. Cleansed. She felt the morning sun streak in and kiss her cheeks, but she was not done sleeping yet and merely turned over and nestled into a different position.

The noonday sun caressed her face and resuscitated her. She shifted onto her back and opened her eyes slowly. Her glance took in the room as she become conscious of her surroundings and remembered everything. She lay there without moving for a long while.

When Fiona swiveled over on her side her eye caught her new and never-used computer which was still covered with its ceremonial drape. She stared at it and then gradually began to uncurl and arise from the bed. She slipped on her robe and moved towards the machine. She reached over deliberately, ritualistically, and removed the covering cloth. She sat herself down in front of it.

Fiona's hands searched out the controls, turned on the computer and brought up the screen. She raised her fingers, poised, suspended over the keyboard. She drew in her breath as her fingers descended, found their place and began to glide gracefully across the keys and find their own rhythm. A story that felt like a dream began to formulate itself and pass though her onto the screen. It was vague and unformed, but contained a germ of substance that she knew would develop into a story. She recognized this old familiar place and reveled in its re-discovery.

Fiona smiled. She hummed along.

Several hours later Fiona continued to write fast and furiously. She printed out what she had written and looked with elation and gratitude at the little pile. She picked up the pages, sifted through them and put them back on her desk. She was past it. Past this particular nightmare. Something had unfrozen her soul and set her writing spirit free. Now she had to deal with the rest.

PART III

EYE OF THE STORM

CHAPTER SEVENTEEN

RETURN

"Keep in your soul some images of magnificence."

AE

Within seven days, Fiona was on a plane heading east with her niece Una sandwiched between herself and Sean. The week had been a flurry of activity as Fiona emerged from her cocoon, made contact with Sean and Declan, talked with Pam and made travel arrangements. The producers were organizing the film crew and hoping that production could start in a few weeks if all went well with the location scouting. Declan had to finish out the week, and Julie had a scheduled doctor's appointment, but Una had begged to be allowed to go over a day or so before them with her aunt Fiona. To Fiona's astonishment Declan conceded. They were to stop off at her New York apartment for a few hours *en route*.

Fiona had shared her experience with Sean, and they continued to consult on the script and fine tune the characters and situations. But she maintained a certain distance and fought against the pull to intimacy. Sean respected her need, and they continued their friendly and collegiate relationship.

As they landed at JFK airport, Fiona told Sean and Una that this had been her first arrival point in the United States ten years previous.

"It was July—hot and humid. And I thought everything was huge."

"Are things a lot smaller in Ireland?" Una asked.

"Compared to Dublin Airport of 1980, New York's seemed like a monolith. The booths were bigger, the people were larger, there was vastly more space, everything was teeming and congested. And I thought the cars were really enormous!" Fiona laughed at her first impressions. "At that time in Ireland, people still drove mostly small cars, smaller American Fords, Mazdas, Morris Minors, and always older models. I thought the airport parking lot in Kennedy was a vast expanse of limousines—big American eight-cylinder gas guzzlers, station wagons, vans—and new, they all seemed to be new!"

As Fiona sauntered through the terminal, Una held tightly by the hand, Sean by her side, her leather book bag on her shoulder, stuffed with a notebook that was active with ideas, she felt a surge of contentment. The film loomed above her; she did not forget for an instant that she still had a formidable task ahead in getting her story to the screen and dealing with family matters, but she was grateful for a small reprieve and dared to hope that she might actually have a chance at happiness.

■ ■ ■

Fiona led Sean and Una in to her apartment building. She picked up her accumulated mail from the concierge, to the sheer delight of Una.

"You have your own doorman!"

Fiona laughed. "A lot of buildings in New York do; it's nothing too fancy."

She felt like she was stepping back in time. After the brightness of Los Angeles, her apartment seemed, small, even cramped. Una zeroed in instantly on the dolls and the doll-making chest.

"Oh, look. Did you make all these, Aunt Fiona? They're really neat!"

Sean went over to look at the dolls with Una while Fiona checked her answering machine. There were a couple of messages from Pam; she was going to swing by and say a quick hello. And then there was a message from Sean. Fiona thought she was hearing things, glanced over at Sean who was completely absorbed with Una in examining the dolls, turned down the volume and started the message again.

"Hi Fiona. Sending my voice across the airwaves to your dreaded machine to break the spell! Am planting great wishes for a fabulous future for the film, and for a fabulous future."

Fiona smiled. She put the kettle on for tea and joined Sean and Una with a tray of snacks.

"This is Grandma Clarke." Una was explaining to Sean. "She's just like in her picture." Sean reached for another doll and asked Fiona. "Is this her also? A younger version?"

"Yes. That's the first doll I ever made."

"And what about this one, a work in progress?"

Fiona laughed and laughed.

"What's the joke, Auntie Fiona? Tell us the joke!"

"Sorry!" Fiona calmed down. "It's just the 'work-in-progress' part is so true. It's me. It's a doll of myself, but I had just started when I broke off to come out to L.A."

"Are you going to finish it?" Una wanted to know.

"I don't know. Maybe I'll take it on the plane. Would you like me to show you how I do it, Una? Maybe you can finish the doll?"

Una was beside herself with excitement. "Really? You'd let me? What if I mess it up?"

Fiona laughed again. "It doesn't matter, really. You can practice, and we can always start another one." She looked over at Sean with a twinkle in her eye. "I'm breaking the spell!" Sean smiled back and winked. Una caught the wink.

"What spell? Why did you wink?"

"You don't miss much, do you?" Fiona joked. "It's just that I'm not taking everything so seriously, Una, not letting everything make me sad."

"Like Grandpa dying. And yours and Dad's little sister all those years ago, too?"

"Exactly. Like that."

The doorbell rang, and Pam made a theatrical entrance. She gave Fiona a huge hug, then stepped back and took in her outfit. "Wow! You look smashing. I approve of the new rags!" Then she shook Sean's hand heartily and greeted Una.

"Fiona is my aunt." Una announced.

"I know, I know." Pam replied. "And you're off to Ireland together. Exciting!"

Pam sat down for a cup of tea.

"Who are you?" Una wanted to know.

"Me? I'm the Wicked Witch of the East!" Pam joked. "But I only scare adults. Children are too smart to be scared. They know when someone is just kidding!"

"Well, I know you're not a witch and I'm not scared."

"Good, we're good, so. And I see you've discovered Fiona's dolls. Aren't they amazing?"

"They are awesome," Sean chimed in. "Works of art."

"Speaking of which," Fiona retrieved a bound bundle from her book bag and handed it to Pam. "A wee bit late, but a story nonetheless. More to follow."

"Great. Way to go, girl!"

"Is that a book, a new book?" Una wanted to know.

"This one is just a story, Una. But the book idea is forming; it will come."

"You see." Pam finished up her tea. "Los Angeles was good for priming the muse!"

"Yeah. Though I don't think it's the location necessarily." Fiona began. "Anyway, it happened." She stole a glance at Sean. "And it might have been your lucky computer! I've had it shipped to Ireland so I can use it for re-writes, by the way."

"Cool! Whatever works! Oh, big news. Sam and I are tying the knot in the fall, date to be decided, but taking the plunge!"

"Oh, Pam!! Fantastic! I'm so thrilled for you." Fiona flung her arms around her. "Let's catch up when I get back. Have a real date?"

"You're on!" She started to go. "And I'm off—and don't you have a plane to catch? Good luck with the filming, Sean. Keep me posted, Fiona—and don't forget your dialing finger!"

Fiona laughed. "You have to admit I'm better than I was!"

"I give you that—I'd say a hundred percent improvement so far!" And Pam was gone. They cleared away the dishes. Fiona gathered a few items she wanted to take to Ireland, and they headed out to find a taxi.

■ ■ ■

"Is this where you live, Fiona? All the time?" Una asked when they were in the cab.

"New York? Yes. Maybe when you're older you'll visit me here?"

Una nodded. "And Sean. Will you visit Fiona here too?"

Fiona blushed. Sean was taken aback and briefly speechless. Out of the mouths of babes. Una was articulating what was unspoken between them.

"Of course," Sean rebounded. "We'll be working on the film for quite a while. Fiona will want to see it before it opens."

As they approached the *Aer Lingus* terminal, the bars and restaurants got busier and louder and there were noticeably more Irish accents. It was 6.45 pm, about an hour before departure. Families and friends were having their last drinks together before going through the final checkpoint and sending the passengers on. Fiona realized she was drawn to the Irish accents. She couldn't help the melting of recognition and familiarity that overcame her at the mere sound of the rising cadences, soft and sibilant, excited and gregarious.

"Would you two like a bite to eat?" Sean asked. "It could be a while before we eat on the plane."

"I'd like Irish food." Una piped up. "Fish and chips!"

"Technically English—but Irish enough!" Fiona laughed, and they found a booth and ordered up some fish and chips.

"Are all these people Irish?" Una asked as she munched on a crispy chip. "Are all the Irish people in New York?"

"Well—there are a lot of Irish here. Not all, but a lot."

"Do you have Irish friends here? I don't think Daddy has any Irish friends."

"Speaking of Irish," Sean joked," shall we have a little refreshment before we board? To get into the Irish mood?"

"Why not." Fiona smiled. "And to help us to sleep on the long flight!"

"What'll you have?"

"A half pint of Harp—for medicinal purposes of course!"

Sean got two halves, and a lemonade for Una.

When they boarded the plane, the *Aer Lingus* flight attendants pulled them further into the Irish vortex.

"What language is she speaking?" Una asked, fascinated.

"It's Irish, Gaelic." Fiona explained. "The national language of Ireland."

"Will people there speak Irish? Will I be able to understand them?"

"Don't worry, everyone speaks English. And the flight attendant will make the same announcement now in English."

"I was there before, you know. But I was five, I think. I just remember Grandma and Grandpa."

When Una spoke it hit Fiona even more forcefully that both of her own parents were indeed dead. A mere two years previous, they were both hale and hearty and young. They lived in the memory of this little girl. Declan and Julie's next child would never know them, and if she herself ever had children, they would never know their maternal grandparents.

Una was full of energy and noticed everything. She admired the smartly designed green and navy uniforms on the attendants. She practiced tilting back her seat and was thrilled with the coloring books the crew brought for her. She told the attendant that she was half Irish and going to visit her grandparents' farm. When a mother and her eight-year-old boy settled in behind them, the boy protesting loudly about the game his mother had forgotten to pack for him, Una was disgusted that such an old boy would act so silly. Fiona and Sean smiled over her head at the sensible little madam they were bookending. Then Una started to read out loud from the Irish book of baby names she had brought. "I'm trying to pick my new sister's name," she explained to Sean. "So, you can tell me what you like. You, too Fiona."

"Thanks!" Fiona laughed. "Okay, go ahead."

"Sorcha, Chiara, Niamh . . . you have to help me with how to pronounce them . . . Shauna—that's just like Sean! Are you Irish, Sean?"

"Part Irish, Una, my grandparents came from Ireland. Those names are beautiful."

"I'll read some more, I'm half-Irish, you know! Then we can pick! Aisling, Sinead, Emer, Maeve. What would you pick Fiona?"

"I love the name Aisling . . . Niamh—that's pretty too."

"Me, too, Niamh is nice . . . you say it with a 'v' sound. Okay . . . Siobhan, Caitlin, Nessa . . ."

"That's beautiful, Nessa." Sean interjected.

"I've always loved that name." Fiona agreed.

"You could call someone Nessa in one of your stories, Aunt Fiona!" and Una continued. "Orla, Eilish, Bridget, Caitlin, Coleen, Grainne, Fionula, Maire, Mairead . . . ." until she trailed off, wore herself out and drifted into a deep sleep. Fiona removed the book from her hands and tucked it in beside her. She and Sean exchanged a smile. Then Fiona opened her copy of the *New Yorker* and immersed herself in a short story. Sean delved happily into reading *The New York Times*. Una slept peacefully between them.

■ ■ ■

When the pilot touched down and the passengers applauded, Una was delighted and clapped along. "It's like a play, Fiona. They're clapping 'cause the play was good!" Fiona laughed and instinctively planted a big kiss on the crown of Una's head.

"Thanks for teaching me that, Una. You're right. It's a wonderfully generous gesture, and saying thanks, too. I think that's it."

Sean had rented a car at the airport and drove them to Cregora—with plenty of friendly reminders from Fiona and Una to stay on the left side of the road. Una squealed when they ran over potholes. Soon they were in the countryside and passing by the farms where the farmers were out on tractors, some of them cutting hay, others stacking bales, still others on foot driving their cows in for morning milking. Fiona pointed out the chapel steeple to the newcomers, and they slowed down as they approached the village and drove up through the main street. They passed Foley's pub, the rival to the Cregora Arms, and Clancy the butcher, and the bookshop where Fiona had worked one summer while she was still in school. They passed Frank's bakery, which looked closed. Fiona did not point it out to Sean and Una. They approached the laneway that led to the farm, turned into the yard, scrunched on the gravel and they were in front of the farmhouse.

"Oh, it's a really old house!" Una clapped delightedly.

Fiona laughed. "It's called Shantiga—which does mean old house."

Sean got out and looked over the farmhouse. "How old is it Fiona?"

"Our family has been here since the 1850's. It was originally a small one bedroom cottage, now you'll see—it has expanded considerably!"

"It's stunning."

Fiona was surprised at Sean's open admiration. She had never thought of their house as particularly special. Una had approached the huge red door and was marveling at the size of the keyhole. "Gosh, the key must be enormous to this door!"

"It was pretty big." Fiona conceded. "Mam and Dad replaced it with a smaller lock just a few years ago, but they left the keyhole intact."

Sean was admiring the construction: two stories of sturdy, reddish brown bricks, a gray slate roof, massive chimneys. The large solid windows were shaded with white lace curtains. "Tradition." She heard Sean say. "Centuries of tradition. That's your heritage." Fiona took this in, stood there a few moments longer and led them in to her family home.

■ ■ ■

Fiona had let Nellie know their arrival time, and she made a great fuss over Una and Sean. The kettle was on, the scones were in the oven and they had had a mini tour of the house. As they sat back down in the kitchen, Nellie had laid out service for five and handed them all a steaming cup of tea.

"Your uncle is on his way over, Fiona. He's mighty anxious to see Una and to meet Sean. He's very excited about the film—well, aren't we all! Of course, we're hoping you'll make us all famous!"

At the mention of Una and Frank in the same breath, Fiona's cup slipped from her hand and smashed into tiny pieces. It was her mother's best china, brought out for the guests.

"Are you all right, love? What's the matter?" Nellie was all concern.

Sean looked anxious too and rose to see if Fiona was all right. She tried to recover. "Sorry. I'm fine. I don't know . . . it just slipped."

Nellie already had the situation under control, was mopping up, getting a fresh cup, pouring Fiona her tea, noticing that her hands were shaking.

"You need a lie down, pet." Nell was all consideration. "Have your cuppa and a scone and then get some rest. It's a long flight that, isn't it, all the way from California?"

At that moment Frank arrived, shouting a greeting as he entered the outside door. He shook hands with Fiona, greeted Sean and bent down and shook hands with Una.

"You're my Uncle Frank!"

Frank laughed heartily. "Well, yes, indeed, I am. In actual fact, I'd be your grand uncle, little girl."

"That's good. I need some uncles." And they all laughed, Fiona pretending she was amused. "I don't have very many relations."

"Well, we are happy to oblige you young lady." And he patted her on the head and sat down for his cup of tea. "Your parents let you off on your own then?"

"Oh, no. I'm not on my own. My Aunt Fiona is minding me!"

Frank found this very amusing. "Aren't you the clever little one?"

They chatted amicably, Una keeping them all amused while they drank their tea and ate the scones, smothered in butter and homemade raspberry jam.

"I'll give Declan and Julie a ring to let them know we arrived safely. Do you want to say hi to them, Una?" And Fiona took Una by the hand, leaving Sean to chat with Nellie and Frank who were vying for roles as extras in the film.

■ ■ ■

After the phone call, Fiona brought Una up the steps she had mounted so many times with Orla. She felt suddenly frightened and protective of her little niece. As soon as Nellie mentioned Frank wanting to meet her, Fiona's suspicious hackles went up. In an entire lifetime of living with the memory of the abuse by her uncle, it had never once occurred to her that he would molest anyone else. She had managed to compartmentalize the entire experience as being about her and him. They were the only two people involved. Now Fiona started to wonder if Frank had ever molested any other children, other girls. She assumed not, as the village was so small that it would have come out—surely it would have come out. Nonetheless, she felt the need to keep Una close by her. They were going to sleep together in Fiona's old room until Declan and Julie arrived, so that should be easy.

Fiona saw that Nellie had made up the bed with crisp cotton newly ironed sheets and the blue quilted eiderdown, and it looked fresh and inviting to her weary body. She glanced at the light wooden lockers on either side of the bed, each with a rose shaded reading lamp. Nellie had already brought up their cases.

Una ran over and sat down on the stool in front of the dressing table. Like the wardrobe, it was antique oak, had a huge oval mirror and two swinging side mirrors, a big smooth surface, and a little jewelry drawer. Fiona sat down beside her, and they looked at their reflections in the mirrors. Fiona and Orla had often sat side by side on this very stool when they were children and played dress up and games in front of the mirrors. They had a game of projecting into the future their relative ages. "When I'm fourteen, you'll be ten." "When you're seventeen, I'll be thirteen."

She'd be thirty-one now. Time Past.

And here was young Una—happy and carefree and on her own big adventure. Time Present. Fiona's reflection confirmed how she felt herself. Wrecked and worried. She unloosed her hair, let it cascade onto her shoulders, and Una picked up a hair brush and began to smooth out the tangles.

■ ■ ■

Nellie had agreed to come over every day and help out with the meals and the house while the family was visiting. Fiona had also proposed that Sean hire Nellie as caterer for the film—and she could get other women from the village to help out.

"When you taste her dinner tonight, you'll see what a fabulous cook she is!"

"I've already tasted her scones—that's a great start! Has she cooked for large numbers?"

Fiona laughed. "Well, she brought up a whole crew of huge lads—each counts for two! And at the same time, she came over here anytime she could when Mam was in hospital. Herself and Aunt Rita helped out a lot."

"Who's Aunt Rita? Oh I remember now." Una added. She gave you *Alice*—she and Uncle Frank."

"You're a good little family historian, Una!"

Fiona was taking Sean and Una on a tour of the farm.

"You know that Nellie is insisting I stay here? I told her I was going to book a B&B, but she refuses to let me."

Fiona was conflicted. She had expected Sean to stay in a local bed and breakfast and drive out every day. For her own sake, she thought this arrangement would be easier, would help her to get some distance and keep her feelings at bay. But she made no strenuous objections when Nellie announced her plan. And now she felt safer that Sean was sleeping under the same roof, at least until Declan and Julie came and she could relax about Una.

"I'll be putting you in Fiona's parents' room, Sean. I hope that's all right? Declan and Julie can have Declan's room, and I have an extra cot for Una if she wants to move back in with her parents when they come tomorrow."

Nellie had the last word.

"Well, it's a lot more convenient for you, isn't it?" Fiona asked rhetorically. "You'd have to drive a good bit to get a decent

B&B—there certainly aren't any in Cregora. And the food could never match this one!"

Una had spied the old treehouse and shrieked with delight.

"Is this it, Fiona, this is the place you told me about?"

"Yep—that's it." And Fiona swallowed the lump in her throat when Una rushed headlong and worked her way in to the carved out wooden enclosure and started to explore.

It was the first moment Fiona and Sean had been alone since their arrival. Fiona had hardly let Una out of her sight.

"Fiona, are you all right? You seem on edge. And what is it with Frank?"

"What do you mean?" Surely it wasn't obvious.

"I just noticed . . . well, you tensed up. You seemed relaxed enough before that."

"It's just so much history, Sean. The slew of deaths around the same time—Rita and the baby, and Orla." She partly lied. "It will always be connected. That's the reason I need to sever the ties."

"But didn't you say you might compromise with Declan and let him keep the land?"

"I felt pushed into that. Making the film became top priority, so I bargained. And it's true that I don't ever have to visit here again."

Sean didn't seem convinced. He looked around at the land, the fields stretching to the horizon, the house in the distance. "It's an amazing place. Full of history."

"Yes. And memories."

At that moment Una shouted out to them from the tree cave. "It's so huge in here. Even you could still fit in here Fiona, now that you're grown up!"

They laughed, and Fiona brought Sean over to peek in to her former hideout. They had planned to reconstruct it for the film shoot.

Fiona and Sean and Una walked a good deal of the land and had a tour of the yard and sheds and machinery. The farm was now rented temporarily and being farmed by locals until Fiona and Declan decided what to do. Fiona showed them the pump at the back of the house—behind the kitchen window.

"This was where we went to get our drinking water in the big white enamel bucket—from the time we were all big enough to reach up to the handle, strong enough to pump up water from the well and hefty enough to carry the bucket of water back around into the kitchen." Fiona also showed them the covering of the well. "When you stood in front of the kitchen sink, you could see out on the yard. Poor Mam spent a lot of time keeping an eye on the three of us when we were little to make sure we didn't get killed by the machinery, eat too much dirt or fall into the well!"

"Are you putting all of this in the film, Sean?" Una asked.

"As much as I can, Una. I want to make it as real as possible."

■ ■ ■

That evening, all of them pitched in to help Nellie with dinner. Despite Fiona's discomfort, Uncle Frank had come over and was acting like part of the family—which of course he was. He had brought over a bottle of Powers whiskey, a bottle of red lemonade and a loaf of his fresh bread.

"Are you a whiskey man yourself there, Sean?" he asked with a twinkle.

"I'm more of a beer drinker, but I enjoy a whiskey every now and then—though I've never had Powers."

"You most likely can't get that over there in America. It's our home grown product! Would you like a wee dram before we eat, to boost the old appetite?"

"Sure. Just a small one. I don't want to shirk my potato washing duty!"

Sean had been assigned to the potatoes. Fiona and Una were cleaning and slicing the carrots and parsnips.

"Shur' this will only enhance your chopping there. Isn't that right, Nellie?"

Nellie laughed heartily. "Well it might and it mightn't. But you're safe enough with us anyway, Sean, if it doesn't agree with you."

"Will you try a wee drop yourself Nell, then?"

Nellie laughed again as she seasoned the leg of lamb. "Not if you want this lamb cooked tonight, I won't! Maybe after dinner I'll have a wee taste."

"And what about yourself, Fiona? Will you indulge?"

Fiona shook her head. "I'll wait 'til after, too."

"Grand." And Frank went to get the glasses from the parlor cabinet.

"What's the lemonade for?" Una asked.

"Why, that's for you, little girl. And for anyone who might want to adulterate their whiskey by adding a touch of lemonade!"

Una laughed happily. "You're funny!"

Frank poured the drinks as they all continued dinner preparations.

"And what can I do, Nellie? Are you in charge of the dinner proceedings?" Frank inquired.

"In a bit you can set the table, Frank. No rush."

"Can I help set the table, too?" Una asked. "I'd like to help set that table—are we eating in the dining room?"

"Indeed we are, and Frank could do with a bit of help." Nellie teased.

Fiona's nerves were on edge. She had hoped to have a reprieve from Frank and wondered if he was spying on her, making sure all was *au fait* with the film, no references to bad uncles. He had also mentioned earlier, as soon as he got her alone, that they should move ahead and finalize the issues of the will as soon as Declan arrived. He seemed to be in more of a hurry than they were. Put it down to wanting to accomplish his legal duties. Fiona had no problem with this as she was anxious to wrap it up in the shortest possible time.

But the business with Una was making her nervous. She didn't want him near her. It was unthinkable that he might try anything. Fiona used to think that what happened with her was an anomaly, a one time aberration. But what if it wasn't? Was he truly a pedophile? Was Una in danger? It made her wish she could have a drink but she wanted to stay alert.

Sean savored the glass of Powers. "Nice, very smooth."

"Good man, yourself." Frank approved. "You've got good taste for a Yank!"

"Well, he's part Irish, Frank, you have to give him that!" Nellie joked.

They were all relaxing and having a good time. It brought back memory waves to Fiona of happy times spent preparing meals in this kitchen.

Sean turned to Nellie as he removed the eyes from the potatoes. "You're a cousin of Fiona's, Nellie, is that right?"

"Fiona's father, James, and Frank's aunt, Jenny, you wouldn't have known her, Fiona, as she died when you were only a wee baby in the pram . . . well Jenny and my mother were second cousins. I think that makes your father, God rest him, and myself third cousins—or maybe third cousins once removed."

"So you're my cousin, too." Una exclaimed as she finished off a carrot. "Oh boy, I have all of these new relatives now. I'll tell Mom and Dad when they come tomorrow."

Fiona laughed. "It's a bit distant, isn't it?"

"Just a bit." Nellie chuckled as she expertly handled the lamb and bundled it into the oven. "But your parents were always good to me and Ignatius and the brood. They got us through a few hard spells when Ignatius was out of work. Those were some hard times."

"You were good to us too, Nellie. I don't know what Dad would have done without you when Mam was sick—and then after Orla died, and . . ."

Nellie nodded. After Aunt Rita and the baby. She started in on the bread pudding she was making for desert. She poured the milk over the bread, added sugar and raisins, stirred it all up. The lamb was beginning to smell delicious.

■ ■ ■

Fiona was washing off the chopping knife in the sink when she saw them. Right out in front of her in the yard, Frank was crouching down with Una and holding her hand over the well handle.

Fiona tried to stifle the gasp and let the knife slip and nicked her finger. Blood began to flow. Sean and Nellie were deep in conversation, and Sean ran over to her. "What is it? Are you okay?"

Fiona was shivering. She tried to breathe deeply. "Just a cut." She held her finger tightly to staunch the bleeding. "Una. I need to get Una."

"She went outside with Frank a minute ago."

Fiona didn't know how she could have missed that. She tried to walk and not run. "I'll just get her in. It's probably getting cold." And she stalked outside.

The air was mild—not in the least cold—a lovely late summer night.

"Una, do you want your cardigan?" Fiona tried to keep her voice steady.

"Oh, no. I'm not a bit cold. Uncle Frank is showing me the old well. He let me touch it but not open it up. It's too dangerous."

Fiona nodded. She didn't trust herself to speak.

"How's the dinner coming along then?" Frank asked. "Is it time to set the table yet?"

Fiona cleared her throat. "Yes. It's time." And hoped it was.

Una jumped up and grabbed Frank by the hand. "Come along, Uncle Frank. We are the table-setters, so we have to go in now."

Frank laughed. "Right you are, little madam. Whatever you say, I will obey!" And they went ahead leaving Fiona to gather herself in the waning light.

■ ■ ■

The meal was delicious, fresh succulent lamb, crisp browned roasted potatoes, juicy carrots and parsnips. And the tasty bread pudding to finish off. They all chatted amicably, Nellie filled them in on what her brave brood was doing. They had all done well for themselves and were now scattered all over the country and a few in England, working in their own construction company. Nellie already had eighteen grandchildren, and her three youngest weren't even married yet.

"I'm the only grandchild of Grandma Anna and Grandpa James." Una offered as they finished desert. "But soon I'll have a little sister. I'm really tired now." Una spoke it all in one breath.

"I'm not a bit surprised." Fiona laughed. "Come on, I'll get you to bed—the men can wash up!"

Fiona had to peel Una's clothes off her and drop her into bed, the little girl was so dog tired. As she kissed her good night, Una managed to ask if Fiona would read *Alice* to her the following night.

"I wanted to read it tonight but . . ." and she was out like a light.

They all put away the last of the dishes and cutlery and then had a final night cap. Now that Una was safely tucked in bed, Fiona felt she could relax. She was still tense from the shock of seeing Frank so close to Una, innocent as it might have been. After all, his touching her on the shoulder during those endless rosaries seemed innocent enough at the time.

Nellie had agreed to a small whiskey with a lot of lemonade. Frank had his own neat—no adulteration as he liked to joke, just straight up. He fixed one with ice for Sean and another neat for Fiona. Frank was going to walk Nellie home then.

"Maybe tomorrow or the day after, we'll fix up the will, Fiona? I'm sure you'd like it over and done with—and Declan, too."

"Yeah—let's see how tired Declan is. If he's up for it tomorrow, then we'll settle it up. Did you need to ring Mr. Stanley?"

"Well, why don't we have our meeting first, around four or so, sort it all out, make sure we're on the same page so to speak, and then we can set up the final meeting with Stanley?"

"Sounds good. Thanks."

"Right you be. Bottoms up then!" And he downed his whiskey. "I'll just pay a visit to the little boys' room, Nellie, and then we'll be off, if you're ready."

"Perfect, Frank. I'll get my cardigan."

Fiona stiffened like a corpse. She was frozen in space. She heard Frank's footsteps on the stairs, getting closer to the top, then couldn't hear them any more, and she sprung to her feet. "Excuse me a sec. I need to get something from my room." And she was gone.

She walked up the stairs as silently as she could. As she got to the top she saw that the bathroom light was on and the door closed. She breathed a sigh of relief. She went into her room anyway, checked on Una who was fast asleep, adjusted the sheet around her neck, waited until she heard the bathroom flush, held herself in suspension until she heard Frank's footsteps descend the stairs, and then she closed Una's door.

After Fiona and Sean saw Nellie and Frank off, they decided to have a small whiskey before retiring for the night. They were both tired. Fiona was emotionally drained with the effort of protecting Una and thus reliving her own past with Frank. She was glad Una's parents were arriving the next day.

"There's something wrong, Fiona, isn't there? Something else."

Both of them were sitting in comfortable armchairs in the living room. Fiona looked despondently at Sean. Her whole being ached to trust him, but she felt the need to hold herself back. There was too much at stake. Sean walked over, took her hand and knelt down by her. All of her resolve melted at his mere touch. All of her pent up frustration and worry. She tried to hold back her tears.

"Sean. I'm really a mess. You would be better off keeping your distance. I can't . . . I need you to direct the film."

Sean stroked her hand gently. "It's not mutually exclusive, you know. Loving you and working with you."

"I'm not so sure." Fiona thrilled at his mention of loving her, and wanted to run the opposite direction as fast as she could.

"Well, I am." Sean pulled her gently down beside him. "I am very sure."

Fiona's body yearned to be touched by Sean, her whole being reached out for his love, and another instinct told her she was fooling herself if she thought she could make a relationship work. She pulled away.

"You don't know me, Sean. Not really."

He drew her back. "I know enough, Fiona. And you'll share as you wish, as you need to."

Fiona knew she had to stop running. It was all coming to a head, converging. "Sean . . ."

"Shh . . ." he placed his fingers gently on her mouth. "No words . . ." And then his lips reached over to meet hers. And his kiss was light as can be, a sprinkle of magic dust, electric and galvanizing. Fiona responded. They spoke in kisses. Easy, slow, lightly landing, tantalizingly soft and gentle. Kisses made to last. To lead to more. To last.

They climbed the stairs together and parted at the top with a soft kiss and went to their rooms to rest and sleep off their weariness.

CHAPTER EIGHTEEN

ENDGAME

"You need to claim the events of your life to make yourself yours."

ANNE WILSON SCHAEF

Fiona slept fitfully. She was awakened several times with thoughts of Frank, memory flashes of the abuse which took place in this very bed, worries about seeing Declan, about Una's safety. Though she dreaded the meeting regarding the will, she wanted desperately to get it over quickly and move on with the film and get that done too. Maybe then she could get back to living her life.

The next morning at 10:30, Sean knocked on Fiona's bedroom door, and, when he heard a sleepy "come in," he entered slowly with the breakfast tray.

"Rise and shine!"

Fiona and Una roused themselves and began to emerge from the sheets.

"We serve breakfast in bed in this fine establishment." Sean joked as the two ladies extracted themselves from the sheets and propped themselves up on pillows. Fiona was shocked when she saw the time and remembered what the day had in store for her.

"I really overslept. I need to get moving."

Sean presented her with a cup of sweet milky tea. "Well, you need a good breakfast." And he handed Una an orange juice. "I played it safe with scrambled eggs and toast—I hope that is satisfactory," he pronounced with mock ceremony.

"This is fun." Una giggled as she devoured her juice.

Fiona relaxed. "Quite satisfactory." She joked. "The cup of tea is the most important."

"I knew that!" Sean replied. "I even made myself one—couldn't find the coffee maker."

"Probably because there isn't one. I bet there's some instant. We'll have to get you a coffee maker and fresh beans."

"And my Mom likes coffee in the morning, too." Una devoured her eggs.

"We definitely need to invest in one, then." Fiona added. "I like coffee when I'm writing."

She finished her breakfast, helped Una wash up and then jumped in the shower to prepare herself for the day to come.

■ ■ ■

Declan had rented a car at the airport, and he and Julie rolled in to the front yard right on schedule in the early afternoon. Nellie greeted them with a light meal and scrumptious scones which they relished. Fiona thought that Declan seemed unusually withdrawn—he didn't rise to his usual level of jocularity in company. When Fiona got a moment alone with Julie, up in Declan's bedroom where their suitcases had been installed, she asked her if everything was all right.

"I honestly don't know, Fiona. He's been withdrawn since you left with Una. When I ask he says he's fine—but he's not."

"Maybe he was worried about Una, being away without you both for the first time?"

"That's possible. I was surprised he gave in so easily. But if that's the case he could have mentioned that to me. It's normal. Of course, we knew she would be fine with you."

Fiona swallowed. She thought of Una outside with Frank by the well. Of him walking up the stairs, and she following to spy on him.

"Maybe Declan's worried about the meeting with Frank. The last one here was fairly contentious."

"Could be." Julie conceded. "But you two have come to an agreement on that, haven't you?"

Fiona nodded. "We should meet before Frank comes over at four, just to make sure we're clear." In her own mind Fiona was not happy about giving in to Declan, but it was worth it to get his okay to shoot the film on the farm. She realized that she hadn't told Frank she was going to go with Declan's wish and had a jolt of fear that he might put up some road block.

"You look pale yourself, Fiona. Are you okay?"

"I'm fine Julie. Let me get Declan, and we'll have our chat."

Sean and Una took Julie on a tour of the farm to give Declan and Fiona a chance to talk. Julie had been there before but never had a real tour. And Una was now the expert on the film locations and, with the help of the director, wanted to show off her knowledge to her mother.

Fiona and Declan were in the kitchen finishing the washing up. Declan was hand-washing a crystal fruit bowl. Fiona was slowly drying the wooden handled knives. She broke the silence.

"We should make sure we're both clear regarding the will."

"Didn't we agree on that?" Declan almost snapped.

"Our conversation was so hurried. I just want to be sure, in case Frank . . ."

Declan stiffened. "In case Frank what? Insists you get what you want?"

Fiona was thrown off guard. Did Declan suspect something? His anger was fierce. Almost cruel.

"We are the ones who decide . . ." she continued, and as she spoke she recalled Frank's urgency about completing the arrangement. Could it be that Frank also wanted to dispel those past memories? Be rid of the site of his violation?

"I admit," her voice quavered, "he seems to want us to sell, but he doesn't have a vote unless we disagree."

Declan seemed to back down. "Una loves the house and the farm."

Una again. All of Fiona's fears came coursing back. She had to warn Declan. If anything happened to her niece through Fiona's negligence, she would never forgive herself. She had just spent her life so far bound up in guilt over neglecting and damaging her little sister, and now that she had been exonerated from any direct responsibility for that death, she felt bound to act to prevent any potential future harm to Una. And she had to release herself from the bondage of these secrets. Fiona realized that she was still holding the knife and that Declan was washing the crystal bowl repetitively. She put the knife down.

"Declan?"

"What?" He didn't sound too inviting.

"Do you remember a while back . . . I asked you about Uncle Frank?"

He stiffened. "What about him. Are you talking about the shoulder incident?"

So, he did remember. "Yes. That. And something else. Something more."

She was aware now of Declan tensing beside her, slowing down the pace of the washing. He didn't speak.

"He used to come up and kiss me goodnight."

"Right, he came to me, too. After Orla died."

"And he'd have drink taken; he smelled of whiskey."

"I think they drank a lot, all of them, for a while."

"And he'd kiss me."

"He was lonely. We were all he had left then."

"On the mouth."

"Near it maybe. He was drunk, Fiona."

"On the mouth. He'd cut off my breathing."

Declan wasn't moving now. His hands were on the crystal bowl, still, arrested.

"And he touched me. Violated me. Every Saturday night. For all of that autumn and winter."

There was dead silence. Fiona couldn't believe she had spoken those words. Aloud. A warm summer afternoon stillness pervaded the kitchen. A faraway buzzing of insects wafted in from across the yard. A gentle breeze lifted the corners of the lace curtains, and they skimmed gracefully across the wooden ledge. Brother and sister were suspended for a long moment in time and space.

After an eternity Declan spoke.

"Fiona." It was like a whisper, hoarse. "Are you sure. Certain?"

"As sure as I am that you are standing there beside me."

"Bastard!" Declan hissed the word. "I remember him, as if he were sleepwalking . . ."

"He was my favorite, well, my only, but my favorite uncle." She managed. "I loved him."

"Fiona. I . . . I think it was totally out of character. I know he was crazy about you—in a healthy way. And after Aunt Rita and the baby died . . ."

"And Mam and Dad went to bits, so he had no support, I know. But that doesn't excuse what he did, does it? He was depressed and drunk and distraught, but that didn't give him the right to interfere with me." Interfere was an old-fashioned word. A word her mother might have used. A word woefully inadequate to describe what happened.

"No," Declan's voice was almost inaudible. "No it didn't."

Fiona was struck by her brother's intensity. He stood immobile, staring at the bowl between his hands. She thought he might crush it. She didn't move.

It seemed another eternity before she could speak again.

"I've made some connections." Fiona found her voice. "I've always had these stomach problems, like a knife stabbing me. But they never could find anything wrong."

"That's a symptom—a sign of abuse." Declan was recovering—trying to sound professional now. "It's usually . . . it's triggered by feelings related to the abuse. It's emotional and psychological, but you can experience physical pain."

Fiona nodded. She felt suspended, like the bowl in Declan's hands. It was strange to be talking to him about this—yet he was there at the time. A room away. And now he stood almost shoulder to shoulder with her.

"When did it start? Do you remember? October?"

"Yes—a few weeks after Orla died. And it ended before Christmas. Two and a half months. It could have been a lot worse, couldn't it? Some children are abused for years on end."

Declan looked over at her. "It's the after effects though, they can be . . ." And he looked away. He seemed to be in pain.

Fiona nodded. She knew now. The pain, fear of intimacy, flashbacks, unexplained anger, self-hatred. She thought of her pounding Declan in the barn and wondered if he remembered. She recalled her mad attack on her own apartment, on her belongings. Her wish for annihilation.

Then Fiona mustered up the courage to continue, to say more. To express aloud one thing she had always speculated about. She had already spoken the unspeakable so might as well push on. She looked over at her brother. Looked him in the eye.

"I always wondered . . . I always, almost from the beginning, wondered if you knew."

Declan did not budge. He stood in front of the sink, the bowl still held tightly, and he stared at it as if he were examining, carefully examining the exact details of the pattern. He stared with an intensity that Fiona recognized. Evasion. She had spent many endless minutes staring at fixed spots, whether moon or imaginary moons, to escape the actual unbearable moment she was living through. She then heard her own voice with an uncanny evenness, as if it were coming from a different body, say to her brother, "You knew, didn't you? You knew all along!"

Declan finally raised his eyes, turned, and met hers. She waited for the dreaded answer that she already intuited. Had long suspected. Even before she knew what it was she felt he was guilty of. She waited.

"I knew."

He went on.

"I think I knew at the time, but I didn't remember. It all came back to me about three nights ago. After you left. I remembered you asking me about Frank when you came to L.A. first, and then something triggered it. I think it started when you had your breakdown, over Orla, but I didn't remember the details, the fact of it, until a few days ago." He paused. "I was able to bring myself back to those nights. In the wake of Orla's death. At first I didn't know what it was, but it didn't seem right, something about his visits to you seemed off."

Fiona steeled herself. "How, off?"

"He began to stay longer, not too long, but longer than it takes to say goodnight."

Fiona waited.

"And then, one night, he left the door ajar. I heard his breathing, and it was . . . not right."

She continued to wait. Suspended. She pictured herself in her bed, the bed she had shared last night with her innocent little niece, the shadow leaning over her, the silver moon, and Declan, awake, in his bed just down the corridor, a few steps away, a world away.

"But I didn't know what it was, the discordance. I was twelve. I didn't have a concept of what it might be, that he might do anything untoward. He was our uncle."

She held back. She wanted him to say all he had to say before she let up.

"I had no words to formulate what I might say, and to whom—to Mam, to Dad? I made up a million sentences. I said none of them."

He stopped. He looked at Fiona, and his eyes reflected pain and devastation. She returned his gaze, recognized the pain and felt not a smidgen of sympathy.

"You coward!" she lashed out. "You lay there night after night in your cozy bed while our uncle molested me a few feet away. You heard him come in, you heard the sounds of his disgusting ritual and you did nothing. Not one thing. Not one bloody thing. You are the one who could have done something. The only one. And you did nothing."

"I wanted them to notice." Declan stated in a dead voice. "I wanted them to know. I kept thinking they'll come to and be our parents again. I was afraid. And yes . . . I was a coward."

"You could have tried—to say something. Gone down to them. Shaken them."

"Do you remember them? They were zombies. And the three of them fed each other, made it worse."

She remembered.

"They abdicated responsibility as parents." Fiona saw that clearly now as she spoke. "At least for that time. And certainly for that endless autumn. They should have been aware. They should have watched out for us. For me. They should have protected me."

"And I kept waiting for them to wake up from their dream." Declan spoke. "To come back to normal. I kept thinking, it will happen tomorrow. One more day and surely they will be back. But I'm not sure they ever did, fully."

Fiona slumped into a chair and felt the support of the wood against her back. She looked around at the room, the house. "It's haunted, with memories. This place is haunted. Do you see now why I want to be rid of it?"

Declan nodded. He placed the bowl carefully in the center of the table and sat down opposite Fiona.

"We'll sell it. I'll agree to sell it. From the minute I started to remember . . . and now you confirming this . . . horror. I'm so sorry, Fiona."

Things were moving very fast. She could hear Una's voice outside, chatting away to Sean and Julie.

"We keep changing our stories. About the farm, the inheritance." She checked her watch. "Frank will be here in about an hour. I really do want to get this over with. Have no more dealings with him."

Declan nodded in agreement. "I am totally ready to sell it. If that's what you still want, I think it would be better all round."

Fiona felt a tug at the finality of giving it up. But it was what she had wanted, right from the start, a clean slate. She took a deep breath. "Good. Okay. I'm ready, so."

■ ■ ■

Fiona scalded the teapot, measured out four spoons of loose tea, covered it with a cozy and let it brew. The meeting was due to start in five minutes, and having strong tea on hand was a necessity. Her stomach was in a knot. She had spent the intervening hour walking the land, soaking it up, revisiting her favorite spots, sitting in the hideout. She had wanted to go alone. Sean had driven into

Mullingar to see about buying a coffee maker. Declan and Julie were tired and had gone up to their room to take a nap, and Una had gone with them. Despite her lifelong conviction never to breathe a word about her uncle's abuse, Fiona did not now regret telling Declan. Especially as it confirmed her long held suspicion that he might have known. She did not worry even for a second that the story would go beyond the two of them. Declan's own complicity would take care of that. Was it inevitable, Fiona wondered to herself, that as she walked over the land, smelled the soil, and even now as she was back in the house and looking out the windows, that she would be overwhelmed as she never had been before, by the beauty of the place and its surroundings? Maybe telling Declan about the abuse had released something in her and made her appreciate as never before the beauty of her former home. Or maybe it was seeing it anew through Sean's eyes, and Una's. It was just as nice as Simon's family home—in a different way. As she took out the cups and saucers, she had the rueful realization that she and her brother now were locked in a diabolical pact, similar to the one she and Frank were embroiled in. They were the keepers of equally unsavory secrets. Bound by equal parts guilt and shame.

As Fiona was sure that Una was upstairs with her parents, she almost had cardiac arrest when, at that moment, she saw her with Frank outside the kitchen window. Frank had his arm around her shoulder and was showing her the old pump. Una as usual was plying him with questions. Then Fiona saw Frank pat her on the head. All innocent gestures, Fiona told herself as she called them all in for tea and the meeting—albeit a few minutes early.

■ ■ ■

The three of them sat at the huge oak table in the parlor. Frank had some papers and copies of the will, in case they needed to check or clarify the language. He was asking Declan about his trip, his work, complementing him on his lovely daughter. Fiona was pouring the tea and trying to steady her breathing. She wondered if Declan had any suspicions at all about Frank abusing other children. Or if he also had compartmentalized the story so that it was an isolated incident. Fiona tried to banish the thought from her mind. She had to focus on the business at hand. Even if Frank might have a propensity to abuse someone else, well, Una specifically, this deal they were going to finalize now would also remove Una from Cregora because the property would be sold to someone else, a stranger. After the meeting with Stanley tomorrow, Frank's main reason to be here would be removed.

"I think Nell and I have convinced Sean that we would be wonderful extras in your film, Fiona. And we'll help to scare up a gaggle of the locals—as long as we don't have any lines, we'll be grand!"

Fiona made an effort to steady her hand as she poured the tea. She handed a cup to Frank who sat across from her, and Declan who sat beside her.

"Grand. Thanks." Frank added two spoons of sugar and stirred. "Will we start then? Formally I think I have to ask each of you what you want. And we'll take it from there if we need to have a discussion. We'll start with you, Declan."

Declan cleared his throat. When he spoke his voice was frayed. "Yes . . . I want to sell it. I . . . want to sell both the house and the land." Fiona thought he was going to cry.

Frank looked surprised, but happy. Relieved. He positively beamed. "Good, Declan. Good lad, yourself. I see you've had time to think it over. Good man. I think that's a very good decision. A wise move."

Frank turned next to Fiona. Of course it was a forgone conclusion that she would say yes and they could wrap up the meeting. It struck Fiona that Frank's question was similar to that of the priest at a wedding, asking the bride and groom separately if they agreed to take the other as their lawful spouse. Unexpectedly for Frank, Declan had answered yes. So there would be no foreseeable impediment to this marriage.

"And you Fiona?" Frank beamed at her. She saw him across the table from her and then saw him as he leaned over her in the bed, covering her mouth, smothering her, stealing her childhood. "Can you tell us what you want, Fiona?"

"Yes." Fiona answered. And Frank loomed over her again, and she saw the moon, the sliver of the waning moon.

Frank smiled and looked at her happily.

"Yes," Fiona continued. "I'd like to keep them. To keep both the house and the land."

She couldn't let Frank get away with it. Declan really wanted to keep the land, and she was, moment by moment, regretting that she had ever considered giving up this precious place.

Both Declan and Frank were in shock. Declan looked at her with concern. "Fiona, you meant 'No,' right? You want to sell it?"

Frank was recovering. Perhaps thinking also that her response was a mistake, that she had simply misspoken.

"No. I know what I said. I want to keep it. And you do, too, Declan. You want to keep it."

Declan was flabbergasted. "Well, yes. I mean I did until we talked, but . . ."

"We can't let him force us into making a decision we will regret for the rest of our lives. I won't give him that power."

Declan stared at Fiona. Frank floundered. "Are you talking about me, Fiona? You know it was your father who gave me this power, but it was only to help you out. I only need to use it if . . ."

Fiona flashed on his touching Una. His hand over hers at the well, his shoulder around hers, his patting her on the head. And she imagined a long line of little girls behind Una. Girls without names or faces. Girls she didn't know.

"You've already abused your power over me far too much, Frank, and I will not stand by and let you do it all over again."

"I don't know what . . ."

"Yes, you do. You know exactly *what,* and if you force me to say it, I will."

Frank looked panicked now. He turned to Declan. "Declan, can you calm her down, can't you tell . . ."

"Declan was there, too, Frank. He remembers. Do you want me to call him officially as a witness?"

Frank looked to Declan again, like a man drowning, desperately seeking a safety net.

"It's true, Frank. I was there, in the next room. I only wish I'd had the wherewithal to do something. Like fucking kill you!"

Frank jumped up. "I don't have to stay here and listen to . . ."

Fiona also sprang to her feet as Frank wound his way unsteadily towards the door. With amazing alacrity she found herself in his path, blocking his escape route. She looked him directly in the eye.

"No, you don't—have to stay. And what's more, you will leave this house and never return, or walk on our land ever again."

He averted his eyes.

"And Frank . . ."

With a huge effort he raised his eyes to hers, the eyes of a haunted, frightened, man. Fiona could see that he was shaking.

"If you ever so much as look at Una, or any little girl, or child, anywhere, anytime, I will go directly to the police and have you arrested."

Frank blanched. Fiona thought he was about to have an apoplectic fit on the spot. Then he gathered himself together, turned and slouched in shame from the room.

Fiona stood rooted to her spot. Then she looked at Declan. He now looked like he'd seen a ghost.

"Fiona?" He struggled to speak. "You mentioned Una. Were you just . . . ?"

"Yes." Fiona slumped back into the chair now. Exhausted. "I was just warning him. Nothing happened. And I think we've seen the last of him."

CHAPTER NINETEEN

EYE OF THE STORM

> "When the soul . . . is born in this country, there are nets flung at it to hold it back from flight . . . I shall try to fly by those nets . . . to live, to err, to fall, to triumph, to recreate life out of life."
>
> JAMES JOYCE—*Portrait of the Artist as a Young Man*

One week after their eventful meeting with Frank, Fiona and Declan sat at the same long table and signed the final papers. They were now co-owners of the house and land.

"I suppose I should get therapy, shouldn't I?" Fiona remarked, after Mr. Stanley had left. "While I'm working through all this. Isn't that what you're supposed to do?" she asked half seriously.

"Only if you need to. You seem like you're doing great. Never seen you better."

"Maybe the film is my therapy—or the whole visit. I'm still working on my hostile feelings for you, Declan!" Fiona was joking—partly. She understood so much more now about her brother and his behavior, but while working on certain scenes in the script she still smarted at some of his childish cruelties.

"I know you're saying that lightly, but I don't blame you." Declan's tone was serious. "I know I felt lonely and excluded after Orla was born, and then hugely powerless during and after the Uncle Frank episode, and all of it resulted in me becoming a bit of a bully. Trying to be a tough guy. Ultimately it all led me to psychology—to try and help myself and hopefully others work their way through these conundrums."

"And I think that's why I would never look for professional psychiatric help," Fiona admitted. "Wouldn't touch it with a ten-foot pole—because it was your bailiwick. Funny, or maybe not so funny, how we shoot ourselves in the foot."

"Yeah," Declan agreed. "And look at me. It took me this long to deal with my own family, too. I mean, I understood it intellectually before, but still couldn't bring myself to deal with you, my own sister."

Fiona laughed. "So, Declan," she teased. "Are all my awful memories of you entirely figments of my own imagination, or what's the percentage—maybe half is truth, half imaginings?"

Declan laughed, too. "Well, there might be a modicum of truth to some of them. But, but . . . I bet you don't remember all the great things I did—like the time I saved your life, for example?"

Julie walked in at this point and joined them. "Oh, I remember that story," she said as she sat down at the table. "You told me that one, Declan."

Fiona stared at both of them. "What? You're joking me. What are you talking about?"

"The time you fell off the kitchen table," Declan said.

"Fell off? When? Tell me?" Fiona was fascinated.

"Okay." Declan began. "You were just a few months old and I was about three. Crazy about you, I have to say, though you wouldn't remember that! Anyway, I don't know where Mam was; she must have gone out of the room for a minute to get something. You were lying on a blanket on the kitchen table, maybe Mam had been changing you or something. I was sitting on the floor playing with my toy car when I saw a movement out of the corner of my eye. I looked up and there you were rolling over head first off the table, like you were diving. I saw it all in slow motion as you rolled right off and were heading for the cement floor. And in that split second I catapulted up and caught you in what seemed like midair, and you dropped into my arms. And the weight of you, though you weren't very big but neither was I, plopped me down on the floor. My bum hit hard, but you were held out in my arms so you were safe though you were screaming at the top of your lungs with the shock."

Fiona stared at her brother as if he had just imparted some earth shattering piece of information to her, like that they really were from Mars. When she found her tongue again she burst out. "But, but, I do know that story. I've known that story all my life but not in that version."

"Did you hear it from someone else or do you actually remember it?" Julie asked.

"No idea." Fiona admitted, except I believe I remember it. Here goes. The first part is the same, Declan. I was lying on the table looking up at the kitchen ceiling. I remember Mam being there and you on the floor and then Mam leaving. Then I remember you jumping up and pulling me off, sort of rolling me along and off the table and me doing a sky-dive for the floor and smashing my head.

I remember hearing this terrible screaming and then realizing it was coming from my own throat."

"But you'd have had major brain damage from a fall like that." Julie surmised.

"Maybe that explains everything." Fiona laughed, and then she laughed even more. She liked the sound of her own laughter—it was a new register that she was re-discovering. It was as if she had lived most of her life in a tragic vein, but had now flipped it around to reveal the complimentary mask of comedy.

"Well, I was always proud that I saved your little life," Declan joked. "Always thought you were a tad ungrateful!"

"And I had you pegged as a murderer! I always thought you were out to get me!"

They both found this hilarious and started laughing all over again. They were still in high merriment when Sean arrived. He had been making phone calls, working on details of the filming. It was late Friday afternoon and Declan, Julie and Una were heading off on a short trip for the weekend. Sean and Fiona were going to try out the new Italian restaurant in the nearby town that evening and put the finishing touches to the shooting script.

"Maybe you should join Fiona as a consultant on the film, Declan." Sean joked, when they filled him in on the disparate versions of the same event.

"Can I be a consultant, too? Can I?" Una also walked in the door that minute—she had been amusing herself outside for several hours.

"Una—is your backpack ready for the weekend? We're leaving in five minutes." And Una bounded up the stairs to gather her belongings.

Fiona picked up on Sean's comment. "If you add your perspective, Declan, then the truth—whatever that is—may lie somewhere in between."

"You could change the title to 'The Crazy Clarkes'!" Declan offered.

"Then you can both continue competing with each other in your respective fields." Julie threw in to the mix.

"Who makes the greatest contribution to the betterment of humanity?" Sean asked in a mock lofty tone.

"Art or Psychology?" Fiona added in the same vein, and they all laughed happily.

■ ■ ■

Sean and Fiona stood side by side and looked out over the land which stretched as far as the eye could see. The fields smelled of fresh cut barley, and the purple hills rose up to meet the horizon.

"You know," Fiona said to Sean, "I've been thinking I might actually want to live here. Even for part of the year. It's so beautiful and peaceful. I never noticed it in that way before."

Sean nodded, breathing in the fresh country air. "It would be a lovely place to write, wouldn't it?" And she knew he was echoing Peter's sentiment to Sheila, which echoed Simon's to her. Fiona's mind turned back to Simon, as she stood side by side with him at the age of seventeen, half a lifetime ago, surveying his family's land. She looked at Sean mischievously. "An idyllic country setting, down on the farm?" She laughed. "You're right. It could be a lovely place to write."

■ ■ ■

Over a candlelight dinner in the new *trattoria,* Fiona and Sean discussed the final re-writes on the script.

"Are you happy with it, Sean? All the inconsistencies you mentioned at the beginning, and the blending of reality and fantasy—do you think it's clear?"

Sean popped a ravioli into his mouth and munched.

"I think it's almost there. You've done great work. I had a feeling the tangles could be sorted out."

Fiona laughed and took a sip of Chardonnay. "How did you know that? How could you be sure? I didn't know I'd be able to sift through the inconsistencies—I'm not sure I'd have even admitted there were any when we started out. So how could you have known before you even met me?"

"I suppose it's the director's job to draw out what's there and to sense it even if it's hidden." He took a bite of salad. The waiter sailed by and topped up their wine glasses. "There's still something missing, Fiona." Sean took a sip. "I don't know what it is. I'm not sure if it's structural, in the screenplay."

"Do you think it's a story element?" Such nice clean words. Such simple terms for such shattering consequences. Time Past and Time Present were converging. She sipped some courage and then looked at Sean across the glinting candlelit table.

"There is something I want to tell you. For you. Not for the script."

Sean caught the look in her eye, the fear and sorrow and hurt and haunting. He reached over and took her hand in his.

"It's something that happened to me, very soon after Orla died." Fiona forged ahead. Her voice was heavy but clear. Sean tightened his grasp as she struggled to find words. "It was in our house, our home, when I was nine . . ."

Sean gathered her other hand across the table and held both of them firmly in his own. "Fiona, I think I know."

She stared at him.

"I think I know what, but not who. Not who it was."

Fiona was flabbergasted. "How could you possibly know, Sean? You just guessed?"

He nodded. "From your novel. I guessed it though it wasn't written. I knew you had been violated in some deep way—I felt there was something else besides the death and loss. But I was confused. I thought it was, that it might be Declan."

"What? How? Why? You saw that in my novel? My brother? I wrote that in there somehow? Hidden? God, no wonder he was scared!"

"As soon as we got to Ireland, I wondered if it wasn't someone else—that maybe you had shifted the blame from someone else and for something you couldn't name, couldn't write about. But the animosity for the brother was so strong in the book that I felt the prototype, Declan, had to have done something dreadful. It wasn't him though, was it?"

"No. It wasn't. Though you're right. I blamed him, unconsciously, and held him responsible."

Sean cradled her hand.

Fiona continued. "It was . . . my uncle, Uncle Frank."

Sean nodded. Paused. "I figured it might be him. After we got here, I began to put two and two together." He was quiet then. He continued to hold her hand. The food was forgotten.

Fiona looked at him. "Did you really know that there was something that dark . . . is that what you meant, just now, when you said . . . ? Sean, you don't mean that this is what's missing?"

His eyes rested on hers. "I didn't know exactly what it was. Just that it was something crucial and unspoken. And when I met you, I knew it was some deep strain in you, something locked away."

The candlelight cast a halo around Sean's blond curls. He looked to Fiona for an instant like a cherub, and she smiled. "Have you ever considered psychiatry? You're good at it you know? Maybe you have to be for directing."

He laughed. "You have to be able to analyze characters and find the inner motivations, the secret lives." He stopped, and a cloud passed over his face. "But I'm not trying to pry open your life, Fiona. I know I have, in so far as the novel is concerned. I had to treat the characters as characters, to get to the bottom of their psyches as much as I could. But this is something else. Painful and private. I really didn't mean to get it out of you, as information. I hope you know that."

"I didn't offer it as information, Sean. Nor to you as a scriptwriter. But as my . . . love, I felt you had a right to know. I know it's my own private life."

Sean raised her hands to his lips and gently kissed them. Fiona had the sweeping sensation again that she had always known him. It was a comforting and exciting feeling. It did not preclude the knowledge that they had a future lifetime to grow together. She dared now to hope they might have a chance.

"What about the script?" She asked. "Can we work it out?"

"Hey, that's my job, and yours. We're writers, we'll figure it out!"

"Okay!" They shook hands as if clinching the deal and returned to the neglected ravioli.

■ ■ ■

Fiona took a long deep luxurious shower and felt she was washing away the debris of centuries. She was still a young woman, only thirty-five, but the grief she carried around for so many years had made her feel ancient. She massaged her scalp and scrubbed her back and slid the soap in all the curves and planes of her body as she worked up a lather and then let the water spray it off. She thought of Sean. He had kissed her goodbye at the door. She had said she might take a bath and soak, but instead, she opted for a vigorous shower. She knew Sean would come. And she wanted him to. Up until now, she had not felt whole and had no desire to enter into another relationship where she needed someone to be her mirror, to give her validation. She saw that her newly developed confidence with Simon all those years ago had been dependent on staying with him; it had not come from her but from his appreciation of her. It had all crumbled away when she couldn't deal with him leaving, abandoning her. In reality, she had abandoned herself.

She was barely out of the shower and vigorously drying her hair in the plush white towel when Sean knocked on the door and called out her name. She wrapped her robe around her tingling body and went to let him in.

No sooner was he in the room than they were in each other's arms. He hugged her tight, and she clung to him. They eased apart and she searched for his lips and he met hers and they hungrily blended their kisses. Then they stood in the center of the room and held each other. Fiona had so much to tell him, a life to relay. At the same time, she felt that he knew. That she had had a catharsis. And that the many strands of her past were now gathering in, and the meaning and hope in them was illuminated. She and Sean looked at each other and smiled. They had not yet spoken. After all of their time spent together, the meetings, the phone messages, back and forth, the separation, the waiting, the return to her homeland, he had found the right time to come to her. The exact right moment.

They slowly moved towards the bed, her bed, and sat down side by side. There was no need to speak. They already knew, maybe had known from the beginning, that they would arrive at this moment. There was an urgency in their eagerness, an excitement to be in each other's arms, yet there was also a sense of timelessness, as if the moment stood still for them. Without hurry, they could ease into their dance of love. Sean reached out and lightly brushed her cheek with his fingertip. She felt the touch of a lover. It fanned out and coursed through her whole body. She reached over and stroked his face, ever so gently, barely making contact. She felt his response in a quivering wave. She knew that her touch, like his, had spread like a mantle and enveloped his entire body. Sean slipped out of his sandals and drew his legs up onto the bed. Fiona curled her legs under her. They now sat facing each other, their legs crossed beneath them. Sean caressed her hair, still moist from the shower. He ran his fingers through the copper threads and slid them down to the nape of her neck. She felt the most delicious tingle and laughed aloud with pleasure. She ran her fingers through Sean's wavy dark blond locks and traced a pattern down the back of his neck and underneath his cotton shirt to his shoulders. Then her fingers traveled back and one by one she slowly unbuttoned his shirt. Sean moved his fingers unhurriedly to the front of Fiona's robe, spread it open and eased it gently off her shoulders so that it fell down to her waist.

"How beautiful you are, Fiona," he spoke, almost a whisper.

The purity and directness of his compliment swept over her like the cool waters of a mountain stream. She placed her hand on his heart.

"You're so lovely, too, Sean." He laughed and laid his palm over hers and then lifted her hand and pressed her fingers to his lips. Fiona felt that this man knew her and accepted her as is. Sean had first fallen in love with her work, which had come from an even deeper place inside her than she knew, and as she trusted her writing and her past to him, she now entrusted her present self. Their lips searched each other out in the sweetness of new exploration as the summer breezes wafted gently against the windowpanes, and the gossamer curtains swayed back and forth to the music of the night.

■ ■ ■

A week and a half later, the crew had been organized, the equipment rented and the filming was ready to go. Sean had assembled a crew, part Irish, part American, and Declan was extremely helpful guiding them around and rallying the neighbors as extras in some scenes. And Nellie headed up the local catering. The American crew loved the fresh Irish food—streets ahead of any Hollywood grub, they claimed! The locals were thrilled no end to be having a film shot in their own backyard, and even more so that they were going to be film stars. The musicians who had played at James Clarke's wake earlier in the summer were happy to provide music. When they heard Declan had taken up the violin again, they tried to talk him into playing with them, but he declined.

"I'm not up to scratch for anything professional, but I'd love to join in an off-screen session, if you don't mind a rank amateur. I think Dad would be tickled if I got to play with you guys!"

A little later while they were having a tea break, Fiona asked him privately, "Is there any one piece, even, that you could play, Declan?"

"You know how awful the violin can be if played badly?" He laughed. "Screeching like a banshee!"

"I know! But I've heard you practicing, and you've been playing all summer. I just thought that it would be lovely if you were a part of this film somehow, in an artistic way, too—but especially if we could sneak a bit of the violin in there for Dad. Writing and music were two of his . . . dreams? Remember how he loved to quote the Yeats' poem, 'I have spread my dreams under your feet, tread softly, because you tread on my dreams'?"

"And he cut himself off from both of them?" Declan offered.

"Yes, or as you said at one point, didn't have the heart for them anymore because of all the pain. Maybe we can give back a little to him, me with the writing, and you with the violin?"

Declan nodded. "And what about Mam? Can we make any gestures to her? Her life was us, really, wasn't it? Her children?"

"I think she'd be happy, as would Dad, that the two of us are talking, getting closer, treating each other more gently. I don't think we could give her anything better than that."

"I agree. And treating ourselves more gently, too?"

Fiona grinned in agreement.

"Okay, good." Declan thought for a minute. Let's see, what do you think about 'The Gypsy Rover?' It's always been one of my favorites, and I've been practicing it a lot. Do you remember it?"

"Oh yes!" Fiona beamed and they started to sing together.

"'The whistling gypsy came over the hill,
Down by the valley so shady.
He whistled and he sang 'til the green wood rang,
And he won the heart of a la-a-a-dy."

"Perfect!"

■ ■ ■

On the third day of shooting, Fiona had supervised the film crew as they set up their shot of the hideout, faithfully reconstructed to reflect the original. Una sat at the base of the ancient oak tree reading the *Alice in Wonderland* that Fiona had given her as a present. There was a huge amount of excitement and bustle. The main house and the grounds were chock full of actors, costume and make-up crew, and caterers. When Fiona felt her work was done outside, she went back to the house to work on the script.

Pam's computer was installed on the huge oak table in the parlor where a few short months earlier the food had been piled high for her father's wake. Sean and Fiona worked there and re-wrote or corrected as necessary. Fiona sat herself in front of the screen and typed out some changes in the upcoming scene that she and Sean had discussed. She had just sent the document to the printer when the storm broke. She jumped to her feet and rushed to the window. The skies opened. Thunder crackled. Rain pelted down like sleek miniature bullets. People raced madly in all directions, taking care of equipment and then running for cover to the house. It was organized chaos.

Fiona stared out the window at the teeming rain. She had a moment of panic and old creeping fear and a streak of sadness as all of the past memories raced through her mind. The eye of the storm, she thought to herself and stared at the leaves of paper as they trundled out of the purring machine. She had a sudden terror of being pulled into that old vortex, where the storm's violence scattered her thoughts and stirred up the unwelcome past. She glanced out at the cast and crew, Sean at the helm. Most of them were now approaching the house where they would sit in the kitchen and eat scones and drink tea and rehearse until the storm subsided.

Fiona fought the pull of her inner demons and forced herself to mentally take control of the journey, to face the true eye of the storm. She struggled to find the courage to carve out a scene of triumph from the degradation and defilement and pollution of a child's innocence. She eyed the computer from her position at the window. Then she marched over and sat down to begin a new scene. She sought out the letters and typed—"*Interior—Bedroom, 1964—Night.*" Her words were arrows, and she would fashion them and send them out to pierce the barriers of silence. "*Nine year old Sheila lies half-sleeping in her bed.*" The walls constructed by family and religion and country and culture and history and fear and a self turned in upon itself. "*A shaft of light streaks across the bed, and a shadow falls on her upturned face."* Walls constructed to defy the true freedom that must precede all others, the refusal to lie down and stay silent as if it never happened, to strangle the scream and stop its penetration into the future. *"She smiles when she sees it's her favorite uncle."* Fiona pounded the keys as she had many times before in an act of banishment, but now the words, though they strained and cracked and screamed as they expressed her pain, proclaimed that she would not be still, be silent, be forced in. Her fingers flew on wings of exaltation and formed her proclamation, as Time Past slipped and slid and soared into Time Present, carving out words that would move perpetually into Time Future.

EPILOGUE

TIME FUTURE

June 21st, 2008

The weather held up beautifully, never a guarantee in Ireland in June, but Una had absolutely wanted to be married on the Summer Solstice. She had also chosen to have the ceremony in the village church and her reception on her family's farm. Fiona and Declan and their families had spent most summers there for the past eighteen years. They had sold much of the arable land but kept several acres around the house which they had landscaped and cultivated.

"It's amazing what you've done with this place." Nellie, now seventy-eight, beamed at Declan and Fiona who sat side by side on folding chairs under a white canopy.

"Well, the decorators did an incredible job in setting up and arranging all the tents," Fiona smiled. "But we haven't done too badly over the years, have we, Dec?"

Declan laughed. "No, I think we can be proud!"

Nellie gestured towards the small guest cottage around the side of the house.

"So, who won out this time?" she chuckled.

Fiona laughed happily. "I believe the bride and her bridesmaids got the prize—as is only right on the night before her wedding! My poor son has to put up with sleeping in the same house as his parents!"

"And uncle and aunt!" Declan added. "It's tough on teenagers!"

"She's something else, that daughter of yours, Declan." Nellie's eyes followed Una as she mingled with her guests. "Turned out very well—all of your children turned our very well, mind you, for Americans!"

"Well, thanks, Nellie! I'm sure we appreciate the compliment, don't we, Declan?" Fiona giggled. "Of course, it's probably the three months every year they spend in Ireland that does it. Keeps them civilized!"

"Yeah," Declan continued the joke, "I'd say they wouldn't stand much of a chance otherwise. They'd be right little heathens!"

"Not to mention that they're actually more Catholic than either of the two of us." Fiona added. "I thought it was supposed to be the other way round, the young ones rebelling!"

"Now, you show your face once in a while down at the chapel, Fiona, don't you?" Nellie commented. "You say the odd prayer, yourself?"

"I do when I'm here, Nell. I like the peace and quiet in the chapel. And I feel close to Mam and Dad and Orla there. I wouldn't hold your breath for canonization, though!"

"Well, God Almighty, I should hope not, colleen!" Nellie

laughed heartily. "We have enough saints to keep us going, I'd say, without adding you to the roster. Look now, here comes the beautiful bride and her entourage!"

Una swept in, a vision in white, followed, in a flash of sapphire blue, by her seventeen-year-old sister Niamh, and Fiona and Sean's daughter Nessa.

"We're going to start the dancing soon, Dad. Are you ready?"

"Isn't the first dance with your husband? I believe I'm second fiddle today!" Declan joked.

"Marcel's all ready for our dance. Just checking on you. You and Mom can dance together during the first one, if you like. Are you going to dance, Nell?"

"Well, I haven't stepped out much since Ignatius passed away, God rest him. But, if I were to get a nice offer from a fine gentleman, you'd never know, I might accept!"

"I'll see if I can find my brother," Nessa offered. "He's kind of hopeless, but we practiced a bit together for today. Just so we wouldn't make a holy show of you, dear cousin!"

"Why, thank you, I'm sure!" Una joked back.

"If you can pry him away from Nicole!" Niamh smiled.

"I thought he was with his father, getting help with the DVD recorder?" Fiona started to look around for Fintan. Nessa laughed. "Well, he was, Mom, but then he was lured away by the beautiful French maiden!"

"And who is Nicole, when she's at home?" Nellie wanted to know. "Surely he doesn't have a girlfriend already, does he? What ages are you two now, Nessa, is it fourteen?"

"Fourteen and a half, Nell."

"Oh, lordy lordy! Seems like the other day you were just born, same year Frank passed away. Lord have mercy!" And she crossed herself.

Fiona and Declan shared a quick glance. It all seemed like ancient history now.

"You're our only hope for a bit of longevity in the gene department, Nellie!" Declan joked.

"It's true, Nell," Fiona laughed. "Poor Declan and I feel lucky to have made it to our fifties! So hang in there for us, will you?"

"Now, does it look like I'm going anywhere? Shur, I'm not even eighty yet. My father lived to be a hundred and one!"

"Is that true, Nellie, for real?" Nessa was fascinated.

"True as I'm sitting here, *macoushla*. And strong in mind and body 'til the end, he was. Swore by the drop of Irish whiskey and a good pipe every now and then. Now, there's a character for one of your novels, Fiona—a right divil he was, too!"

"We should sit and chat about him someday, Nell. Maybe during our teatimes?"

"Not that you're short of ideas. I can hardly keep up with all your books these days."

Fiona laughed. "I'm always on the lookout for new ideas!"

Sean arrived just then, sat down beside Fiona and took her hand in his. "One minute I had Fintan in my sights, next minute he's vanished."

"Well, it's a bit early for haystacks this time of year, or is it?" Una joked.

"And what do you know of haystacks, my innocent daughter?" Declan joked back.

"Father, I'm a married woman now, quite experienced. Which reminds me, I'm going to look for my husband. I think he's talking to Mom. And don't forget your violin. I talked Fintan into playing with you!"

"Now he has someone he wants to impress!" Nessa added impishly.

Una gave big warm hugs to them all and swirled away.

"We must follow and serve our lady!" Niamh proclaimed dramatically as she grabbed Nessa's hand and dashed off after Una. They caught up with her, each took one of her arms, and the little covey flounced off, laughing and giggling, into the crowd.

"Bless them. They're like sisters, aren't they, the three of them?" Nellie murmured.

Fiona and Declan exchanged another glace and smiled. He reached out and squeezed her hand quickly.

"Am I missing something about Finn?" Sean asked.

"I wouldn't worry!" Fiona laughed. "He'll be fine. They'll all be fine. It's a beautiful midsummer's day. A perfect day for a wedding."

"Nothing would do for our Una except the Summer Solstice." Declan added.

"She wanted the longest day of the year, when the sun is at its zenith, so she could stretch out her happiness." Fiona offered.

"The old wisdom was that the sun stood still on the solstice." Nellie told them.

" 'At the still point of the turning world.' " Fiona remembered T.S. Eliot. " 'Neither from nor towards.' " She continued softly. " 'At the still point, there the dance is.' "

ABOUT THE AUTHOR

Gemma Whelan is an Irish-born theatre director and educator. After moving to the San Francisco Bay Area, she directed more than sixty stage productions and was founding artistic director of GemArt and Wilde Irish Productions. Gemma is also an award-winning screenwriter and film director. She graduated from Trinity College, Dublin in English and French, and has graduate degrees from University of California, Berkeley in Theatre and San Francisco State University in Cinema.

Gemma Whelan lives in Portland, Oregon.